D0860141

PALE

PALE

A NOVEL

EDWARD A. FARMER

BLACK
STONE
PUBLISHING

Copyright © 2020 by Edward A. Farmer

Published in 2020 by Blackstone Publishing

Cover and book design by Kathryn Galloway English

All rights reserved. This book or any portion
thereof may not be reproduced or used in any manner
whatsoever without the express written permission
of the publisher except for the use of brief quotations
in a book review.

The characters and events in this book are fictitious.
Any similarity to real persons, living or dead, is coincidental
and not intended by the author.

Printed in the United States of America

First edition: 2020

ISBN 978-1-982673-86-4

Fiction / Literary

1 3 5 7 9 10 8 6 4 2

CIP data for this book is available
from the Library of Congress

Blackstone Publishing
31 Mistletoe Rd.
Ashland, OR 97520

www.BlackstoncPublishing.com

For Sister Lewis

CHAPTER 1

Young people see cotton as beautiful, something to roll around in until their eyes bob like apples and they become dizzy. A cool place to hide their feet on summer days, along that base where weeds grow, but never too long before the chop of a steady hoe. Let Daddy tell it, those white stalks were no different than the white man, a devil he'd known all his life out in Crenshaw, Mississippi, the place of his birth.

"You don't know that white face until it works you," he'd say, coming through the front door tired and sore, his hands knotted like ropes as he wrung out the tension through cracks of his knuckles.

But Daddy left this world to be with the Lord a long time ago, and only Henry was left by my side. When Henry left, I had no one. He was supposed to send for me but never did. Together, we were going to live out a life far away from this wretched place we knew as home. On the first day, all joy I had for his journey faded just as fast as mop water on a sun-licked floor, as I feared his passage had met its end somewhere out in the black heart of Mississippi. Yet, slowly, as the days dragged on, those images were but pebbles inside my mind that rattled around whenever my spirits sank low. I knew he'd somehow made it and was now starting a life for us, and that I would soon join him. After two months, I knew my letter would arrive any day, and that we would be free in that place we'd dreamt about together. We'd lie barefoot on the sand, feeling it clump between our toes like the red dirt that chipped along the countryside and made the pathways muddy. We'd open a basket of figs and natal plums, and we'd eat selfishly, never fearing the weight of that white hand pressed over our lives again.

At three months, the sorrow came once more, along with visions of his death. At four months, I checked for his name in the obituaries almost daily. At five months, I wrote to the bus station to no avail, and at six months I just gave up, not on him but of any hope I had of ever leaving—for with him went all of our money. At night, I dreamt of his face merged with the countryside, the rounds of his eyes in perfect harmony with the passing fields as he watched through bus windows a land that had betrayed him. On other nights, I dreamt he'd died by the hands of the Klan and his body was strung up like a welcome banner for everyone to see. I watched as my strong husband fought then bled and died on the streets of Sumner with no one there to mourn him, his blood a hot trickle along the cracks in the gutter curb as it coagulated into a cold clay and became the earth.

Nonetheless, on other nights, not so troubling, when the soft winds blew the sweet smell of jacaranda trees into my window, I pictured more simple thoughts of him resting by the ocean, content and dreaming of his bride, his apparent death nothing more than part of his plan to sneak back to my bed. These dreams continued every night until the time of the dog-day cicada, when my brother sent for me to live with him near Greenwood, Mississippi, down in Leflore County, because, according to him, "Ain't no woman should be livin' by herself at times like this. Plus, they treats us far betta down here."

Floyd knew those parts better than most and, as such, knew the good from the bad like he knew the back of his own hand—and mine, too, let him tell it. Although it was late summer, it was still hot, the date on the calendar meaning nothing when it came to Mississippi and heat. The plantation went for miles in both directions, one of those places where there was nothing, then something, then nothing again for acres at a time. Ninety miles from Jackson, thirty miles from the nearest interstate, tossed out there amongst the coyotes and armadillos, the Cotton Capital of the World, they called it. It bears a starkness that can only be said to exist in the furthest reaches of one's imagination, as one would picture hell to be if it were an actual place on this earth that one could see and feel. A wolf in sheep's clothing, Daddy would say—an aphorism that for only that reason remains a jewel. The rain dries quickly, the ground a pillowed bed, the marsh a thirsty bowl, those cotton sheets a white covering for the night, lulling so gently and quietly into my ears. Nothing ever happened except for the rain and plows, or maybe a loud truck occasionally came roaring down the street or, if they were lucky, a car passed with blaring music, but nothing stirred in the fields.

Plantation life was often a slow and steady process with little to do between planting and harvesting except maybe check for whiteflies or squirrels on the bolls. On the day I arrived, the grounds sat completely void of any human life until we'd actually made it inside the house.

The cool air met us at the door as Floyd gave a shove to my backside with his wide hands.

"Don't mess aroun' an' let out the cold," Floyd barked.

We walked quickly into the kitchen, where a woman stirred up something awfully good, especially to one in my condition, having traveled most of the day and foolishly packing very little to eat. The woman was of a sturdy build and not fond of smiling and, as such, gave nothing more than a nod in my direction when Floyd introduced us, continuing her duties in silence while we continued through the kitchen and out toward the parlor. Floyd had mentioned her in previous letters to me. Said her name was Silva, and she had family in Lafayette and some parts of Jackson. Said she was a snitch and couldn't be trusted with a secret around a deaf or a mute.

"You stay 'way from her," Floyd said as we entered the parlor, quitting his speech right quickly as we came upon the Mister of the house.

The pleasant breeze inside all but faded when we entered that sunlit room attached to the side door. On all sides large windows sat cracked to let in the humid air that rushed through like tempests while old Mr. Kern sat beside the window with his legs crossed and a cigarette hanging from his lips, that white stick having grown soggy from the moistness in the air.

"Sir, I'd like for you ta meet my sista Bernice," Floyd said.

The stern man turned from the window to face us, his nose a pointed peak that pierced just as sharply as his eyes. From his forehead fell beads of sweat while on his nose, or those parts that were wide enough to collect moisture, clung oily drops that caused his entire face to shine. He removed his cigarette from his mouth and placed it on the tray beside him. Taking his handkerchief from his breast pocket, he wiped the sweat from his upper lip and forehead then placed it onto the arm of his chair, the smoke from his cigarette curling beside it as he watched us.

"We all like family here," the old man said in a gruff voice, hiking his pants and coughing loudly. "You good with the Missus, you good with me."

I had never encountered a man like him before—mean as the day was long yet gentle toward a negro he'd only met once and need show no kindness toward. I watched him intently, forgetting I was there to complete a job and instead studying him as if I worked at his side. Floyd nudged my shoulder, having waited long enough for my response and refusing to wait any longer. The old man turned back to the window, done with me all the same.

"Yes, sir," I finally said, noting right away the old man's inherent shortness of speech, in addition to the lack of patience that seemed to touch everyone in these parts. "I'm very grateful, sir."

Floyd led the way back inside the house, that cool sanctuary where the curtains never parted and sunlight never touched a crack on the wooden floor. Like spurs our shoes hit the floorboards with a firmness that urged us closer and closer to the Missus's upstairs quarters. She spun around as we entered, her skin the palest I'd ever seen on a person, its thinness like that of paper that was translucent and easily torn.

"Floyd!" she gasped. "You know not to be so loud inside the house."

"Yes, Miss," he said with his head low. "This here's ma sista."

"Even so," she said. "There's no need for all that noise. Gonna wake the dead, I swear."

She stared at Floyd until she was certain he understood her severity. Then, when his head sank the lowest it could go and his eyes were infantile and teary in nature, did she finally turn to me.

"Welcome," she now said kindly, her youthfulness evident in her mild stare.

She had to be at least a generation younger than Mr. Kern, who appeared to be in his late sixties, his skin the thickness of rubber and the color of used cooking oil. She possessed features softer than any Mr. Kern could ever imagine, her forehead plated milk and her hair golden wheat out over the plains. She was pretty, even if slightly anomalous, her one eye offset from the other, as it could never quite follow in the right direction until she had blinked several times, and then it caught up, only to trail once more.

"This here's Miss Lula," Floyd said to me.

"It's my pleasure, Miss," I replied.

"I look forward to you carrying your share," she said distantly.

Her eyes were half closed and her gaze stuck on some item along the dust ruffle of her bed.

"Silva knows the house and will show you the rest."

And with this unusual greeting, the young woman turned away from the door and back toward the dim space where she knitted silently, making the loops without ever looking at the work of her hands.

Floyd spent that evening acquainting me with the lay of the house and its rules, as he saw them.

"There's talk of them out there," he said, his cupped hands juggling pellets he spread for the chickens. "They's sayin' all types uh nonsense. I believe them as much as the next. But I don't dare bring that foolsness in here. Mista Kern be good an' you smile an' say thank you. Here makes a good home. See it so."

With this final order, he dropped the remaining pellets and slop for the hogs. He jostled their pens and was quiet again, if only for a few seconds, before returning to his duties and leaving me to trail behind and await his next lecture.

CHAPTER 2

The abandoned skins of the cicadas were left on the trees after that summer, and the children used them to chase each other. The countryside was filled with their screams, yet the Kern Manor sat quietly in its own blockade. Along the farthest reaches, the children's laughter invaded, though never reaching the front porch. There hadn't been milk-laden breath in this home for years, the little Miss of the house passing one winter, well before I arrived, as told to me by Floyd in one of his many letters.

With no children to rear and Silva to care for the family indoors, Floyd assigned me duties in the fields with him, preparing for the cotton harvest, except for at night when Silva returned to her family and I would care for the house and the Mister and Missus during her absence.

"You're gonna need plenty of patience to deals with her," Silva told me on that first night, awaiting any bit of dissension I might have so that she might run back and inform the Missus, I was sure.

When I merely nodded, her face turned to stone.

"Just know," she said, "things that typically keep well in other homes don't keep well here."

"I keep all my things in the icebox," I replied fiercely. "Even the flour."

After this, she knew me and I knew her, and our paths rarely crossed, and if they did, it was pleasant. Still, when the Missus fell ill that September of 1966, Silva undoubtedly blamed me. For it was during that hot stretch of summer that Miss Lula fell victim to the strangest sickness I'd ever seen on a person, as in an instant she had gone from her normal position beside the curtained window with her needlework in her lap to one of pure anguish, doubled over on the floor. It had been only minutes since I'd checked on her when her cries rang out, as delicate as the mouse whose squeaks we'd hear echo throughout the halls at night. I did swear she was one of those creatures as I found her shivering helplessly like a rodent trapped inside the corner, and me with the broom in my hand.

"Miss!" I cried out. "What's the matter?"

With one hand I gathered her elbow and with the other grabbed the thinness of her waist, lifting her from the floor onto her feet. She sagged in my arms, sinking like stones in the river as she took a seat in the nearby chair.

"Bernice!" she called while lurched forward and panting.

"Yes, Miss, I'm here," I assured her.

She was whiter than at any other time since my arrival, although in her hands burned a color that swore she had made contact with the bright flesh of a beet. Floyd barged in with a look of terror, wildly throwing his arms in front of the Missus. She could barely gather the strength to shoo him away as she slumped farther in her chair like some hand puppet now done for the day.

"Hold 'er up," Floyd said with his large palm against her shoulder. "Expedishously!"

Floyd had learned a new word recently: expeditiously, and he had taken to using it at any chance he got. Notwithstanding, we both lifted the Missus until she was seated upright and had slowly returned to her normal breathing. Floyd excused himself to go wash up, as he was still dirty from his work and would surely be scolded if seen inside the house or tending to the Missus in this condition.

The doctor came quickly and guided Miss Lula from her quarters into the Mister's bedroom, where he laid her down. With her nightgown removed and her feet elevated on the bed, he wrapped her sickly body in towels and bade her not to move or else she might reawaken the monster.

"Miss Lula done suffered a heatstroke," he said in serious tones. "Makes you take relief in the fact it wasn't her normal ailment, but could've been—believe me, it could. Just make sure she rests. Ain't no need of chancing it for some silly wish to get out of bed and stir about. Not in this heat."

So this was how I would come to know her, this helpless creature, this mindless thing, this porcelain doll that we coddled and babied and wished would just fall asleep already. No detail of the doctor's delivery was lost as, when Mr. Kern later discovered his wife's impairment upon his return home, he blamed the staff for having left the doors wide open while running in and out. Silva then blamed me, her words coming across as clearly as whiskey on a sinner's breath as she repeated quite viciously, "Some things just don't keep well inside this house!"

Despite the Missus's condition, Mr. Kern spent that evening inside his parlor as usual, insisting no less that the doctor's orders be followed scrupulously, that the Missus rest throughout the night and that I look after her for the remainder of the evening, replacing towels and retrieving water whenever she requested it.

It was during this time of my care that she woke in a fit as frightful as the first and tossed the towels from her chest and forehead, sending them falling like wet sheets on the line caught in those nasty winds that rushed over the plains.

"No, Miss!" I shouted, pinning her down as best as I could although her strength was that of ten men. "You can't."

"I hate this heat," she insisted. "If it were up to me, I'd leave right now, I tell you."

She pouted and appeared even more childish than when I first met her in that dark room, with her lily hands that had seemingly never lifted an object heavier than a spoon to her mouth and were so soft that they reminded me of wadded silk. Her tantrum was short-lived, however, and thank you, Lord, for as soon as she lay back, there was a faraway look in her eyes that I had only seen once before in a man right before he died, that blankest of expressions that made her appear either lost or dumb and signified defeat. Her eyes wandered for a bit in this confused state before settling permanently on the wet towels upon the floor. She then closed her eyes and moaned.

"Guess I'd be lucky to leave this world anyhow," she said.

"Don't talk that way, Miss," I said. "It's so nice here."

"I should know," she said prudishly without ever looking up.

She didn't speak any more after that and urged me not to as well, unwilling to even fuss as I replaced the towels with fresh ones and forced more water down her throat. She lay there helpless like an infant for the remainder of the week, requiring that Silva "get this" or "move that" or "keep it down, please" or else she might be sick once more. Needless to say, Silva placed even this on me, repeating, "I don't knows how else to say it, but some things just don't keep inside this *house*!" Silva found need to remind me of this each time we passed. Whether it was the kitchen or outside the back stables or on that front porch and indeed along those gravel parts just beyond the back shed that led to the walking paths near the outer gates, she was a constant foe.

"Missus gonna need lots of care," she said, "and you can't go forgetting it."

By the weekend, however, when the weather cooled and the smell of honeysuckle sat thick in the air, like children's arms reaching and grabbing at one person then the other, Miss Lula showed renewed strength as she took her needlework to the porch for the first time that season. Indeed, the young woman had never stepped a foot outdoors in the weeks since I'd met her, at least not intentionally, that is, and definitely not in my presence, yet here she was all naive and untested as she marched proudly out the door with her tote underneath her arm.

"A right old 'weekday doctor, I'm not fine,' but 'weekend doctor, I'm well,'" I said jokingly as I spotted her on the porch.

She returned a stiff smile then requested by way of a shooing hand that I return to my duties. Silva had also spotted this bit of humor and gave a stern glance in my direction, saying, "Bernice, the eggs!" She then shook her head disapprovingly and trotted off. Still, she needed to say nothing more as I knew my work inside the stables begged my attention and chatting would not see it so, although a bit of laughter seemed exactly what the doctor ordered.

The coop was a mess if I'd ever seen one. Floyd had been off in town with Mr. Kern all afternoon tending to men's business, his handprint surely missed on that coop where several chickens pecked their neighbors and rodents attacked the feed. I started with the nest box, removing the hens then applying a bit of white vinegar to the soiled area. Any noise caused me to sit up and take notice, as I strained to hear the sounds from the front porch. But surprisingly there were none. It seemed that even with the Missus's usual fussiness she was at peace, sitting for several hours uninterrupted on that porch while Silva and I carried out our chores. When she finally grew bored of the sunshine, she returned to her dim quarters, where she spent the rest of the evening until dinnertime. Silva left the house reluctantly that night, aware that it was the first day of the Missus's full recovery and afraid that I would somehow return the Missus to that wicked state. Silva couldn't shake the pervading sense that something awful was on the horizon since I'd first arrived, bringing with me those cicadas that everyone knew was a surefire sign of impending bad luck. And sure enough, just when I'd thought I was in the clear and my mind at some semblance of peace, the Missus woke. Sick again.

"Silva!" Miss Lula shouted just when the house sat empty, Mr. Kern retired to his parlor room and Silva nearly halfway to her home by this point.

"She's gone for the day," I said patiently.

The Missus looked up to find only me there as a look of disappointment settled upon her.

"Can I help you, Miss?"

"I swear that girl leaves earlier and earlier every day," Miss Lula protested. "I wonder why we even pay her."

"I'd be happy to help," I said. "She's shown me most everything."

"I don't want any help!" she said.

"Should I get Mr. Kern?"

"No babysitter either," she scoffed.

She looked around the room disgusted, her cheeks red with a desire that seemed more than mere fickleness, a translucence that shone in them as if her skin allowed what flesh and blood she had to shine directly through.

"Go on, excuse yourself," she said exhaustively. "And don't bring him, either. I'd rather be alone than take his pity."

Her face was morbid, her lips a cold, barren blue—not like those corpses you'd see, all made up and ready for the grave, but rather like a skeleton, lifeless and bare. It was this expression that stayed with me more than any other, more than any whimpering she'd made throughout the night, as I closed the door and allowed her to rest, hearing her mumble a few additional words under her breath.

CHAPTER 3

I was affixed to the fields by day and the house at night. My quarters adjoined Floyd's, in an area out back of the shed and coop's wafted smells. Tall oaks made the small space bearable, as the main house relied on shaded windows for coolness while my room required I only raise the square pane for a pleasant breeze.

If the plantation was empty before, it was not now. Mr. Kern had hired some thirty cotton pickers for the harvest, and they worked each day from sunup to sundown with their canvas sacks trailing the mile-long rows, their arrival having been signaled by the hiss from that Flagstaff Motor Coach every day at dawn. The driver dropped them at the entrance to the gravel drive then returned each evening when the sun sat at its lowest, and Mr. Kern handed each man, woman, and child their day's keep as they then boarded the bus and it grumbled away.

Silva's boys, Jesse and Fletcher, had joined the crew that year. Floyd took it upon himself to ensure the boys stayed in line and kept good numbers like the rest, reporting to Silva each day of the boys' progress and impressing upon them that same Christian work ethic he'd been taught as a boy. Jesse was eighteen and had a spirit of defiance about him that gleamed through the slight flicker in his eyes that made him appear somehow wiser than most boys his age. There was a handsomeness in his face that extended to his broad shoulders and chiseled frame. He was stout and stood proud, nothing like those scrawny youngsters you'd see around the market as bag boys and clerks. Fletcher, on the other hand, was created in their likeness. At sixteen, he had not the muscles nor boldness that his brother possessed, although he was just as handsome and quite possibly prettier, people often commented, noting right away the boy's thin nose and lighter skin, his large eyes that sat beneath those dashing eyebrows that occurred naturally with him. He was special and was, as such, treated that way, his slight stutter a perceived innocence that led many to coddle him and his brother to, at all costs, follow his mother's insistence that he take care of his younger brother.

Both boys adored Floyd, I quickly noticed, never poking fun at him, which could be an easy task, given Floyd's fussy nature and rambles that often ended right where they began. No, the boys were instead like his own children, each of them following his orders without ever questioning and never giving backtalk no matter how stern the lecture was. When I found them on this day, Floyd was deep in one of his sermons as the boys took their lunches under the shade of the magnolia trees, the two of them stretched like fat cats on the grass to relieve the crooks that formed from having bent for hours. The countryside looked the same all around as I approached—the pushing up and down of white heads from the wind's fuss, that cotton a sea of foam witnessed only at the water's edge that pooled and lapped in constant thrusts.

"Now, King David was small, too," Floyd began, taking in their eyes as he spoke. "An' look at what he done. An', Jesse, what ya don't know is that ya were named for his father who was also

Jesse. Now, outta all the sons, Jesse never figured David would be the one that'd be king. But he was. An' he defeated a giant an' had the Lord's favor. So I don't wanna hear ya poke tease at ya younga brotha. Ya both got power. It's from the Lord."

This sermon was in no way an atypical lesson for Floyd to give, his knowledge of the bible as well versed as his knowledge of those fields, as keen as my own training for housework when I was younger—when I was blessed to read books by Dostoevsky, Woolf, and Chopin during my free time. Each of these distinct skills was reared in us since we were little and never went away, like the mastery of learning to ride a bicycle. The boys seemed partially entertained by this story, Jesse taking it upon himself once the story had ended to show his complete lack of understanding as he shoved Fletcher's arm and sent the boy falling into the dirt. Fletcher brushed off his sleeves then took chase after Jesse who, although bigger, was not necessarily faster. The two ran wildly amongst the blooms and around the piled sacks near the middle of the field, the dust leaving a trail behind them that eventually curved in our direction and caught Floyd's nose just as he reached me.

"Boys!" Floyd shouted then sneezed loudly. "Don't let me tell ya agin."

The boys slowed their pace along the outer edges. Floyd turned to me with his handkerchief in hand as he used it to wipe his nose and eyes.

"Damn sun's gonna get 'em faster than the fields," Floyd said, still sniffing as he dabbed once more.

"They just boys," I acknowledged.

"But this here ain't no playground," he said. "An' this ain't their home, either. Ain't time for that. Now, ya come out here for what, ya say?"

"Silva needs Jesse at the main house," I said.

"Ya can't take one uh my workers away," he argued. "What's he gonna do there?"

"We need him to help with moving the Missus's wardrobe," I said. "Should only take a few minutes. Miss Lula won't have it there another second. You know how she gets."

"Since when ya get so weak, Bernie?" he said teasingly, now turning to the boys who walked inside the shaded area. "Jesse, ya go wit' Bernie, but come right back, ya hear."

Jesse rushed over, bringing with him that towering presence.

"Come on," I said. "Your mother's got a task for you at the house."

Jesse smiled, relieved to be out of the sun and perhaps even happier to try his hand at something new. Honestly, who knew, but his smile cast as something permanent even if it was just housework.

Although he sailed leaps and bounds above me, he still appeared juvenile, that energy he had unable to be contained like most boys his age. He kicked at rocks and picked up sticks wherever he saw them, leading me to constantly direct him to "put that down" or "don't do that" or "don't get so dirty."

He sighed a huge relief once we'd entered the house, that coolness always welcoming when coming from outdoors. He looked around him curiously, walking loudly as he clumsily bumped into this or that, unaware of the silence that home demanded. Silva turned the corner and shushed him immediately, her pointed finger raised to her lips as she blew.

"Be mindful, Jesse," she said. "You ain't at home."

"Yes, ma'am," the tall boy replied.

The three of us tiptoed into the bedroom where the wardrobe and dresser were located. Miss Lula rested in the adjacent room where the items were to be placed, not necessarily her usual quarters but an equally dim space where she often sat, dependent upon her mood—usually a foul one, as it was on this day. Jesse bent down and lifted the heavy dresser by his own strength, his arms wide enough to secure both sides without any help from Silva or myself. Silva guided him as he carried it from the room into the hallway while I remained behind to remove the remaining clothes from the wardrobe so it might be just as easy to carry.

With my arms loaded, I turned to see their swift return.

"Damn thing can stay right where it is for all I care," Silva muttered. "Ain't worth a dime anyway."

There was time enough to retrieve one final blouse and slip from its sliding door before the two stopped my efforts completely. Silva pushed Jesse in front of the wardrobe, where his frustration instantly met similar chides from next door, as I could indeed hear the Missus fussing from within her room.

"What's going on?" I said.

"Ain't nothing," Silva swore. "Jesse, just get that thing and be done."

Jesse did as she said and lifted the wardrobe, Silva leading him once more into the hallway while I followed with the remaining clothes to be placed inside.

As we entered, Miss Lula sat rigidly in her chair. I followed her eyes, expecting them to sicken at the sight of our dirty shoes on her pristine floor, or for her to insist Jesse place the wardrobe near the window instead of the bed, or near the mirror where she could reach it more easily, or just over by the cabinet as that location made the most sense to anyone with half a brain. Yet she displayed no annoyance at all and made no sound of disappointment. It was completely silent as both Jesse and Silva inspected the wardrobe and dresser for any nicks or handprints the Missus might discover in her persistence. I made myself busy arranging the clothes. This went on for several minutes when I suddenly turned to the Missus out of fear of that continued calm.

"Silva," I called with my sights set on the Missus. "Look."

Silva turned. The Missus remained stock-still with her eyes placed in a vacant stare, her body stuck like some wood carving lettered and trimmed by a fishtail spade.

"It's okay, Miss," Silva said.

Silva soothed the Missus, stroking her gently.

"She's goin' to be alright," Silva added to us, speaking with a softness that brought life once more to Jesse's face. "She's just having a seizure. She's goin' to be just fine."

As if given permission to finally let go, Miss Lula began to convulse and shake with the protection of Silva's guiding arms around her.

"Bernice," Silva commanded in full control, "you get that side. Just make sure she don't hit nothing."

Beside the flailing child I stooped with my arms out, not necessarily sure of what I was guarding against. It was long, this one, longer than any other fit I'd seen the Missus have, which made that day appear all the more cumbersome in comparison to other days in the fields, where not much happened besides the cotton and the heat as we picked and chopped and sang and grunted the repetition all day long. What seemed an eternity was no more than a minute, although the Missus's body remained a trembling wreck that still hinted of the fit she'd endured. Over the chaos of her involuntary spasms and kicks and screams, which still emerged every so often, came the sight of Jesse's face tucked far in the distance, his warm eyes awash at sea and panicked, a timidity in him I had never seen before, although I knew it to always be present in children.

The convulsions lasted for several more seconds before they finally ceased for good, and the Missus fell limp to any cause. Silva then eased the Missus back in her chair, Miss Lula's arms falling over its supports as her head reared back like that of a drunk. When the Missus did finally open her eyes for the first time by her own cognizance, she looked about the room wildly.

"It's okay," Silva insisted, holding the Missus's shoulders and soothing her gently.

"Silva," the poor woman called out wretchedly. You couldn't help but feel sorry for her.

"Yes, Miss," Silva said.

Silva turned to Jesse and whispered sternly, "Jesse, you gets back to your duties."

And like that, just as Jesse turned to leave, I saw it, that momentary fix they had on one another, which Silva did not see, that chance meeting of their eyes as Jesse and Miss Lula encountered each other for the first time in years, separated by only a decade or two, excited like passing puppies on the street. Jesse noticed my attention on him and left the room quietly without another peek, his feet much softer than they had been when he'd first entered the house.

Silva later described to me the regularity of those attacks as we sat alone inside the kitchen. She told me they were brought on by stress and that the Missus often skipped her pills, which increased their frequency. There was no need to inform Mr. Kern, Silva insisted, adding that he would only blame the staff for his wife's misdealing. That these attacks happened every now and then but were nothing to go panicking over. That we could pretend it never happened, and so we did. Then, possibly to ensure my silence, Silva spoke freely about the Missus in a manner that she had never spoken in before, gossiping to me, and I did not turn her away.

"She tolds me about the attacks," Silva said in a whisper. "Said she ain't never felt something so strange before in her life, but that it's always been there since she was little. Said it's a feeling like she's far away and she can't get to herself. Said it's like death, she could only imagine. She swears that when she comes to, she's more relieved than she's ever been to just be back in the land of the living and see and taste and hear things again. She thinks every time it happens, she's finally gonna die. Said nothing like it in the world."

Silva nodded her head with these last words as I nodded back my reassurance that she could indeed trust me. Neither Silva nor I mentioned the attack to Mr. Kern and neither did the Missus, who would surely be chastised by the old man for having forgotten to take her medicine.

Only Floyd mentioned the mishap when he complained about Jesse's absence in the fields just before Silva and the boys left for home.

"He's all yours tomorrow," Silva assured him, waving Floyd off, as was her way, I soon discovered—that hand a welcoming or dismissing entity, to say the least.

CHAPTER 4

The next day was just as busy as the day before, and it would be that way for several weeks to come. The cotton sat high on the horizon, yet so did the dried bristles from the pickers' work as that once-colorful spectrum shrank to mere quadrants of the fields. The heat that had worsened over the summer did not fade as everyone hoped and instead lingered in the plastered walls of the kitchen following breakfast and the baking of biscuits. It sat stout in certain hallways that allowed in such boisterousness from the sun with their uncurtained windows, and it particularly bothered the Mister's parlor, which seemed to be hotter than the actual outdoors.

The Missus was smart and avoided these areas, whereas Mr. Kern foolishly walked directly into them, his temper roused and heavy with curses that fell from his lips like the running of bathwater when that tub would at first be too hot to sit comfortably, but later the water would mellow if just left alone.

Silva and I located outside tasks to complete during his riots, finding joy in the trimming of hedges that seemed to grow each second of that summer or the milking of cows, even if they protested our frequency. There seemed to always exist this trade-off between the Mister and Missus that when she was content he was angry, and with his joy came her sorrow. Nonetheless, these weeks saw her in considerably higher spirits as she took her needlework to the porch for days at a time, which allowed a slight color to return to her face and natural highlights to dance upon her golden locks. From her position, she could see the workers in the fields, although she rarely looked up for more than a fleeting glance in their direction. She'd often smile when Silva brought glasses of lemonade or other delicacies, which the young woman accepted then continued without a fret in the world. Her beauty during those days was how I imagined her to be when Mr. Kern first married her, her cheeks of a certain color and her face animated to a smile by more than chance alone.

Silva returned to the house with an empty glass and saucer just as Mr. Kern barged in. The two circled each other before Silva finally eased away inside the pantry, placing the Missus's bussed tray within the cupboard.

"I swear there's no beating this heat," Mr. Kern complained.

Silva rolled her eyes then calmed her face before she continued.

"Well, I fixed some cold lemonade if you'd care for some," she offered.

"That there's too sweet," he said without even tasting it. "I can't stand it syrupy."

"I can fix you one separately," Silva said.

"No, don't bother," he scoffed. "It'd probably come out the same way. Just have the Missus come in from that porch. Last thing we need is another sickness on our hands."

"Yes, sir," Silva said.

Silva walked stubbornly to the porch with a slow, tiresome gait that seemed more like an ornery child set to some unwanted task than a servant charged by her employer. We all dreaded disturbing Miss Lula during these moments of contentment, as her joy brought peace to the house that did not exist otherwise. There Miss Lula sat, her eyes the deepest blue, her dress the color of sunshine as it clung to her slender frame. Upon hearing Silva's footsteps, the Missus looked up and smiled.

"I swear I can't eat or drink no more," she said kindly.

"No, Miss, I ain't here for that," Silva said.

"Good, 'cause I thought you were gonna make me, I swear," Miss Lula joked, chuckling at her own bit of humor, which was rare to say the least.

"Mr. Kern was just wondering if you wanted to sit inside for a bit, rest your eyes for a blink before supper."

"No, I'm quite fine out here," she said. "This heat's not nearly as bad as what's inside."

"Well, I can't force you, but Mister's real concerned you might grow ill again and I must say, I can't blame him."

"Tell him I'm not coming!" she yelled. "And that's final."

It turned out that when she did return to the house, she was pleasant again and smiled just as brightly during dinner, to which Mr. Kern looked away and focused on the lack of seasoning in his food, smacking his lips loudly as he tried to distinguish the source of that bad taste.

"Silva!" he called nastily, watching as she turned the corner into the dining room. "Something just don't taste right here."

"It tastes fine to me," Miss Lula chimed in before Silva could apologize. "In fact, it tastes even better than it normally does. I loves Silva's fried chicken."

Mr. Kern scowled as Miss Lula grinned bigger than a naughty child, holding her cup to her mouth to keep from completely laughing out loud.

"I told her she should start a business," Miss Lula continued. "Call it 'The Best Darn Fried Chicken This Side of the Delta.' Sure did."

Mr. Kern smiled a slow grin that cracked along the lines of his face and seemed altogether sinister once it was completed.

"I guess you're right, Lula," Mr. Kern assented.

Possibly he'd hoped his agreeableness would deflate her ego or maybe this trick would get her to shut up and quit that foolish behavior, but either way, he did not add to her childishness, saying simply, "That'll be all," and watching Silva leave the room.

Miss Lula's eyes brightened, the repetition of her fork hitting the plate seemingly awakening her thoughts in the silence that crept over and under and through.

"I tell you, you're sure on a rampage," Miss Lula said looking solely in Mr. Kern's direction. "This food got good flavor. It's probably something in you that's spoiled."

She waited.

"Anyhow, I thoughts you liked Silva," she said. "Guess I was wrong."

Mr. Kern ate his meal quietly, poking his tongue with his fork yet never delivering a word in opposition or giving her a reason to continue. He lit his pipe then sighed a loathsome expression that covered his face and eventually faded into lasting fatigue.

"I just never understood it," the Missus said. "You been good to her for years, and now you can't stand her. You know, George?"

She looked into his eyes but gave up when he remained silent.

Following supper, Silva and I cleared the table and washed the remaining dishes. The boys had returned to the house from the fields and waited by the side door for their mother just as they did each night. Silva gathered her hat and purse as well as a small bag of leftover cornbread and chicken from dinner, which was always allowed by the Mister and Missus if there was enough, when suddenly Miss Lula appeared at the doorway.

"Miss!" Silva jumped. "What ya need?"

"Don't worry, Silva," Miss Lula said. "Just thought I might rest on the porch tonight and figured I'd stop here for a bit of coffee to take with me."

"Sure thing," Silva said, removing her hat and purse while grabbing the pot from the stove.

"You go on home," Miss Lula instructed. "Bernice can manage."

Silva looked at me fearfully then placed on her hat once more and took her purse from the nail and her bag into her hand as she opened the door to the sounds of her boys' laughter.

"You have a good night, Miss," Silva said.

At that moment, a spark reawakened inside the Missus as she looked out toward the sound of that laughter and caught sight of the passing culprits just as the door closed, their silhouettes crossing before her like flashes amongst the shadows at dusk, as brought about by those occasional cars that did pass along the isolated road. She turned to me and smiled, a contentment having built in her that replenished with each breath she took then gave away in heavy sighs. It all seemed so childish, yet with her it was often this way, and we all dealt with it. She giggled and twisted in her chair until I finally presented her coffee, which she marched outside like some teenager who had been given extended curfew for the evening. There she sat for only a few minutes before dumping the coffee in the grass and returning to her quarters. Still, at breakfast the next morning, she remarked on how great it was to sit outdoors at night, how the air was much cooler and the crickets just dazzling as they croaked and hopped all around her, how the Southern summer was like no other, not that she had ever experienced another. She bade Silva to sit with her a while longer, since Mr. Kern was not keen to listen to her ramblings, leaving me to command the regular household duties in Silva's absence. Needless to say, Mr. Kern did not like it one bit, yet he tolerated it for as long as he could, as long as that season allowed or his stomach could manage the turmoil of her content, until alas, the cold came once more to that small town.

CHAPTER 5

By November the harvest neared its end and so did the collection of pickers. Only a handful of workers remained, although they, too, would soon be gone. The fields were once again as bare as that eternal damnation that spread during this time of year, where the long running of a picket fence met the sparseness of trees and their bald exteriors cast out over the plains and that flatness. Fletcher worked beside me in the barn, feeding the hogs and collecting whatever eggs the chickens reluctantly laid, while Jesse remained in the fields with Floyd. There was increasingly less work to do, and the boys would soon move on just like the other workers, to farms farther out that still held scattered blooms in the fields or find work in town if it was indeed available. Fletcher had grown fond of me during those weeks following the harvest and took to calling me "Miss Bernie" like his brother, relinquishing that formal title of my first and last name that he'd held to so firmly.

Fletcher had been at my side the majority of the day, his young mind troubled with questions that, if only a year or two older, he would surely never ask. Still, I indulged his curiosity, as he was a sweet boy and meant no harm, and there was no need to break his inquisitive spirit so early in life, though any other adult would surely have him mind his manners.

"Miss Bernie," he started on this day, his hand twirling a piece of yarn he'd found amongst the stash of hoes and rakes. "Where's your husband?"

I stared into his young eyes for a moment, allowing the shock of his question to settle into a smile before I continued.

"Someplace far from here," I said, picturing him now.

"Heaven?" he asked honestly.

"Not that far," I laughed.

"Well, why aren't you with him?" He scrunched his face as he pulled apart the yarn into strips.

"That's a good question, Fletcher. But only God knows."

Fletcher found a stick to break once the yarn was completely torn apart. He looked down and used the stick's pieces to scoop a metal shard into his hands then flipped the jagged square into the air from the perch of those twigs.

"So do you stay once the picking is over, too?" Fletcher asked, now using the shard to scratch lines into a piece of wood, having left the stick on the ground.

"I reckon I'll be here for a long time," I said.

"Me too," he smiled. "Mama says both me and Jesse can work here from time to time as long as Mr. Kern don't mind. And as long as we stay outta his way and be nice to Miss Lula."

Fletcher dropped the shard and returned to the stick as if it were something new.

"Well, if you wanna stay, you gotta do less talking and more working," I said, patting him on his bottom and sending him inside with a basket of eggs. "Take it straight in," I instructed. "Then come back."

His shadow followed him as he ran, that stubby stranger that knew not the height the young boy would soon obtain. A rustling grew in the trees and stirred the chickens inside the coop, yet nothing so unsettling as to warn me of approaching trouble, as within minutes of Fletcher's departure the Missus's screams made their way from within the house. The Missus had been in one of her moods lately, and I feared I'd sent the boy smack dab in the middle of her tirade. By the time I'd entered, Fletcher was already in tears.

Miss Lula stood near the sink where Silva dabbed her dress with a damp rag. Broken eggs covered the floor and seeped along the tinted caulk between square tiles while the basket sat upside down at Fletcher's foot, the smoking gun resting in plain sight for everyone to see.

"Bernice!" Miss Lula shrieked once she saw me.

"Yes, Miss?" I answered, fully aware of my crime.

"Don't you ever send someone inside the house for something you should be doing yourself! If you don't want the job, then we'll take it away."

"Yes, Miss," I replied even quieter than before, merely gathering the eggs and their yolks into the basket.

Just then Mr. Kern entered, his hands at his side like a gunslinger and eyes poised for the draw. He surveyed the calamity in silence then watched Silva's efforts with the rag. Yet in the corner where the culprit stood was where his eyes remained the longest, locked on Fletcher and the boy's tiny sniffles, which wavered in their intensity like a puckering flame when caught in the wind. For indeed Fletcher's entire face burned a deep red, his fair skin unable to hide the surge of emotion that built and burst through in long sobs that left his nose somehow redder than his face as he nearly rubbed it off in his fits. Given the boy's innocence, no one could dare stay mad at him for longer than a second, although Miss Lula seemed quite intent on doing so.

Mr. Kern observed the boy closely, a look in the old man's eyes that seemed more wistful than angry, a kindness toward the youngster that I was sure stemmed from that ripe beauty the boy possessed.

"I'm sure he didn't mean it," Mr. Kern finally said.

He continued to watch the boy, ending the standoff with his final decree, saying, "Bernice, clean this up."

The Missus gathered the soiled parts of her dress from Silva's hands and shoved her way past Mr. Kern.

"Fletcher, go on, get out now," Silva said to the boy.

Mr. Kern watched him leave, turning to Silva once Fletcher was gone with nothing more than a squint of his eyes as he left the kitchen for Silva and me to clean.

"I swear he just don't pay attention," Silva fussed once we were alone. "Sometimes I don't knows how's he gonna make it in this world. I swear they eats folk like that alive. Don't make it past the start line."

Silva and I both knew the world she spoke about and the dangers it held for those who were unaware of its malice. We'd seen it in the land and men's hearts and our dreams and now our nightmares.

After taking several deep breaths that staved away whatever thoughts or images she had just seen of her son adrift in this world, Silva took to her duties once more in restoring the kitchen to its previous sheen. Then, when the area was tidy, she went to find Fletcher, eventually spotting the boy near the stables, where

he sat alone. She lectured him for nearly an hour before returning to the house and placing the tree switch by the door. Floyd
heard of the mishap and lectured the boy as well, taking that same
switch in his hands and leaving the house right when the sun sat
as a red afterthought in the western part of the sky and the stars
had started to sprinkle upon our heads in light showers.

CHAPTER 6

Dinner was quiet that night, the Missus's glare as sharp as a prick from a rosebush thorn. Her eyes remained on the table where her food sat unconsumed. She constantly resettled in her chair, that noise being the only sound other than Mr. Kern's fork falling to his plate. The old man was the gentlest I'd ever seen him.

"Thank you, Silva," he praised as if the meal was prepared in a more extravagant manner than it was every other night. "This sure is good," he commented. "Got any more of them rolls?"

Miss Lula dropped her glass to the table, sighing a strained breath as she watched him fiercely. Her stare was capable of chopping off his head if he met her eyes even once. Silva returned with more sweet tea and lemonade, which Mr. Kern accepted, swearing it was the tastiest drink he'd ever had, insisting it must have taken hours to prepare, and proclaiming how lucky they were to have a servant like Silva in the house. They couldn't pay her enough, he insisted. Silva, however, showed no extra care toward his benevolence, merely bowing courteously before gathering their empty plates and returning with slices of pound cake for dessert, which Miss Lula only nibbled at, turning up her nose and frowning distastefully. As Silva left the room with their glasses, one empty and the other not, Mr. Kern cleared his throat, an act that gathered the attention of everyone seemingly in a mile's radius and indeed Silva as well who returned to the dining room to see what was the matter.

"I've been meaning to tell you," Mr. Kern said to Silva, "I think we'll have your older boy stay on and help out throughout the winter if he wants."

"Thank you, sir!" Silva replied graciously.

"He's a good worker," Mr. Kern said. "And Floyd likes him."

Surprisingly, this bit of news saw not one sad expression as I looked around to find smiles on everyone's faces including that of Miss Lula, who was never one to smile simply because of a happy ending.

"I know Fletcher was hoping to come by after school and maybe help out as well," Silva soon added.

Yet before Mr. Kern could reply, Miss Lula had already quit that bit of joy and protested quite fervently, saying, "It's already too much noise around the house as it is! Now, two servants is enough. This place ain't no schoolyard, everybody's children and brothers and sisters coming whenever they please!"

Mr. Kern acquiesced. "Lula's right. Should be enough work for the one but maybe not the other. But if he wants to stop by sometime, he can."

Mr. Kern watched the smile return to Silva's face. They both watched each other, their eyes indulgent and irrevocably joined. I looked to Miss Lula's eyes, which were quite different.

"No, George," she said. "You make your exceptions all you want, but this is not one."

The young woman had never appeared so grown up in my presence, staring without blinking, folding her arms across her chest while waiting for any sound to slip past his lips that she might pounce on it.

"What do you know of my exceptions?" he said meanly. "I'm not a man of even one."

She steadied her eyes. Her body was stiff, and her voice lowered to a snarl.

"I can sure think of one," she said. "And what I remember, it's the only thing you love."

The room fell quieter than any disagreement or typical reversal of mood, the Mister's fork tapping his plate in the same vibration as his trembling body, which made for the only movement in the space around us. Seated there, he appeared to inflate like a growing balloon made taut with venomous air, possessing a mass that could crush any person, place, or thing if it got in his way. Silva left the dining room without a further peep in the Missus's direction, gathering her hat and purse and meeting the boys at the fields instead of the kitchen door as usual, leaving the tension inside the house to persist like a surging wave that built in size as it traveled.

"What's the darn meanin' a this?" Floyd argued when she arrived, knowing he had at least another hour with the boys before their work was done.

"Boys!" she shouted, taking Fletcher by the hand and leaving Jesse to apologize to Floyd.

Floyd's explanation of these events was simple as we sat in the backhouse with a cup of coffee between us and the remnants of our meal scattered about the table.

"A house of cards," he began, "they bound ta fall down eventually. Ya see, the Missus was promised ta Mista Kern. Although she loved him, problem was he didn't love her. Married her at seventeen when she was still a child. Both her an' Silva pregnant at the same time. Gave birth almost together, Silva wit' Fletcher an' Missus with Elizabeth. Practically raised the boy in the house till the girl fell ill, 'bout age three. Then Missus never wanna see Fletcha agin. Can't stand the sight a him. Buried Elizabeth up at the church. Missus was never the same agin."

Floyd's words lingered in the space as he and I sat a while longer with the smell of coffee and sweet rolls thick upon our breaths, his mind lost mostly in memories of the house when the Missus and her daughter filled that place with laughter and a curtain never sat unparted in a single room.

CHAPTER 7

For days no one did speak or listen to a single thought outside of their own. Each moment fell into another, and for weeks I could not answer surely what time or day of the week it truly was. Jesse had remained on at the house as planned, working with Floyd in the fields, while Fletcher did not show his face nor have any mention of his name after that heated dinner. I thought of him often, any joy I felt clouded by his troubled face, which would come to me like a bad dream and persist despite my attempts to wake up. Silva went about her duties with no extra spark of kindness, retracting from me even that slight warmth she'd started to show. Indeed, she served me pancakes with cold syrup. She gave me butter for toast that was not softened enough to spread. She made me lunches that were not concluded with a slice of her warm 7 Up cake.

Still, some things did continue as usual. Most days following that evening and its dinner, the Missus took her needlework and a slice of pie out to the front porch as she sat for hours in view of those languished trees and fallowed fields that surrounded their home this time of year. For the Southern winter was indeed a cruel monster, we all knew, not necessarily colder than most but just as punishing with its lack of color—the once-green grass now a pale yellow, the leaf-covered trees that made tolerable the torrential rain now stripped of all life, the iced-over ground a pathetic reminder of the sleet that never turned to snow. It was heart wrenching, the loss we felt, the voids that reached so deep into those dark places that existed when nighttime came, and we were alone with our thoughts and our God. Still, the world continued in all directions, and the Missus sat in full view of it all despite its insipidness, her thoughts known only to herself, although her eyes did hint at their meaning.

It was during these times that the plantation could seem so lonely, when we were left to our inhabited minds, until a passing car or truck on the road reminded us we were not so isolated and that others did exist, even if we knew not a single one on a level deeper than the absence left by their passing. Nonetheless, during this time of sadness, the Missus showed signs of life. As the months dragged on, she'd glance up every so often to see Floyd or Jesse pass with a load of mulch or new planks for the fence, and she'd smile and wave. She'd bite her bottom lip, tucking it under the top, and exhale loudly, blissfully. For weeks it remained this way until the cold finally came and the Missus fell terribly ill under the weight of her own insolence.

There was to be no more needlework outdoors that winter, Mr. Kern made certain to inform all of us. For weeks the Missus remained laid up in bed with Silva or myself bringing her food or a magazine or puzzles to rework, although Mr. Kern never visited even once. Even in her sickly condition Miss Lula was a hell-raiser, at one point locking herself in her bathroom and refusing to come out until I finally threatened to summon Mr. Kern to her room. She suffered every minute she sat inside that house, seemingly forgetting that she had once secluded herself indoors and would not bear the outside for even a second. During this time, Silva and I became her tormentors, as she put it, and this home her prison.

"Just one minute outdoors," she'd beg. "I swear, the sun would do me some good."

"No, ma'am," I'd argue. "It's ice-cold out there."

"What about a walk?" she'd say. "Anything to gets outta this bed."

"No, ma'am," I'd reply. "There ain't even a hint of sunshine today. Frost out there could kill you."

Then she'd finally turn over, mumbling and groaning until she'd fussed herself into an even weaker state.

"If it were up to me I'd leave this very instant," she'd say right before her mind fell blank. "I swear, Bernice, I'd leave right now, if the Lord would let me."

Then she was peaceful again, her soft skin lay gently over her forehead, her hair a golden crown that seemingly marked her territory as queen of this manor. As I watched her, I hoped she could at least dream of some distant place, even if she would never find it in this lifetime.

Still, that illness did not fade as the doctor had hoped, and within several months the fever had embedded itself deeper in her lungs, and she now lost most of her mobility and indeed all coordination in her legs, not to mention the color that summer had brought. Mr. Kern prepared for the worst, having us ensure the Missus was as comfortable as possible during these final days, as he put it.

"Don't talk like that, sir," I said. "The Missus gonna pull right through. Be just fine."

"Only time ..." he replied, leaving me to wait for the rest of his sentiment, although he made no further point.

Fields once again turned green as those early cicadas sprang from their dens and could be heard around the plantation during the evening hours just before the sun set, and the grass stiffened. Mr. Kern seemingly relished his quiet dinners alone with Silva each night, the sum of their thoughts compiled in polite gestures they'd share, through smiles he gave, and those infrequent slips of his fingers when she'd pass his glass or issue his plate—a moment to breathe her scent as she hovered or leaned closer.

All, that is, until the Missus quit her foolishness and rose from her bed in good spirits. With time she had lost that fever that had kept her down for so many months and now just sat spoiled rotten with expectancy that someone would care for her every need.

"You better shame the devil and stand up right now," I'd insisted. "Tell the Lord you want to live before He believe your act and take you on."

"Bernie!" she screamed once she'd stood from her bed. "I can feel my toes. I can wiggle them!"

"Yes, ma'am," I replied, "I see," sure as hell she always could.

"Lord willing, don't ever let me sit again," she declared.

"Well, sometimes, at least," I corrected her.

"No, never!" she screamed back. "I swear, I'll never stop moving."

She danced around the room like a possessed person, twirling to a song heard only inside her head.

"I think I'll even eat supper downstairs tonight if that's okay with you, dear Bernie."

The Missus had a sense of humor that I'd grown tolerant of in her company. For indeed during that time we both grew fond of one another, the Missus now calling me by that shortened name and certainly feeling a strong sense of attachment to my care and no longer that of Silva's, although with so much time together we had no choice but to grow closer. Miss Lula and I had developed an intimacy that bade upon her a proclivity to speak of those personal matters of the heart when only I was around, things she had never told a soul, as she'd close her eyes each night and fall into recollection of her previous life.

"I did love him," she once told me as she rested from a feverish day that almost saw her meet the Lord. "I wouldn't marry him if I didn't," she swore. "But a woman's love can only pull so far. A man can only stretch it so thin until it finally breaks."

She paused, opening her eyes like a child who peeks to be assured of a parent's love, relieved to find me still seated there as she glanced around to see the empty plate placed by the window, the hairbrush I'd used to smooth her hair full of golden shimmers. Tiring, she nearly closed her eyes again, but not before she'd found me once more and gently sighed, lay back, then continued with my hand in her hand.

"I knew he didn't love me," she said even weaker than before. "I could tell by the way he held my hand, like he was afraid or something, like he was my brother and I was his sister. He called Silva 'Silvi,' but had no name for me, only calling her by that name when he thought I wasn't listening. She never loved him back, and that made me happy. I thought he deserved it for treating me so bad.

"When Elizabeth was born, I just knew he'd have to love me. But there was Fletcher, and George had eyes for only him. Poor Elizabeth would just be there. She would call out to her pappy, and he would wave her away, kiss her forehead, then send her to me, and she would come running all happy, thinking her pappy loved her too. I prayed she would never know any different, and that prayer came true for when she died, she was as dumb to his indifference as ever. But I still knew, and I swore he would have not one happy day as long as I was here. I cursed that man and sent his beloved ape from this house—Bernie, please don't think any different of me. I done always done right by negras, but that boy remind me too much of what I lost. Anyhow, I allowed Silva to stay because she had no love for him and that alone made me the happiest in the world."

A contentment fell over the Missus's face with these words as she closed her eyes and curled up beside the warmth of my hip. She fell asleep instantly, waking only once throughout the night as she mumbled some indiscernible name then fell back asleep just as quickly as she had woken.

———

With her face a brushed application of crimsons and blues, and her hair fluffed to pageantry perfection, she was now ready to hobble downstairs for her first dining room meal in months.

"How do I look?" she fussed. "More or less?"

She panted, pointing to her flushed cheeks covered with translucent powder.

"You look just fine, Miss," I said, not sure which person she was trying to impress, as no one downstairs wanted or anticipated her arrival.

Although the house was fairly large, one could still hear voices from downstairs in the upstairs quarters where the Missus and I resided during those months of her illness. The house seemingly underwent a transformation during that time, as there was a sudden increase in the frequency of both Floyd and Jesse roaming the halls, yakking some foolish nonsense that came across as mere murmurs to our ears. The Missus never acknowledged their presence, although her eyes did seem to elate at the idea of newcomers, her stare fixed on the door, as if she'd hoped they'd enter. She'd wait until the voices passed then once again work whatever puzzle or needlework she had at hand. More often than not it was Jesse's voice we'd hear, as he had a gentle tone that caroled softly and faintly throughout the house.

Once the Missus finished dressing on this evening and felt certain she was flawless before the mirror, she defiantly wrapped her shawl about her and went charging for the downstairs area. Silva looked up from the porcelain set with surprise, the first to see the Missus as that scarlet vixen turned the corner, her ruby shawl like that of a seductress's whips and ties as it billowed listlessly around her collar.

"Miss, you're better," Silva said, drawing the attention of Mr. Kern, who looked up immediately.

The young woman indeed looked remarkable. Although she had not fully regained that previous summer's color and her hair was not as danced upon by the sun, she still exuded a heartiness that made her appear supple and as beautiful as the next. Mr. Kern rushed to her side, taking her hand as he eased her into the chair. She accepted his assistance, though she was not as impressed as me by his efforts, as was evident in her strict glance around the room at the subjects she had not glimpsed in months. I first thought I saw inattentiveness in her gaze, but upon closer inspection I soon discovered it was more of a discarding of those objects that had been placed there at one point, to appease her, as if the woman no longer needed anyone or anything. Truly, it seemed no trifle bothered her, no word stuck upon her tongue, her thoughts set on some specific idea that she mulled over without need for company.

"Let me fix your plate," Silva said, as the Missus had indeed entered in the middle of dinner when Mr. Kern's meal sat mostly consumed.

Silva rushed to the kitchen as I followed, their voices trailing us from that brief distance away, choppy conversations where neither answered more than sufficiently necessary to respond to the other or complete their own thoughts. The Missus laughed loudly on several occasions, although we hadn't heard the precipitating joke. These haughty snickers seemed greatly exaggerated, though no one knew what to expect from the Missus now that she had returned from the dead. One might so easily believe without a second thought that the young princess had indeed morphed into a pleasant being overnight, as if that knocking at death's door had made her want to live again.

"What miracle brought this?" a voice soon said. "I never thought I'd git the pleasure agin."

Before any thoughts were with me, I fled the kitchen and made my way inside the dining room. When I arrived, both Floyd and Jesse stood at the opposite door, Floyd with that look of startled joy still upon his face and Jesse unmoved by the unfolding situation, although he still smiled politely in the Missus's direction. Astonishingly, that good spirit the Missus had developed was not short-lived, and she now smiled and even blushed before Floyd and the boy.

"Thank you, Floyd," she said, her eyes far from him. "I feels much better thanks to your sister and her care."

Mr. Kern glanced up with a look that was neither grateful nor relieved, for the first time making it easier to decipher his wife's emotions than his own.

"I just thanks God that ya here," Floyd said, clasping his hands together and looking up toward the sky.

The Missus kept her eyes stayed on Jesse, this powerful creature before her, a boy of such substance that he commanded stares and forced even the bravest soul to cower in fear if, upon accident, he or she stepped too close. To touch his frame was to meet a structure so solid that it seemed almost indestructible, fully encased in flesh that burned warm on contact and hinted at the fire that blazed within. Indeed, he was always warm, even in winter when all around had the protection of heavy coats and gloves, he wore none.

Miss Lula seemed not to breathe in his presence, as if she feared some type of retribution for these actions, and I feared the poor soul would surely faint from having held her breath for so long. If before there was said to be a lack of purpose in her eyes from that day I'd first met her, then today she was a woman renewed, for from that wretched spirit now came compassion and kindness and, dare I say, love.

Remembering his business inside the house, Floyd called to Jesse who turned and followed him down the hall without a second glance toward the Missus. Miss Lula seemed unaffected as well, turning her attention toward the door as Silva brought forth a plate of okra, lima beans, and pork chops. The Missus ate quietly with no need for attention, her supper acquiring all her thoughts as she examined the beautiful porcelain that showed at the end of her meal. And though I didn't condone it, part of me understood the Missus's wrath for Mr. Kern, recalling that tidbit Floyd divulged to me that evening before he slouched off to bed muttering half awake and half asleep. "Mister didn't even cry when young Elizabeth died. I don't think he ever cried a day in his life since tha day he was born. Never will."

The Missus, however, had cried on several occasions in my

presence. Woefully, she'd sunk her head into her pillow and sobbed, then muttered lonely words and cursed the Mister's name, but not tonight. No, tonight she wrapped her shawl tightly around her neck as she delighted in the evening's chill, trapped here like some princess inside a tower, lost in a luxury that came at such an expensive cost, yet she did so with a smile and a conviction that needed no words to define its cause.

CHAPTER 8

"Bernie, be pleased," Miss Lula said as we sat together on the front porch some days following her recovery, her eyes taking note of my repressed tears as I'd glanced at the newspaper she read and noticed the front-page article: *Burning*.

Her with her needlework and me with a basket of snap peas that I'd picked and washed, the sun burning hotter every day as summer approached in just-noticeable increments over the cooler morning, drowning it slowly in shorter nights. Darn humming-bird came by, and we watched it for nearly ten minutes, Miss Lula resting her head on the cushioned part of the rocker while I sat directly on the ground with the basket to my side.

"Seems like every day there's something new," she said with the newspaper opened, her thoughts having careened like this for several days as we'd sat together on that porch. "Don't make no sense. Wish they would just end it all and everything go back to normal. That's what I pray."

She looked to me for confirmation that I felt the same. But Miss Lula had prayers much different than my own—her prayers born of her circumstance, and mine born from mine, as if there was a white god and a black god depending on the petitioner. And while I knew there was no need of beating your head on the same stubborn stone unless you planned on learning something from it, and that I should just smile like usual, her words still brought nothing but pain to me, as those memories of Henry and our past came to mind as swiftly as his life had likely departed, that life he'd given to me in song and time and love. I said nothing to her, my anguish bursting from the seams and running down my sides, pressured like firemen's hoses within my pursed lips. I was lost here, forever confined in today and yesterday with no future, a clear view of the trails that bus left behind as my soul swept up in the smoke from its exhaust. Unseen in rearview mirrors, invisible to them like black faces on the pavement, like buoys lost at sea, I could no longer keep quiet.

I knew very well that the negro controlled almost nothing in this world, having that white hand strangled around our necks so tight, with our sights in constant view of what little we had—our toil and our souls and our God—His land a bounty stretched in front of me, belonging only to the white man. That surge of blood coursed through my brain and caused those few cars on the road before me to burn red hot beneath the sun as it cast mirages over the fields like a sea of watery graves out amongst the cotton and peat moss, graves that ran for miles in both directions and caused the soil to sway just like that vast ocean it mimed, those graves placed out there for the just folk, I knew, someplace my Henry most likely laid.

For here, the negro worked, his hands grown harder and his heart just the same, his hair not flowing and dainty but rough, his eyes a darkness that grew to handle the sun, and his feet a plagued callus he stood upon. Looking up from my seat of discontent I found the Missus still in her frustrated state and felt my stomach sour, my tongue water with urge to speak, and my hands tremble from that struggle to hold it all down. I could say so many things at that moment but knew Floyd was right, and so I kept quiet, forcing those thoughts back into the depths of my mind for God's watchful eye to keep. Instead, I remembered Henry as I did each night, and his smile gave me peace. I thought of Floyd and acted like the good nigger I was supposed to be as I watched the land along with the Missus, the cotton a misery to me that she prayed would always be present in our lives, something my daddy knew and his daddy before him, too—that whiteness to be a devil.

CHAPTER 9

The Mississippi summer seemed to grow hotter each year, and that summer of 1967 was no different. Lord willing, we would make it through. The buds of the pagoda dogwood hung low, fanned out over the horizon in a white pageantry of pomp and dance, circumstance enough for us to walk amongst the fields in admiration of their splendor, which the Missus and I did almost every morning before the sun rose too high and suffocated us in its grief. She'd taken to having two showers a day, yet even then the heat was unbearable, that lasting kindness of a spring day long gone while in its wake stood the bearer of oppression. Even during the night we stayed out from under covers, as the sun never fully retired, even if it did turn its head.

In slow succession we made our way from the kitchen to the front porch, Miss Lula unwilling to sit indoors on any day now that there were workers in the fields. She was excited by the work of those men, insisting to me how she could just *never* spend so much time under that hot sun, how she could live a hundred years and never grow to like it one bit and how those people just got it in their blood. She had kept her good spirits since her recovery and seemed to strengthen each day we watched those men, calling for vast amounts of time in my company, which kept me from the fields. On occasion, Floyd would toss a wave or send over some piece of fruit he'd plucked from a tree out back. Missus never ate any, yet she enjoyed it all the same, that feeling of connectedness that grew just by being present with those around her. Often Floyd would join us on the porch once his gift was presented, resting his dog-tired feet and exhaling loudly as he took in the shade and a cold glass of water, the remainder of that glass's contents serving as a cool bath over his head as he stood and went back to work. When Jesse returned after having taken a week off from the house, some excuse he'd given about a trip to Jackson or thereabout, Floyd sent him over with the plucked item that still bore the leaves of the tree on its stem.

"Bernie, go wash it," Miss Lula demanded as Jesse presented it.

Ain't never eaten one bite a day in her life and now she wanted to try it.

Jesse placed the fruit in my hand and watched as I walked it inside, his hand having been confiscated by the Missus who prevented him from leaving. I hurried to the kitchen with the fruit nearly falling to the ground in my haste. Nonetheless, by the time I'd washed it and returned, Jesse was seated by the Missus with her hand upon his shoulder to keep him there. My attempts at catching the boy's eye were blocked each time by the Missus's protruding knee.

"Jesse," I called in a voice that screeched from my body like shoddy brakes.

His eyes met mine in a state of panic.

"Take a piece back for you and Floyd," I instructed him.

Jesse attempted to stand but was stopped immediately by the Missus's grip as she squeezed his shoulder and he eased back to the ground.

"If only for a bit," she said slyly. "Floyd does it all the time."

Jesse settled at the Missus's feet, a stiffness in his movements that never allowed him to get too comfortable, I was happy to see.

"So how's it been so far?" the Missus asked.

"Just fine, Miss," Jesse said.

"Well, I don't see how you manage with this heat," she continued.

"It's not so bad, Miss," he said. "Once you get used to it."

"I tell you, I'd just melt in a minute," she said. "Can barely keep up with Bernie as it is in the mornings."

"Yes, Miss," he replied.

"So tell me, how's your brother?" she asked, that bit of devilment finally peeking through as she lifted her lip and flashed her piercing fangs. "We sure do miss him around here."

"He be fine, Miss," Jesse said.

"Wished we could've kept him," she swore, placing her sights on me now. "Just ain't enough work sometimes. Nothing you can do though."

"He understands," Jesse said. "Mama sent him down to Jackson this summer with my aunt and uncle."

"This's no place for a smart boy like him anyway," she said with a smile.

"Yes, ma'am," he replied.

"But, Jesse, you gonna stay, right?" Miss Lula asked.

"Of course, Miss," he said. "I likes it here."

"Good, then we'll have to have you stop by more often," she said, her smile growing larger. "Maybe let you help out in the house as well."

"Thank you, Miss," he said warmly, oblivious to her undertones.

"Well, I best not keep you or else Floyd will pitch a fit," she said.

"But be sure to stop by tomorrow and we'll see what work we have for you inside."

Jesse stood and took the pieces of fruit from my hand, the Missus watching this exchange as if she were a referee awaiting some action that was against the rules. Jesse turned to her, their eyes meeting just as they had on that one day inside the house. Jesse was young and knew beauty, but he also knew not to stare at a white woman too long, and so he quickly made snug the fruit in his hands and took off at a slight jog toward the fields.

The Missus exhaled then turned to me, having lost that smile or any bit of encouragement that would assure me she was still in good spirits.

"Don't be mad, Bernie," she said. "It's just a bit of fun."

Miss Lula then returned her eyes to the fields and the workers there, later adding once things were much quieter and the sun had completely passed away, "I think it's a change of heart I'm having, but who can know for sure."

I didn't believe her as much as I would a drunk in a bar pleading for another round. That night I took Floyd inside the backhouse and disclosed to him the events of that day. I told him about the Missus's lust for the boy, as I saw it, and insisted we keep him away from the main house as long as possible. Whatever she was planning, it would happen soon, I said, and could possibly cost the boy his life. It was decided between us to keep this bitter knowledge to ourselves, forcing Silva to remain in the dark a while longer, at least until we knew for sure what the Missus would do. In the meantime, Floyd would take Jesse farther out each day and have him work where the Missus had no chance of seeing him. Floyd would still bring fruit by the house as usual, so as not to draw attention to our deceit, but only at certain times when the Missus was not present, and he would place it on the front porch as if he'd somehow missed us so that she could never inquire about the boy. We would keep this up until further details of her heart were known.

CHAPTER 10

The next day we walked, the Missus and I, around the tulip trees and the magnolias that stretched high up. We followed the paths the tractors left then crisscrossed the fields' narrow rows. We found a shaded area and slowed our speed then hightailed it to high heavens within a hotspot that had no trees to block the sun. We walked faster until we'd cleared that devil's beloved playground before finally slowing to our normal pace as we continued toward the sticker bushes and other shrubs outside the house.

The Missus was a thing of beauty, her shawl wrapped around her hair like a turban, her golden ringlets falling in atypical places that made her seem almost thrown together with an effortlessness that befell her like rain. Her eyes looked about her with a sense of expectancy, somehow aware of the future, with no need to wait, hope, or pray as us regular mortals. For her eyes were bent to God as one who commanded His armies and walked with the conviction of that One who had breathed life into every man, and with this she knew her power.

Once our walk had ended beside the shaded porch, she insisted we take another, that omniscience she had leading her to see things I couldn't, as she declared more animated than at any other time that she just wasn't tired yet.

"Another?" Silva protested, emerging from the house with drinks to conclude our stroll.

The Missus smiled.

"Here," Silva said. "At least drink this so you don't turn to stone."

Miss Lula took the glass and sipped it slowly, turning to me, for I had not yet accepted mine. Her gaze was sinful, having trapped all that Tree of Knowledge had to give and possessing it now fully in her sights.

"You two, I swear," Silva fussed.

"Better know good advice when you hear it," the Missus instructed me.

I reluctantly lifted the glass and drank, the coolness rushing down my throat just as the condensation fell along my wrist and forearm, that chill meeting almost immediately with the sulfur that encases a coconspirator's heart. I couldn't stand the sight of Silva, knowing my deceit, yet couldn't stand the sight of Miss Lula either. Once our glasses were both empty, I was eager to return to the fields, where Miss Lula and I sat with our backs facing each other, feet in the grass, alone in our plots.

The heat provoked a shorter route this time, just around the white flowers and bull bays east of the plantation. Miss Lula picked at their buds while I sat with my hands at my ankles and fanned the flies that dared approach. The Missus looked around for some specific target yet never seemed to find it, her eyes darting wildly and never settling even once in my company. I spied her movements like my very own shadow that bent then spread then covered the world around me. She walked with her hands clasped tightly as the wind kicked up dust, pushing it before her as if it somehow steered the way. Around one corner she met the contempt of a thousand gusts, while around another sat a wind sent straight from the swells of Hades, leaving her blinded for minutes at a time as she marched with one hand out front and the other covering her nose and mouth. Once the blustery assault drew tears from the Missus that were too numerous to continue, she gave up her mission, and we both returned to the house without a single word.

At the porch the fruit awaited us, bundled by a single thread of yarn and placed inside a bowl beside the Missus's chair. She looked at it furiously, having lost that bit of omniscience that would have surely warned of such an occurrence.

"What's this?" she said. "What am I, a dog? Some beast that has its food left on the ground until it eats? I would think I'm better than that. Wouldn't you say?"

"I reckon they were busy today, Miss," I tried. "Floyd never means any harm."

"I don't like what it implies, Bernice," she said. "Ain't no decency in it."

"Yes, Miss," I replied.

"I won't stand for it," she said. "Tell him not to bring it anymore if he's gonna do it like this, or we'll just chop the whole damn tree down. Fine with me either way."

The Missus stamped off and was not seen outdoors for the rest of the evening. Silva snooped to discover the motive for the Missus's foul mood yet quit her efforts when she deemed it best to stay out of her way or else she'd get an earful, too.

Mr. Kern had settled in his parlor beneath the murky light. He sat with his paper and his pipe, his eyes a magnet to those words even as the Missus crept in, easing by him with the tote containing her needlework and a blanket in case she got cold. She sat in a corner of the room opposite him where her frustrations could be clearly seen, although it still took several minutes for Mr. Kern to actually acknowledge her presence.

"Guess I might tell Floyd to watch the pigs tonight to make sure they don't fly away," Mr. Kern said without looking up.

"He should be told many things but not that," she said sharply.

"What's that supposed to mean?" he asked, finally placing aside his paper.

"Nothing," she swore. "Just some of his workers should be more careful, that's all."

"Then I'll tell him tonight," he said. "Anything I should know?"

"No," she answered before drawing her next words more kindly than she'd uttered any other. "Just some things out of place I noticed this morning during my walk. Nothing too important, but it still bears telling."

"Good," he said.

"But let me tell him," she insisted. "I wants to make sure he knows exactly where we saw them so that he knows for next time. You knows how I hate having to repeat myself."

"If you wants to, handle it," he said. "But tell me, how is it this heat don't bother you no more? Walking every day now."

"It's not so bad," she answered playfully, scrunching her face and rolling her eyes. "Once you get used to it."

These words brought a smile to her face that lasted longer than the amount of time it took for her to say them, as if a thought had latched onto her heart and wouldn't let go. Later that evening, she found Floyd outside the stables, still with that smile blatant as ever.

"Evening, Miss," he said as she approached.

"I swear it is," she replied. "Can't be nothing else."

"Yes, ma'am," he said.

"Tomorrow we'll have work for Silva's boy Jesse inside the house," she said. "Shouldn't take all day. I meant to tell you earlier but you weren't around. Just send him to the main house around noon. Should have him back within an hour or two before you can even miss him. You can send him with fruit, too, if you like."

The Missus turned and walked toward the house, a scowl covering her face as if it hurt her to breathe. Then, without a single thought to make it reasonable in the world, she turned and smiled as she waved to Floyd in likeness to a beauty queen on a parade float.

"I swear she crazy!" Floyd protested later that night as we sat in his back quarters. "Done gone plum mad. That boy can't come back here. Ain't safe."

Even if I agreed with him, there was little we could do aside from telling Silva who would rave stark mad at our theories of the Missus's attempts to taint her boy or, even worse, bring him harm.

"If we tell her, I swear it's only going to bring more problems for not only Jesse but Silva too," I said, as I was sure Silva would have no patience with the Missus and would go and get herself killed. "This thing involves a lot more people than just those two. It's all of us now."

It was for this reason that I agreed to watch the boy while he worked inside the house, never leaving him alone with the Missus and "never givin' 'er a chance ta ruin him," as Floyd insisted.

Jesse was sent for around noon the next day, that coldhearted being taking no chances the boy would not show and instead sending Silva to claim him. Silva left the house to me as she ventured outdoors to the back stable. Miss Lula and I sat at the kitchen table, the young woman's chatter a breathless assemblage of words and sometimes mere guttural sounds as she reviewed her plans for the work to be done. She would rearrange the entire house, she insisted, as long as it took.

"You mind your business and be done," I said to Jesse as soon as he entered, taking his ear privately when Silva and the Missus weren't looking. "You got one job to do, and then you get back to Floyd to help him out. Cool air doesn't mean a thing if everyone can't enjoy it."

Jesse smiled with that look of trouble, kidding as he normally did, although my pinch to his arm straightened him right up.

"You make sure you mind your manners around Miss, too," I said.

"Yes, ma'am," he finally said, fixing his face rather quickly.

"You do your job and be gone, or else I'll box your ears."

Miss Lula seized the boy's arm, pulling him to the table, although she was halfhearted in her reproach.

"We have work to do, son," she said. "Standing around'll see you passed up at heaven's gate. Now you don't wanna be left behind with the rest of them, do you?"

Silva noticed the boy's eyes still on me and prepared him for a lecture.

"Jesse," Silva said sternly, "you listen real good and pay attention now."

Miss Lula smiled at this bit of chastisement.

"It's okay," she promised. "Work inside the house can't be that exciting for a boy like him. Most boys prefer to be outdoors anyway. It shouldn't take too long."

"Still," Silva demanded.

"I'm sorry, ma'am," Jesse said to both Miss Lula and Silva respectively.

Jesse started his work inside the kitchen, forcing both Silva and myself to find duties elsewhere. During that time I took up chores in the barn, staying as close to that outside portion as possible, where you could hear a fluff of cotton fall from its stem if you listened closely enough. Silva kept busy in the upstairs quarters while the Missus walked about the outer stables, passing me every so often, yet never saying a word. She hadn't spoken to me or the boy since he'd entered. He worked a decent shift that day. By the evening, Miss Lula sent him back and promised she would call if need be.

"But ma'am!" he protested. "This here's barely done."

"It's okay, Jesse," she said. "Floyd needs you too. He insists you be back early."

And with this the division was drawn, as the next day Jesse came sneaking around the house in hopes the Missus would see him. And even though she did, she spoke not a word and allowed him to leave without ever knowing of her presence. When Floyd asked him where he'd been, the boy lied and said he'd gone out back for some water. Next day I caught him again poking around the bushes near the front porch when he thought no one was looking, telling me he'd wanted to see if there was landscaping that needed to be done because a handful of workers had finished their jobs and could use some more work.

"How about you worry about your own self, Jesse," I told him. "I see what you're doing and I don't like it one bit. If there was work to be done then you'd know it because you'd be doing it."

The boy smiled, still looking toward the main house just past my shoulder. He then laughed playfully, asking, "The Missus complained about the kitchen being in such shambles?"

"No, son," I told him honestly. "The Missus ain't seen the

insides of that kitchen since you last saw it. She couldn't tell you what color it was if you asked her today."

Jesse laughed, still defiant as ever, although the brunt of his defiance was saved for Silva when she discovered him one day circling the kitchen door at the height of the workday.

"Jesse, you done lost your ever-loving mind!" Silva said.

Her body trembled to a feverish pitch as the folds along her neck released their sweat.

He stood up tall to her, saying, "Miss Lula wanted me to finish the job, but Floyd won't let me, wanna keep me out there with him all day when I can do both."

"Floyd can't stop Miss Lula from doing a damn thing!" Silva insisted. "If she want you here, you'd be here."

"Floyd just wanna keep me out the house," he pouted. "Want me to work out there with him forever like I ain't got a brain."

"You ain't got what the Good Lord gave you if you expect me to believe that. Floyd ain't the master of this house. Now, you know better, Jesse."

The worst of his contempt, however, was said in private, my ear just happening upon those words as I drifted past the garden. Silva accused the boy of being a silly nigga, and he rushed off with his chest puffed up.

"I ain't no nigga!" he shouted back.

"You ain't no man either," she said.

"I *am* a man," he said quietly, these words uttered more for his own acknowledgment than anyone else.

"Then be one," she said. "You are what you do, Jesse."

"I work harder than any worker out here," he said.

"And if the Missus wants to bring you in, she will," she replied. "But you can't makes her."

I overheard them continue their arguing and name calling in hushed tones out by the back porch, when by a slip of my eye I spotted Miss Lula at her upstairs window, her hair at her shoulders and her eyes looking down, her cheeks a faint color that blushed and made her complexion appear alive and fervent.

CHAPTER 11

"I'm going!" Jesse fussed to Floyd one day following that argument with his mother, insisting that the Missus had sent for him despite Floyd's claims that she hadn't.

Just before noon, Jesse charged out over the rye grass, those wilting greens that had grown a solid foot after the rains and now reached the heights of the fescues that grew down by the Yazoo River. When he'd made it to the main house, the Missus awaited him, having taken her seat on that porch with her needlework in hand every day since observing the boy's disagreement with Silva, knowing he'd be coming sooner or later.

"Jesse!" she said, feigning a sense of surprise.

"Yes, Miss," he said. "Floyd give me permission to finish."

I cut him a stern look, but he turned away.

"I don't know," Miss Lula said, watching both our faces. "There's lots a work out there, and this house don't run on decorative wishes. We cotton people. Always have been. Always will be."

"I can do both if you like," he said. "I just thought you want it finished. Mr. Kern said it'd make you happy."

A lie if I'd ever heard one.

"You're an angel," she praised. "But work outside comes first, then you can help in here."

"Yes, Miss," he accepted.

"And no more running off without telling anyone," she said. "I heard about you coming to the house without Floyd's permission. You come when you want now. You have my permission as long as your work is done."

Jesse smiled at these words, returning to the fields that day with a weightlessness about him, his arms swaying freely and his legs lifting his body some ten inches above the ground. He would make amends with Floyd, yet each time the boy left for the house the wound would grow deeper.

After that encounter, Jesse found himself at the house every day that summer. Silva and I did our best to rearrange the results of Jesse's work, returning the house to some semblance of a home before Mr. Kern sat down for dinner, or at least shading parts of the boy's destruction as much as possible until Jesse returned on the next day or the next to finish it. However, it seemed that once Jesse was inside the house, the Missus forgot about him. He was only noticed by Mr. Kern, who'd spot a nail on the floor and howl. He'd look toward his usual sights at dinner to find them covered in plastic and ram his hands so forcibly that it shook the paintings from the wall.

The Missus's fickle mood was not surprising as she had family visiting from Little Rock, who had arrived the morning of Jesse's first week inside the home. Blindness could have provided more sight than those skewed headlights outside the car window as Floyd waved the family in just before the stroke of dawn.

"Let me take you to your rooms," I said as they emerged sleepily from the vehicle. "I know you dying for some rest after that long drive."

"Just the little ones," a stout woman said, mean as ever.

The three boys followed me inside as the woman and her husband met Miss Lula on the front porch. Miss Lula gave the boys kisses before leaving them to follow me to their bedrooms, the smallest one just barely making it as he fell asleep in midstride, requiring that I carry him and place him into his bed or else he would sleep right there on the hallway floor. The other two were not so easy, the middle one insisting that he have his own room and the oldest child demanding the same, although less adamantly.

"I don't have to listen to you!" the middle one shouted. "I'll tell my mama."

"And I'll tell Miss Lula," I replied. "She told me to have you boys sleep here. Now be a good boy and get to bed."

"Aunt Sissy don't control me," the middle one spat just as mean as he could. "We control *her*."

Either unable or unwilling to continue this fight, the older boy hesitantly obliged, leaving the middle child to continue his grief just long enough for that heaviness of sleep and a long journey to finally settle as he climbed into his bed with a fading insistence that he have his own room tomorrow.

Silva and Jesse arrived just as the family unpacked, Floyd taking Jesse to the fields right away while Silva began her work inside the kitchen. With this brief distraction, I stole off to Floyd's quarters and closed my eyes for a minute. Dreams were never hard to summon, and this time was no different as I pictured some far-off place where Henry awaited me beside the sounds of an infinite ocean that tapped and gurgled and lobbed its soft song. Those sounds met those of our own heartbeats, as I imagined the children's voices I heard to be those of our own. That I had nursed them to my breast and they'd known my inner touch. But still, there was something different about this place, and I saw it in the tide—the white surf a static motion that did not reflect some endless possibility of distant lands but instead the sights I'd seen every day out here. The air was harsh and brought tears to my eyes as I became painfully aware that I was alone in the cotton and nowhere else but Greenwood.

The children's voices came again, their footsteps racing about the stables wildly as I jumped to my feet and went to find them. John, Simon, and Matthew—mine for that weeklong period of the family's visit while Silva managed the house and Floyd the fields, and Jesse roamed in and out unchecked and unnoticed by all who were around except the Missus, who kept tabs on us all.

CHAPTER 12

There was no way to watch the three boys *and* Jesse. In the evenings, I would return to the house to see some new project he'd completed or just started, his presence announced only by the work he'd done or some tools he'd left in the kitchen. One day I found him chatting with the Missus as I passed the back stables with the three boys following me like the trains of my housecoat. His eyes showed remorse when he saw me, and he ended that conversation right quickly, the Missus turning to me then sauntering off toward the house, a devil in a white dress with satin hair.

Because of those three boys and their constant energy, I couldn't tell you which mission was more taxing. John, the oldest child at thirteen, was a smart boy, well-dressed and considerably better behaved than his middle brother, Simon, who at age eleven was a firecracker, cunning yet as simpleminded as a flea, round and plucked straight from his father's image, his pug nose sitting proudly on his face as he often scrunched it up and poked out his tongue at whomever issued directives that were not of his choosing. Then there was Matthew, age six, a sweetheart who had not yet learned the ways of this world, too young to see or understand this society's distinctions and, as such, was as loving toward me as he would be to his own mother.

The boys followed me during each of my duties around the farm and the back stables where I worked the cattle and kept the pen and chicken coop tidy.

"Can I do it?" John asked as we stood at the pigpen this day.

"Yeah, me too," Simon interrupted, not waiting for my response before he'd stuck his hand into the mix of cabbage and tossed it over the fence.

John then followed, having seen his brother's example and learning from it. Still, while John placed the food gently for the pigs to eat, Simon threw it directly at them, laughing each time they drew closer as he'd rear his arm back to get them again. He had some type of devil in him, chasing the chickens and smashing their eggs and pulling the cows' tails when he thought no one was looking. Then his father would merely pass and laugh, that proverbial thumbs-up the boy needed to continue his rampage.

Jesse had completed the entire kitchen and dining area by the time I saw that space again. It was beautiful, adorned with framed cabinets and matching doors, as well as fresh paint in both rooms that still smelled like new. He'd built a shelf by the kitchen door that stored the Missus's preserves and now started work inside one of the downstairs bathrooms, as she'd requested.

When I entered the house, the silence that once plagued this place when I'd first arrived had swiftly returned. Mr. Kern sat in his parlor and the Missus upstairs in her usual room, almost making me believe that these months of frantic haste and her deliverance had never occurred. If it were not for the Missus's revived color, I would be assured that they truly hadn't.

"Why, Miss?" I heard a voice ask from within her room, as I stood in the hallway just outside her door.

I counted the number of people inside the house. Silva remained outside with Floyd, Mr. Kern sat inside his parlor, and the Arkansas clan was gone for the afternoon. I recoiled then slipped back as a snake would when inclined to strike.

"There's no need even thinking about it," the Missus replied, her back to the door and the stranger's face veered toward the window, although the shades remained drawn and the dimness in the room was nearly impossible to see through. "There's nothing you can do about things like that. God's will be His will sometimes."

"But don't you miss her?" the man said.

"Sure," she replied. "I'd be fool not to. I think about her every day. She would be Fletcher's age about now, ready to go off to school or get married."

There was a sudden rustling inside the room as her voice abruptly stopped, a sound of two bodies moving amongst the darkness toward one another. And it was there, just within the outline of the window and closet door that they stood, embracing one another innocently enough to get him killed. The embrace was quick, consoling whatever tears the Missus had, for she now regained her composure and sent him from the room to continue his duties elsewhere. She sat at the window a while longer, her body a deflated shell of self-pity and wrath, her youthfulness an ever-fading casualty to that scorn that ruined her from within. She did not move for hours at a time, standing only when her guests had returned to the house and their voices reached her in that upstairs room, the boys returning with that same vigor they had charged the house with on that very first day after their rest. They rushed upstairs with gifts to place at the Missus's bedside, for it was indeed her birthday.

The boys then found me near that upstairs window, ready to once again race the fields. The three of them leapt wildly while my gait trailed slowly behind. They turned a deaf ear to any heeding to be careful when climbing the fences that had just received new posts, that might insist they not go so high when swinging from branches of the tallest magnolias. Floyd found us just as we neared the white heads of his cotton fields, the boys using this bit of distraction to rush along those patches as Floyd pulled me aside.

"I ain't seen him all day," he said. "Guess he been workin' at the house?"

"He's been there, but I can't say he's been working," I said.

"What d'ya mean?" Floyd asked.

"Missus had him in her room talking as usual," I said.

"Talkin' 'bout what?" Floyd insisted. "That boy ain't said a wise word since I'd know'd 'im."

"Missus got him in there talking about Elizabeth," I said. "All types of things."

"If I hears that name one more time …" Floyd shouted, "I swear that child in heaven just beggin' ta be left alone. Wanna live out the rest of her days in peace, not draggin' up the dead. Been fourteen years an' she still can't rest. Listenin' to those carrying on down here."

Floyd stamped his foot, which sent dust to both our eyes.

"I'll have words for him," he said. "Lest he forget …"

The children rushed back with guilty looks on their faces, the smallest one holding his knee, which was bruised, although the other two would not say how it happened. I marched them inside with the little one over my shoulder, Floyd taking to finding Jesse and scolding him good.

Although it was the Missus's birthday, not even that occasion could bring a smile to her face. As Floyd put it, not even the second coming could seemingly lift her mood. Her family was to depart Greenwood that evening, the little ones having their final go at wreaking havoc on this place as they ran past the kitchen window screaming while Silva prepared the cake inside with the help of the youngest boy, who piped icing messily.

When this was done we all sat down to eat, the little ones, their mother and father, the Missus and Mister, and Silva and myself.

"I sure hates to eat and leave," the boys' father said. "Way things going back home, make you wanna stay in places like this, where people make sense."

The stout woman smiled and nodded her head in agreement, a mass of blue icing in piles at the sides of her mouth.

"Scott will tell you," she said. "He know'd a man who owned his shop for fifty years. Folks come along one day and wanna show him how to do it. I tell you, ain't no place the same. But I'm sure you've got your own problems down here, too. Ain't nothing perfect no more."

"It's all these damn excuses!" the boys' father shouted. "Been one way forever, ain't nobody complaining till now. Ask Sissy, she'll tell you."

The stout woman turned to Miss Lula who sat quietly beside Mr. Kern, the old man never looking up from his half-eaten plate a minute during the meal.

"Sissy done run a good home all this time," the boys' father continued. "Ain't nobody crying or complaining. You get some people come in from their parts and they say you doing it wrong. Do it like this or that."

"We all believe in doing right by our negras," the woman

said, shaking her head at Miss Lula, whose thoughts were persistently elsewhere.

The boys paid no attention to this talk, now pleading for more cake, which they received by Silva's hand.

"You gotta chop off the head," the boys' father said. "Then the rest will fall."

The stout woman nodded, licking the icing from the tips of her fork. The family sat for a short time longer while Silva and I cleaned the mess around them, and the boys played outdoors before they gathered to sing another verse of some birthday song that was familiar to only them. The family then departed, kissing Miss Lula kindly as they tried to load those unwilling boys back inside the car and pry the smallest one from my knee.

"They prolly do better takin' this one with 'em," Floyd said as he pointed at the Missus, who watched pitifully, her eyes cast down like some sick child kept inside on a sunny day.

This bit of juvenile madness prevailed in her as she sulked for days after their departure and indeed until the very moment she rejoined them some three weeks later in Little Rock after all of Mr. Kern's attempts at helping her regain her mood had failed and he just gave up.

Floyd was to drive Miss Lula to Greenwood Station, and I would accompany her on the platform.

Floyd remained in the grumbling pickup as he awaited us, turning a disinterested glance away from the Missus and her pathetic attempt at sympathy as we approached the car door. Floyd would not give her the pleasure, his eyes stayed on some lump of cotton that inched across the road as the thump of luggage hit the flatbed and the passenger side swung open. The interior cabin filled with light but was dark once more as the door closed.

Floyd placed the gearshift into first. He remembered each turn toward the station by blind sight, a combing of catacombs inside his pressed mind that, with great skill, he navigated thoroughly and alone. We sat in prickly silence as the Missus stewed and Floyd fumed. The silence lingered for the duration of the drive as we peered through the expanse of bug-splattered windshields. Floyd then stopped the truck and said not a parting word to the Missus as I gathered her things and we moved to the platform.

———

It's funny how a train sounds if it is not wanted. It carries with it no awareness of its hulking presence or the sharp scrape of metal during those slight turns through the countryside. It makes not that shushing sound that children love, achieving to impress no one. It is invisible and carries not the weight one would give a passing stranger who has little to distinguish himself from the person to his left or right. It is, indeed, unnoticeable. That this woman of fine descent, who had all the life left of an infant born to the care of seventy servants, had heard nothing of its approach, saw no car or coach or occupants as they scurried along the platform at Greenwood Station just after the screech in the dead of night, says it all. With sad eyes she surveyed a note scribbled on wadded paper from some purchase she'd made a long time ago, indulging her fancy in rereading the not-so-legible script as she imagined the hand that had scribbled it, for that hand and its handsome owner would not leave the safety of her thoughts the entire afternoon and subsequent journey from Greenwood to Memphis and on to Little Rock, she would later tell me, and that says it all.

I had seen the two together, not just that afternoon of her birthday but several times during that three-week period before the Missus's departure for Little Rock, when her spirit was at its lowest. I daresay they were friends, even though that simple notion was frightening in and of itself. They'd walked like lovers through the paths and in those wooded areas that kept private their secret affair, finding use for all those nooks and crannies just beyond the fields that stretched into the forests, although they had not yet shared a single kiss between them, as far as I could see. Still, they laughed with great frequency, although never too long, as even that bit of happiness was met by the Missus's own wretchedness that precluded her from ever straying too far. Mr. Kern remained true to his nature too, tiring of her moods and paying no more attention to her dealings, which left her with ample time to scurry off amongst the wild columbines and irises of the far fields, finding some quiet place where she could be alone with Jesse and they could talk and whisper and behave like adolescents away from the prying eyes of adults. Part of her must have enjoyed his youth, the invincibility he possessed that came with having his entire life stretched before him and the possibilities that awaited his every footstep and how endless it all seemed, that even in a young black boy it was still present.

Although she'd been given the world, during these times together she still wanted more, more lingering stares, more tempting hands at each other's sides, more gut feelings of want and reciprocation of love. Yet, as always in this life, there were those moments that pulled them apart, when finding heaven was not so easy and running away from this Dixie life was an impossible task, as the afternoon was not so long amongst the turnip flowers as they would've wanted. So, Jesse would merely scribble some note where the Missus could find it and once again be pleased as she cradled it to her chest like some silly schoolgirl unaware of the world and its schemes. I watched her do this every day and reported these sightings to Floyd, who had already spoken to the boy, yet Jesse continued his actions. And so, on this night, I would inform Silva, I told myself, as I was to have dinner at her home after we'd both been granted the night off by Mr. Kern by virtue of his wife's departure.

CHAPTER 13

Floyd restarted the loud monster that had never quite cooled since our drive to the station. The ignition clicked then stopped, bringing all types of curses from Floyd's lips as he climbed from the truck and filled the radiator with water from a jug in the back. He allowed the hood to slam as he tossed the jug back into the flatbed and offered similar curses, mostly toward the Missus, whom he blamed for us having to travel so far. The rumble of the engine started once more as the headlights peeled from the windows of the station. With the Missus safely aboard her train, we now headed to Silva's home down by Route 82, just adjacent to the jailhouse, that place you never wanted to be, especially as a negro in the South. My cousin Levi could sure tell you that, if he still had breath in his body. Floyd would not stay for dinner, only offering to return to drive me home that evening. He still did not trust Silva and urged me not to as well, though he later conceded that women were of a different nature than men and, as such, our friendship made sense to him.

Silva's home sat at the end of a dead-end street, a small neighborhood of clustered shacks longer than they were wide, all lined up beside each other like battered soldiers in formation, where at the end was a black-owned grocery whose exterior showed the charred edges from previous fires.

"That white paint turn gray long time ago," Floyd said as we arrived. "Never stood a chance wit' what they did to it. Mostly the smoke got to it, but had no life after all them times. Why folk won't let that place stand, I don't know."

Floyd fussed until Silva met me at the door, her hair worn down in observance of her day off, her face the loveliest I'd seen it as, outside of that home, she could now smile and show glimpses into her true character. She took hold of my arm and guided me inside the house, waving a pleasant goodbye to Floyd, who mumbled something under his breath as he drove away. Inside the living room sat Jesse with a bowl of knickknacks, his eyes about the size of half-dollars when I entered.

"Miss Bernie!" he said in shock, immediately dropping the bowl to the ground, which saw those items fall in every imaginable direction.

"It's good to see you too, Jesse," I replied.

He sank in his chair, a weight upon him like that of bricks stacked upon his shoulders. He appeared sickly as he showed a look of desperation, panic, and surrender all in one turn of his upper lip.

"It's good to see you too, Miss," he finally said, standing from his seat to welcome me properly and indeed clean up that mess. "Mama didn't tell me you were coming."

"Last-minute plans often work that way," I said, finding a seat near him on the sofa where I rested my legs from that cramped ride. "I'm sure there's lots she doesn't tell you. Kids nowadays wanna know everything."

Silva laughed as she returned from the kitchen with a plate of sweet rolls before dinner.

"They think they grown," Silva said. "Especially the little one."

It was at that moment that a voice called out from behind me, low and refined, saying my name with an ease that rolled from the tongue as if the person somehow knew me and was accustomed to using that shortened name I went by. I turned and standing there some eight inches taller was Fletcher, smartly dressed and looking just as handsome as he did when he was a boy. It was amazing how fast children could grow, as if they were just waiting for our heads to turn that they might shoot up some ten feet taller and lose their childish ways. His voice was deeper too, his hands a tool for work now as he reached out to me.

"Fletcher!" I exclaimed.

"Miss Bernie!" he called out with the same excitement in his voice, his words a low bellow that never quite emerged until that last syllable when they finally sounded louder than any other words in the room.

His embrace was kind and his linger a side effect only of those stifled memories that could come crashing down at any moment, and indeed all at once, from the mere sight of a familiar face and the thoughts of where one saw it last. For I'm sure at that moment Fletcher recalled that large plantation out amongst the rye grass and wild iris of Leflore County, that smell from their bitter shucks that stung his nose on cool mornings when they'd arrive for work in the fields, the whites of those cotton bolls still fat in his hands as he filled his sacks with the soft buds out there amongst the endless powder. And no matter how he felt about it now, that place and its memories and that negro calling were still a part of him, those scars just as deep today as they were only a year ago. For, truly, no one grows out of it, not the pain of childhood or that lesson into who we are—not the fear it deals or that constant curse of waiting to get out, attempting to progress toward some semblance of your true purpose, regardless of that heaviness right there in the pit of your heart, a bottomless torture that repeats for an eternity as that mere act alone causes us to push and pull and never truly free ourselves of that previous person, place, or thing that has brought us harm.

We each sat around the living room with our rolls and tea, Fletcher settling into stories of his summer in Jackson and the people he'd met. According to Silva, he was worse than "this one over here," she said, pointing to Jesse who hid his face behind his hands and, in silence, bade me not to speak.

It wasn't until we'd each had our fill of stories and laughter that Silva led us to the kitchen table, showing the way through a home that, although overflowing with affection, still sat as a sparse collection of rusted items not numerous enough to give that home sufficient warmth or character. Their poverty was evident, the emptiness beginning in the living room where only one sofa and chair dressed the room. A coffee table sat in the middle and a cabinet in the corner, a wooden cupboard simple in design and construction adorned the hallway, with family photos displayed on top, and the kitchen sat as an open space with merely a table and chair—the other chairs being carried from the outside by the boys who wiped them clean before sitting on them.

Dinner was no surprise, given Silva's usual meals at the Kern house, and it was just as good. Jesse sat quietly while Fletcher, although grown-up in appearance, rattled on as a child would, leading Silva to end those discussions each time he went on too long. He was still just as innocent, glimpses of that young boy recognizable in his large eyes and feral smile, his gaze staying on anyone who would give him praise. Yet when he spoke, his tone was not that of a child, that tenor sounding as if he merely mimed some adult nearby. He was no longer the young boy in the stables. He was a man now, with a voice that didn't belong to the boy at all; it belonged to Mr. Kern.

"They gave me my own room down there, too," Fletcher continued as we ate.

"He ain't been there since he was little," Silva interceded. "Ain't seen his cousins since he was like four or five."

"Everyone kept calling me 'light-skinned brotha,'" he said proudly. "Marshmallow, too."

"He think he handsome now," Silva joked, winking at the boy who smiled back. "I told him he goin' ta get darker; just look at his ears. They were the first thing to turn when he was little."

"It ain't happened yet," Fletcher said, clearly still waiting for it to occur.

Who knows how many people in her family knew her secret, but one thing for certain was that her boys did not, the little one even now still uncertain as to why he looked so different than everyone around him, even willing to give up that perceived beauty that came with lighter skin just so he'd look the same.

"I joined the rally down there, too," Fletcher said.

"That's the first thing he says to me when he come home," Silva spat, her words a condemnation. "All this time, and he still don't know how to talk."

It was in her eyes, that fear and fire, that anguish that only a mother knows from the emptiness of her womb and now her arms. Lord knows I had placed these thoughts far from my mind, that hearing them made it even more difficult to bear.

Fletcher shrugged his shoulders.

"Ain't nothing wrong with it," he said.

"I see you've outgrown your britches," I said to him. "You got a larger pair of shoes and somehow think you're wiser."

"Miss Bernie, you don't understand," he said. "Mama did it once."

Fletcher's glance in Silva's direction was stopped by her wall of reproach. His eyes lowered to the floor, yet no amount of sneaker gazing could evade Silva's stare. He was changing and she knew it—that awkward age where innocence bears a lonely pot, those vines of change hidden behind the shades of adulthood, although they would soon require a larger area to grow. Yet still he was unwise and didn't know it, stuck within that ignorance or recklessness that often sat betwixt childhood and adulthood.

He looked to me and smiled daringly.

"We have to," he said.

"Fletcher!" I chided.

"Miss Bernie, it's what anyone would do," he said.

"Still, that's no way to walk in the door. Miss Silva worried sick about you, and you come home talking like that."

"But—" he started.

"But nothing," I said. "You been gone off to the city, and they missed you like crazy. And you don't even think to ask how they're doing or tell them you love them."

"They know I love them," he said.

"Then act like it. Your mission means nothing, son, if you don't take care of home. You take care of the people you love and the rest will fall into place."

"Yes, ma'am," he finally said, still that wide-eyed boy with sticks in his hands and curiosity in his heart.

That from toys to tools, that vigor had reared inside him and would eventually lead him away, just as it did every child, leaving Silva to pray like every black mother during those times. This simple prayer saying, "Dear Master, let Your grace be upon this house on this day. Teach my children to pray, Lord, and keep them in Your will. Deliver them from those wicked ways and all those who would mean them harm. Save them from the hands of man and give them Your peace. Grant them access to Your kingdom, Lord, and allow them a full life. That they would know who and whose they are. If it be Your will, let it be so."

Seated beside Fletcher with her eyes already in mourning, I knew Silva prayed this prayer and that her heart sat painfully aware that the battles she'd fought now belonged to her children, and she cursed all those things that killed the dreams she had for them.

———

It was not in Jesse's nature to be so meek yet he was a frightful thing at present, his mouth a burial place where words seemingly came to die. He did not utter a single sound that entire meal other than his hesitant bites of food, which in truth were nothing substantial enough to fill his stomach and would surely see him in the kitchen for a late-night snack after I'd left. Jesse found me just as I'd pulled Silva aside at the kitchen counter.

He took my arm and spun me so forcibly that it garnered the immediate attention of both Silva and Fletcher who stood nearby.

"Jesse!" Silva admonished as the boy's grip remained upon my wrist.

"Miss Bernie gotta see this before she go," he insisted.

"Jesse, you ain't old enough to have company," Silva said. "Now stay outta grown folks' business and go on now."

"It's real quick, Mama," he pleaded.

"Jesse, you heards me," Silva warned.

The two stared for a minute. Jesse then squeezed my hand, and I felt the tension in his fingers quiver like the glint in his eyes. I nodded that it was okay then followed him into the living room where we sat, seeing Silva's eyes stayed on us.

"Miss Bernie," he spoke softly, his voice nearly a whisper, "I wanna explain."

He settled further on the sofa with his hands at his side and his eyes a timid shell as he looked back to ensure the sounds of Silva and Fletcher continued before he said another word.

"You see, I don't love that woman, and she don't love me," he said. "I was just being good to her. I hope you understand."

"And you think she needs you to be good to her?" I said. "She's a white woman, Jesse! She doesn't need anything from you. That, I hope *you* understand."

"Well, I just give her attention," he said innocently. "And she comes to me for it."

"And you don't turn her away either, do you?" I accused him.

"No, ma'am," he said.

"Then you're both wrong."

Jesse stared as if he somehow watched all those times they'd been together now displayed before him, finally opening his mouth to speak once he'd viewed enough of his shame that he could bear it no longer and needed to confess.

"See, she first came to me on her birthday," he said. "I was working in the downstairs bathroom, and she said she need help upstairs. When we went into her bedroom, she just start crying. She told me not to leave her and just to stand beside her so that no one else could see. She said she was sad about Elizabeth. And I told her I remembered her and how Elizabeth and Fletcher used to play when they were little. She told me she hates to think of that time, and when I asked her why, she say she didn't wanna talk about it and there was no need bringing it up, and so I didn't make her. She swore there was no need to."

"And then?" I asked.

"Then I saw her again after her family left for Little Rock. She seemed so sad again, crying about them leaving and saying how alone she felt in that house. She said Mr. Kern don't love her and that she wishes she had someone to love. She said he took the only thing she ever had when Elizabeth died. Then she took me inside the kitchen when no one was there, and I thought she was gonna kiss me or something, but she didn't. She just stand there holding my hand and saying how she was gonna make Mr. Kern pay, that he was gonna be sorry for what he did. We didn't meet for a few days after that. She just stayed up in her room crying, but she found me on that third day and asked if I would walk with her because she was scared to go out alone with the workers out there, you know. I didn't know what else to do, and so I did it. We walked around the fields, out by the east road, and then down by the swamps, close to the Yazoo. She just talked, and I listened. That's all she ever wanted."

"You ain't telling me nothing I don't already know," I said sternly.

"Well," he continued, "I finally knew something was wrong with what we were doing when we started out as usual down by the fields one day, you know, the parts where they already picked and cleared. Because she turned to me and just start laughing. She smiled and said she had figured it out. When we got closer to the house, she begged me to write notes to her instead of us meeting like we did. She said Mr. Kern didn't like it that she wandered off so much, but that we could still talk and write letters, but only if nobody saw, and that she would keep it secret. Now, I know secrets are bad but I did it, afraid of what she would do if I didn't. I knew it was wrong, but I had no choice. It was gonna be her word against mine. She made me say all those things I wrote to her. She told me she love me. And so I said it back. But I ain't never touch her. And she knows it."

Jesse looked up, frightened, his eyes a well of tears that had spilled over and poured down his face. I took him outside immediately, in the dark of night where no prying eyes could catch sight of us. There I told him of the Missus's wrath, omitting that troubling notion that Fletcher was indeed Mr. Kern's son but instead telling Jesse of how the Missus had it out for everyone, myself included, a lie I had to tell.

"You can't see her anymore," I said adamantly. "When she returns from Little Rock, you stay away. You hear? Let me spend time with her, but you stay with Floyd at all costs. Don't ever stray from his side, Jesse."

Just then Floyd arrived, his grumbling truck signaling to both Silva and Fletcher that he had returned. Fletcher shot out the door, a bolt of lightning, white-hot, with sights on that steel contraption.

"Lord, when did this happen?" Floyd shouted. "I thoughts ya were ya brother, how talls ya are!"

Floyd embraced the youngster as if the boy were his own son. He held him tight and didn't let go, the veins in his arms snaking like vines on a dogwood that encased the boy in its reach.

"Why, I bets ya growed every time ya ate something," Floyd continued, proud of him for those same inexplicable reasons we all held.

Floyd raised his hands well above his head as if showing the height of a giant.

"Ya goin' let 'im beat ya, huh?" Floyd cackled to Jesse who was still in no condition to laugh although he did appear in better spirits than he had mere seconds before.

"People says I eat like I got a tapeworm in me," Fletcher bragged.

"That's how it always is," Floyd laughed. "Ya goin' get even taller, I bets, God willing."

God willing, I thought. God willing a lot of things would happen. God willing, we'd find peace in this miserable land. God willing, that home wouldn't confine us to hate and disgust forever. God willing, we'd forgive and finally let die. God willing, we'd make it to see tomorrow. God willing.

"Come on, Fletcher, before Mama start yelling," Jesse finally said, pulling Fletcher by his shirt collar and stretching it just slightly, which left a large portion of the boy's shoulder exposed.

The two of them turned toward the house quietly, older and younger both appearing just as juvenile as they returned to the poverty that awaited them, and Floyd and I returned to the plantation under the resolution of night, its blessings bestowed upon us by the half-moon, God willing.

CHAPTER 14

The Missus was gone for three weeks, finding her temporary home in Little Rock more than accommodating to her mood. The house sat empty most days with Silva in the back stables and my duties leading me to the fields where I assisted with the final picking of the season. Fall approached and that coolness could be felt in the air just before the sinners woke, that time of morning when only the righteous were up so early and stirring about the fields in preparation for the day. The Lord must have lent us a smile for His grace could be seen in the roundness of the sun, that pink mass that sat out over the oaks and made the rest of the sky as some watercolor canvas that sank upon us in slow, steady drips. Truly nothing in Mississippi happened swiftly and this, too, was a sight that none of us wished to hurry, especially not with the noonday heat fast approaching.

Mr. Kern lay dead to the world, had been that way for a while, unmoving for several days in his parlor. He had grown fussy during those weeks of the Missus's absence, and that temper of his as quick as lightning and just as hot too. Floyd mostly conducted the duties of the house during this tantrum, as he was the only person the old man could stomach. Although Mr. Kern reserved nothing but kindness toward Silva, her indifference toward him made her insufferable in his sight and did nothing but stir his anger. Soon he became that which he hated, wandering the fields, indeed, just like the Missus, as one who had lost something in perpetual search for anything to replace it.

For a spell, I assumed it was religion he had found out there, Floyd insisting to me that one could only avoid the Lord for so long before He somehow finds *you*.

"It's at the strangest time," Floyd vowed as we watched the old man wander, "it binds ya helpless ta the floor, exposin' your vulnabilty for the whole worl' ta see. Makes ya like a child all over agin, turnin' ya ta that age where ya jus' learnin' ta walk an' talk, that it might mold your entire thinkin' till even your words are no longer your own."

He swore Mr. Kern had somehow found it that night as the old man gazed up at a sight that could have surely been the Rapture, for how long he stared. At the middle of the field, the old man rested, the small of his back pressed against the smooth stone as his head rested against the bark of that oak or magnolia, as it was hard to distinguish this time of evening when everything looked the same underneath the persistent shroud. Over the whine of cicadas came the sound of distant tractors. The sun had long disappeared to that place it always ventured, and the clouds were colors of orange and gold out toward that fading direction, leaving the rest of the sky dark as that minute right before sleep. The old man watched and waited, never knowing when that sliver of light would completely disappear but convinced it would, out of repetition or habit, I was sure. Mr. Kern rested in this state for hours until the sky gave birth to distant galaxies and the wind sat too cool upon his skin to feel contentment, for only then did he return to the house and Floyd's company there.

Inside, the two sat around the fireplace, the crackle of splintering wood growing louder before them, its red heat filling the room and indeed slowly causing their arms and legs to back away from those glowing embers. Mr. Kern stared distantly, waiting, waiting for death to come, waiting for judgment to reign, waiting for his friend to finally give up on him, for God to send some ultimate decree that would see his empire fall. It was as the fire quelled and the cold returned to the room that he finally stood and gathered a log to his chest, removing that burned cinder with a swipe of his foot as he then replaced it with the other, acquiring that bit of chewing tobacco from his back pocket and placing the lump inside his cheek, tissue and all, as he sat again. Then he was quiet, and those thoughts paved a swift return to his mind as the heat grew once more in the room.

Several days later, I would spot the old man down by the lake, his fishing gear with him and a sense of calm about him, even if his line never moved an inch in the water other than by the toss of those waves. In the week that followed, I would often see him in this position, his tackle box opened and a small fish tucked inside. He'd rest it entirely in his palm before beginning with the head, following that crescent curve around the gills with a sharp knife. *Snap!* it'd cry. The body he'd then cut into eighths, big enough pieces to attract those bass or crappie or maybe even a catfish, if he was lucky. It was always wiser to go larger rather than smaller, and so he'd cut the pieces big enough so that his hook fit entirely within the fleshy parts.

The sun was a fixture on its own, even without the sky, an ever-growing mass that swelled around us and caused our eyes to squint and our hands to shade those affected parts, although Mr. Kern seemed quite content to indulge in its pervading light without a flinch or peep. His lure dangled from the head of the fish like some fanciful tail as, with his reel baited, Mr. Kern approached the more shaded area along the southern end of the lake and cast his line there. This corner he loved more than any other, an area that was mostly brush and known particularly as a spot to avoid by novice fishermen because of the poison ivy that grew rampant. Yet Mr. Kern walked freely amongst it, having fished this spot many times and innately knowing exactly where to step in order to avoid troublesome areas.

He felt good there, like some people feel in church and others in juke joints and some with their families at home around a warm meal. He cast his reel and watched it fly to the center of the lake, a beautiful sight for any fisherman and especially one of such low spirits as he was lately. *Plop!* it shouted as it hit the water, creating the tiniest splash, which rippled along the banks and eventually back toward him as he watched contentedly.

Down it immediately went. He tugged at his spinner, cranking its handle until a stalemate occurred between the line and the fish, that point where the old man's strength met with that of the fish somewhere in the middle and caused them to both stand completely still. He held the line, continuing to pull although he was well aware that a broken line would do him no good, and so it was then that he eased up from his current stance.

"Yer gonna lose her," a voice warned, seeming to emerge from the lake itself.

Mr. Kern turned, as limping toward him was Floyd with his own pole and tackle box by his side. Mr. Kern appeared pale and his clothes as sickly as death, although everything about the old man seemed to fall to the weight of gravity nowadays, his sweater drooped at his shoulders and his pants layered around his ankles.

Floyd positioned himself alongside Mr. Kern with his own line cast into the water.

"Don't you worry," Mr. Kern said. "She ain't going nowhere."

"If ya pull thatta way she will, sir," Floyd insisted.

"She's fine," Mr. Kern barked back.

The line drifted just slightly as Mr. Kern attempted to hold it steady.

"Either ya pull 'er, or she gonna pull you," Floyd fussed, completely disregarding his own line for that of Mr. Kern's. "Ease 'er to ya just slightly, sir."

The fish tugged as Mr. Kern yanked back, easing the fish toward him in that manner Floyd had instructed.

"They can be tricky little devils can't they?" Mr. Kern said.

"She won't get 'way from ya," Floyd replied. "Just take 'er slow."

The line now stretched toward the opposite side of the lake, dangerously approaching a log that waded amongst the brush.

"She knows what she's doing," Mr. Kern said.

"She wanna tangle ya," Floyd acknowledged.

"She got some fight in her," Mr. Kern said, now pulling the line even harder.

Both men watched with fearful eyes as the line darted beneath the log, holding their breaths as it eventually stopped moving altogether, and Mr. Kern knew it was over. He pulled, yet his strength was useless as the more he pulled the more that line wrapped around the log and refused to budge.

Mr. Kern scoffed, holding the line steady as it now dragged him toward the water's edge.

"She's got ya now," Floyd snickered.

"Seems like it," Mr. Kern replied.

Mr. Kern retrieved his knife from his back pocket, that same knife he had used to dissect the fish earlier. Then, with that ever-present sun watching from above, he cut the line, seeing those ripples spread along the opposite side of the lake as the fish swam away.

"You'll get 'er next time," Floyd said.

"My hook back, too," Mr. Kern fussed.

"Just like ol' Mason down there," Floyd cackled. "He ain't seen that hook ever since."

"He ain't found his johnson either," Mr. Kern added. "That old blowfish gottem good."

The two were like this all afternoon, sitting in the peace of each other's company as the fish bit or did not bite—it didn't really matter. They had conversation and that was enough. They had sunshine and wind and laughter and of course more stories of old Mason down there who was said to have once been stung by a jellyfish on his manhood, or so they say.

There was nothing left of the morning as they sat, no lingering minute to break the fixed spirit of conscious thoughts and make it last longer, no moment that could be recovered to stop the pecking click of that incessant clock on the wall. The cold descended rapidly, yet they found peace in this world where time did not matter and calamity sat far away. Neither of them did move until the sun was almost gone, when Mr. Kern finally pulled his line from the water, or what was left of it, laughing as Floyd also retrieved his line to find a tiny fish clinging to the end along with that flimsy worm that had died a long time ago, if it was ever alive to begin with. Mr. Kern laughed even louder. Floyd then pulled the fish from the hook, adjusted the worm's soggy body, and once again cast the whole thing into the water. Floyd repositioned himself on his overturned bucket and watched as Mr. Kern repaired his broken line.

"Have some?" Floyd said as he removed a bag of peanuts from his tackle box and began to chew loudly, the dirt from his fingers mixing with the nuts in the bag.

Mr. Kern reached in and ate the portion he gathered.

"Ya need your strength out here today," Floyd insisted. "Don't starve yerself 'cause the fish surely won't."

And with this, he continued to chew loudly, licking the salt from his fingers and adjusting his line.

CHAPTER 15

Whatever ailment Mr. Kern suffered, Floyd during those three weeks delivered him from it. In his recovery, Mr. Kern took to his parlor once more, finding no more need to spend all his day in his upstairs quarters. He found the outside air refreshing and once more delighted in walking the grounds both at sunrise and just after the blistering sunset, right when the humidity subsided yet it was still warm. He found contentment in song, humming a tune that was familiar to these parts as his stroll lingered and his eyes lagged amongst the trees. All, that is, before the Missus returned.

A stiff wind struck the fields, lifting the mulch that Jesse had placed that very afternoon and tossing it wildly. Silva yelled from within the main house for Jesse to close the back shed or else the hogs would flee, and there was no easy way of getting them back if they got spooked in this wind. Jesse rushed to the double doors and spread his arms as far as they'd go. He pulled one side then the other, glancing above his head at the windmills that spun like fans and seemed to propel the wind forward. His arms quivered as he placed the middle latch, coaxing the long, wooden board into place between two handles that just barely fit the wide mass.

He then pulled the rubber strap around the fat end and pressed it hard into the dented cavity.

Within the shed, the hogs and chickens amplified their back-and-forth rampage, kicking up dirt that rose where Jesse stood.

"Quiet, Jubba!" he shouted, pounding his fist on the door. "You too, Roxy."

The shed fell silent, if only for mere seconds, as the wind increased, and the hogs fought the invisible enemy once more. In the house just yards away, Silva rushed to the kitchen with her arms loaded. She placed the handful of dishes in the sink then turned to the counter with a large spoon. There she gathered the remaining pills into a pile and crushed them because by this point, Mr. Kern would not swallow them whole even if the doctors insisted these pills be adhered to daily, the old man just did not care, concerned even less whether he came or went.

"Jesse!" Silva shouted from the window, her drawl lapping in the wind several times before it reached him. "Don't forget that outhouse! Make sure them locks on there real tight!"

She leaned forward, searching the mix of flying objects when she finally spotted him by the water barrel, his contorted body bracing against its steady base as he placed a wooden board over the wide mouth and knocked whatever was loose on top onto the ground. He sucked in a deep breath then tore himself from the drum, pushing toward the outhouse that sat at the very edge of the farm.

"Jesse!" I called, meeting him halfway. "You get one side, and I'll get the other."

It was completely dark as we walked. The countless rows of cotton rose beside us with full, fat blooms opened to reveal their white hearts. Yet, even with their glow, it was amazing how dark this place could get, how the stars seemingly sprinkled, as if we were sitting in heaven. The rocks crunched loudly beneath our feet, that final stretch of road seemingly the only place on earth that could keep up so much noise.

Beneath the awning of magnolia trees sat the frumpy outhouse that should have been condemned a long time ago, a place now empty except for Mr. Kern's tools and some broken trinkets the old man's father found on the sides of the road.

We discovered the door already opened, the mess meeting us outside where all around once-filled boxes lay spilled, many of the items now broken, although some had already been broken well before the storm. Mr. Kern's carpentry work lay in ruins, a craft the old man toyed with every so often when a neighbor needed something built, and they called on him because he was just that good. Jesse pressed the lock while I took charge of the other door, turning the squeaky latch then pushing the handle forward alongside the doorframe that jammed with any change in the weather. Jesse stood there for a moment once this was done, somehow as aware as I was that Mr. Kern's life's work was all but over and any remnants of that life he had was now destroyed. Jesse sighed, kicking the broken items at his feet. He then looked above him at the heap of stars all gathered together in one place.

"I ain't never been outside Mississippi before," he said. "But I swear looking above me now I would bet you stars were only here, if I didn't know no better."

"Sure enough?" I said to him. "Makes you believe that?"

"Yes, ma'am," he said. "Like they blinded by the Hollywood lights and some reason they like it here."

Jesse looked around him innocently, the windstorm having cleared the clouds and left only precious sky.

"For me, Mississippi the only place on earth," he said. "Anybody leave is as good as falling off the face of it."

He walked toward the house. He had not spoken of the Missus since that night following dinner at Silva's yet his eyes seemed to think of her now, that same look I'd seen watching from the corner as Floyd and I drove away. In his eyes was a look of shame, and he dared not glance up from his moving feet to meet my sight. Jesse walked with the stars falling at his head like fireflies, climbing the steps onto the front porch where he grabbed the fly swatter, as requested by Silva, and stood outside that front door as he awaited her, not daring to enter the house with his shoes as muddy as the ground itself.

Silva met him at the door, the dark tree line etched across the fields behind him. He must have had dreams at some point, I considered, although he never spoke of them and, even worse, never seemed to care about anything outside of his work and that bit of praise he received from the Missus, who stroked him like a pet with her exaltations. Reaching the screen door, Silva grabbed the swatter and told him to complete his chores before they returned home. He sighed a deep breath, taking one final glance at the flickering, stained porch light and lurking stars. He had changed this bulb some hundred times yet each day this light flickered on and off, day in and day out.

The Missus arrived on the late train, the leaves shuddering wildly as we left for the station, flapping like hands clapping in the dark. Floyd was once again angry despite his quiet mood as he pulled the turns from his memory. It was impossible to see any light or darkness through the fog. He drove until we saw her there, her shape cradling a pillar beneath the weathered awning and her arms almost fetal as they clung like an infant to its mother.

"Come on, Miss," I said to her, pulling her slightly. "This weather won't kill you."

She eased to me as if there was danger my direction, and I was convinced at that moment that she thought me to be a stranger, she cowered so badly. Floyd rolled his eyes at her attempts for sympathy. The fog worsened, and I could make out my companions' faces beside me only because I knew it was them. The world outdoors was a shapeless place, marked by dangers we could not define until those tires hit a pothole or branches in the road, and we knew vaguely the things outside our window from the feel of each impact.

CHAPTER 16

Miss Lula's first day back was a day of resettling. She checked the flowers for water. She made decent her wardrobe. She unpacked her needlework and followed these tasks by compiling a list of duties for Silva to attend to. She read a few letters then saw that they were refolded and put away before she cleared her dresser, which had not seen her attention in three weeks and now met the arrival of those weeks' worth of clothing. She read a handful of recipes that were delivered by Miss Clementine to all the church-women, even if they did not attend services regularly or pay their tithes as they should. Miss Lula commented here and there as to the quality of those domestic rules before she finally retired from these chores and ventured outside to check on the tricks of her favorite pigs Roxy and Corrine. Sadly, Mississippi never felt like home to her, and Mr. Kern never much like family, and so returning to this place was nothing more than a return to some miserable incarceration.

Arkansas was her real home. I'd spotted her love for that place during her family's visit, Scott's love for his "Sissy" just as strong as mine for Floyd and his for me, and how we both felt the same for Gloria, that final sibling in our chain. Gloria was the wild child, never feeling the sting of Daddy's belt a day in her life, although he never spared a curse word toward her either. Indeed, Floyd was the only one who'd actually felt it, that belt with the holes along the center that sucked up pieces of his skin like a vacuum before releasing them with a fiery snap. Daddy was not soft with his belt either, a man of few words and quick-tempered, whose stance was like the roots of the magnolia trees that grew in our front yard, their protruding mounds leaving that entire front enclosure bumpy and grotesque. He swung hard and meant every lick, his arms moving like those branches, thick and sturdy, his belt like the flimsy leaf-covered ends that pelted us on windy nights as we'd walk home from night watch of the farm, down by the old water tower and pecan grove where Floyd and I once played as children before we moved from Sidon. Daddy had little reason for his beatings. Windy or not, they came.

It was with these memories of Sidon and Floyd, along with that water tower and pecan grove, that I understood Miss Lula's loneliness. For at least I had Floyd, and Silva had Jesse and Fletcher, and even the Mister had Silva's disinterest, yet the Missus had no one besides those distant relatives and that on-again, off-again affection of both Roxy and Corrine, which could hardly be considered love, although the Missus now accepted anything they had to give. She liked anyone or anything who would like her back, and she'd check on those pigs daily to determine their mood and whether she'd be accepted on that day or not.

The steady trickle of water from recent rains had produced a ringing in the air, a measured counting of the morning that eased by under gray skies and cooler temperatures until it was at last afternoon, and the clouds still looked the same, leading me to believe the weather would continue like this all day. Miss Lula sat alone on the porch with her needlework, a return to that woman who'd once seemed so indifferent to this place and its fatigue. She looked up wearily yet made no shouts for Silva to fetch this or that. No, in silence she simply sat with her feelings, poised to do so the entire evening if Mr. Kern had not stirred her from this rest.

"What's this nonsense about you taking a hatchet to my parlor?" he fussed from the opened screen door, its hinges still squeaking and popping even as the door stood still.

Despite these words she sat quietly, as it took her a moment to return from whatever imaginary world she'd ventured to and remember this earth and its duties. And so it wasn't until she'd settled and showed about her a sense of peace that she looked up and smiled, that revived woman once again coming through in her assured countenance.

"That room needs some changing," she said in a voice kinder than any she'd ever used with the Mister.

He prepared his lips to attack yet deflated rather quickly as her tone settled upon him, and he could no longer bring himself to yell so loudly. He instead made his case as plainly as he could. Simply put, he loved that room for what it was, and it was the only place he still had to himself, and he would have no changes be made to it, refusing the Missus's insistence that Jesse provide just a few touch-ups to certain areas to make it look nice.

"Just look at the other work he's done already," she said. "The entire house looks better, like an actual home now. Like people actually live here."

"All I've heard is a bunch of noise," Mr. Kern barked back. "Now, I've put up with a lot but ain't nobody gonna change my parlor. And that's final. If I wanted it changed, I'd do it myself."

So it remained that from that day on, Mr. Kern cringed each

time he spotted Jesse inside the house, the boy performing a job the old man could have surely done in his youth. He loathed the sight of tools left on the table and our miserable attempts at covering those works in progress. His blood boiled each time he smelled sawdust in the air, as its pungency overpowered the robustness of food at his table, the scratch of some newly finished cabinet or dresser bruising his hands so easily in his older, weaker state. Indeed, Silva and I smoothed each wrinkle from his bedsheets, as if even that elevated surface could somehow harm him. The Missus, however, smiled her usual grin, demanding projects that took more and more time, and were vastly noisier than ever before. She beamed with a maliciousness that adored the assault on the Mister's once-quiet parlor, now turned into a roaring construction site—even if the work did not take place there, he could still feel it.

The Mister stalked about gravely, hating the heat and hating the cold. He despised any laughter that was not sought after and was intolerant of those coming in and out of the house, letting in flies, as he declared. He would have no talk at all and was a pain to all he saw, that is, to all but the Missus, who welcomed his foul mood and saw his temperament fitting for that house.

The harvest had seen its last days with those final rows completely cleared. Still, outdoor duties remained, keeping me away from the house during this critical time of the Missus's deceit. As promised to Jesse, I needed to regain the Missus's trust. In truth, I needed a way back inside that house, a thought as unlikely by anyone as some soul attempting to bribe its way back into hell. She'd grabbed Jesse privately several times since her return, leading him through the house with her hand upon his shoulder. She'd whispered in his ear and touched his cheek with her lips, sitting him down, where she caressed him softly.

With the cooler weather, the Missus no longer took her needlework or coffee outdoors, instead sitting in her quarters and listening to the work below that signaled Jesse's presence and brought a smile to her face as she ran to collect him. In my efforts, I hovered at the breakfast table, yet she did not bite. I sparked conversations we'd had during our walks, yet she still felt no certain need to talk, her thoughts remaining only on the work to be done. Yet one day when there was enough time in the afternoon and the birds chirped at a consistent enough level, I invited the Missus outdoors in the rare appearance of the sun and that calmness of the pestering wind that so often kicked up loose soil and made it unbearable to sit in the open air, let alone have an open window. She gave reason not to but, just as quickly, she obliged my offer and brought her needlework onto the porch with a blanket, not that she ever used it. Her mood was pleasant and her eyes casually glanced around her at the fields she hadn't viewed in weeks. Still, she was quiet.

"We might finally thaw today," I said.

"Hmm," she replied, not really taking in these thoughts but feeling a need to respond.

She made several more stitches before finally looking up again.

"I think you might be right, Bernie," she said, a certain warmth returning to her skin that brought with it a sense of peace to her eyes.

And with this I knew I had her.

"I bet those fescues and rye aren't nearly as hard as they were a week ago," she continued.

"Not warm enough for you to walk through barefoot, that's for sure," I said.

"The mud would stop you, but I'm sure it's warm," she replied.

"Ain't enough sun in the world could warm them about now," I said. "I already miss it. That grass started turning a few days ago. By next week, it'll already be yellow. Still ain't worse than the trees, though. They change from green to yellow to orange to red, and then they die before summer's even out. Swear it's a blink in the night. A nap and it's over."

"Don't be so down," she insisted. "It's not that bad. I done seen lots of green out there, Bernie."

"I walked it just today!" I protested. "You'll never see such a sad sight in your life."

"Then you show me," she said, placing her needlework in her chair as she stood and packed her loose yarn into her carrier.

With our covers about us, we walked toward the east end of the plantation, not an area we typically visited but a sight I knew would get the Missus talking. The trees had started to lose their leaves yet nothing as dire as the situation I painted.

"Where are these hellish sights?" she insisted.

"There!" I pointed, picking out a small tree that had already lost most of its colorful parts.

"It's a baby," she insisted. "Of course it's lost its leaves, if it had any to begin with."

"Your cup is too full, Miss," I said.

"And yours too empty, Bernie," she said.

We had been amongst the graves for several minutes before she noticed, our location settling upon her like a chill that starts small then spreads over one's entire body, as I hoped it would on this day. She looked around solemnly at the field of gravestones along the churchyard.

"Maybe not so full," she finally acknowledged. "At least not as full as it might seem."

Patience being a conspirator's best friend, I waited, allowing her to come to me before I said another word.

"I swear it's been years," she continued. "Ain't been here since it happened, Bernie. Makes you glad you're alive, I guess. Until you realize what you lost."

"Elizabeth?" I prodded.

"Yes," she caved. "She rest right up there on that hill. The prettiest one up there."

The Missus pointed to the church at the very top, a white wooden structure with graves that extended down like tiers of a woman's petticoat and cascaded to their final resting place at the side of the road. It was a pale-yellow sun that guided us up that hill and indeed sat directly above the steeple. The Missus walked ahead as I satisfied my curiosity in observance of the multitude of forgotten graves: *Robert Kindsman—A Loving Father*; *Julie Sinclair—A Wife and Mother*; *Mary Givens—Beloved*; *Oliver Capps—Remembered Always*.

When I'd arrived at the last gravestone nearest the top, Miss Lula sat at the youngest, Elizabeth's gravestone being simple—her name, date of birth and return to the Lord, and the word *Angel* all on a gabled slab of stone that sat crooked in the ground. I dared not disturb the dead or the grieving, or else face judgment myself when that time came for my sins, and so I sat in silence as the Missus mourned. At that moment Miss Lula possessed a delicacy about her like that of a cut flower, an evanescence to that life in her veins that was only present for a certain amount of time before it withered, as it often did, only to reappear later before she soon lost it again. I pictured Elizabeth to have her mother's same beauty, yet conversely that same unsoundness of life that Miss Lula suffered from and that plagued her even now.

She sat with her legs crumpled beneath her, the uselessness of her arms in full display as she sobbed. Her tears could have scratched the eyes of God, I swear, as in her despair she looked up to that place where God's kingdom reigned, yet pitiably she saw only the rising moon in the dead of day—bad luck, as anyone knew. She had been cursed once and now felt that sting again, willing to surely kidnap the moon as ransom for her love. Still, truth was a whisper spoken softly beneath the chaos of it all, as a voice barely heard in her grief and friendly as any I'd ever witnessed came now from a man who crept by slowly, saying, "You'll see 'er agin." Or maybe he hollered it over the madness of her sobs, for his words were mute to both our current conditions.

The Missus soon turned to me with renewed willingness to depart as she reached for my hand. Wobbly, she woke from her prayers to find her legs numb, my arms easing her to her feet and back to that awareness of this present time and space. She wore a look of resignation, as was often the case in places like these. And so it was that we walked in silence nearly the entire road home before she finally spoke again, her heart a matted cacophony of sound that now spewed from her lips in miscellaneous wanderings.

"Bernie," she said painfully, "you got children?"

"No, Miss, I don't," I replied, a sense of care in my delivery, as she was still grieving, and I dared not anger God. "But I do have nieces and nephews that I love like they were my own."

"Floyd?" she asked.

"Yes, Miss," I said. "And my sister, Gloria, too. Floyd with Arnold, and Gloria with Janice and Steven."

"I don't even know the first thing about you," she said with a slight smile that grew to be as big as her head and showed all of her teeth. "Other than you're Floyd's sister, I don't even think I know where you come from."

"You know people by their actions and how they are to you," I said. "Everything else means nothing."

"I guess I don't know too many people then," she laughed.

"I'm sure you know enough," I said.

"After Elizabeth," she began, "I don't think I wanted to know anybody else."

"And how about now?"

"I don't know, Bernie," she said. "I got a plague in my heart."

She stopped at the side of the road and leaned against a tree, taking her eyes with her wherever it was she'd drifted.

"I see Elizabeth all grown-up in my dreams sometimes," she said. "I see her running around the house and through the fields just as happy as all the other children out there. Then I wake up and she's gone, and I'm furious I even saw her in the first place, because it breaks my heart to lose her all over again. I hate that she'll never grow up and get married and have children of her own to love. She'll never see my face or hear my voice, and then I wonder if she even remembers me, wherever she is. And then I feel selfish and foolish for even wanting it. You never wanna lose something like that again, you know. It hurts you too much."

My mind prepared a speech about how life's just like that and you live with it every day, yet my heart beseeched stillness as the Missus soon regained her footing, and we started down the road without a word between us until the main house was in sight. Falling at our heads were wondrous magnolia blooms, as those giants never gave in to the stern commands of winter or parted with their leaves even if it meant a less vibrant display of their grandeur than in those summer months.

"Seems like it's gonna be a cold one," Miss Lula acknowledged, morose in her delivery as she looked up to the sky.

"Yes, Miss," I said. "Ain't no running from it, although you can try."

The Missus and I were close after that, a closeness I would use to purge the secret from her plagued heart. This, I swore.

CHAPTER 17

The next day the Missus and I walked by the marshes, as the warmth had surprisingly lasted another morning and afternoon and could be seen in the retracting frost on the rye and fescues.

"How's Jesse been?" I pried as we sat amongst the turtles and water moccasins whose splashes could be heard behind.

"Very good, Bernie," she said. "He's really making that place a home. Done everything I asked for."

"That's nice, Miss," I said.

"Reminds me of a boy I once met on the riverboat cruise in Memphis," she said. "Beautiful, Memphis is. You been?"

"No, ma'am," I said.

"Well, I promise it's gorgeous," she declared. "Anyhow, the *Queen II* it was called, that boat. Had a nice fella working there who smiled a lot. He was a nice negra and made our trip the most pleasant I'd ever had.

"The Mississippi," she lamented. "It runs wide and mean, but we didn't feel a thing on that boat. We didn't even feel it rock at all really. And they had all kinds of seafood for us to eat, and we ate like kids, sure did. Cotton and cotton and more cotton for as far as you could see on either side.

"I think I've never had so much fun, riding up and down the river on that boat. You feel like you're going nowhere, but you know you're going somewhere, and then you look up and you're in Tunica or back in Memphis where you started, with those lights from the buildings all around you. I never seen something so special in my life."

Her head fell to these thoughts, bobbing like the lights on the water she'd described. Then she looked up again and caught sight of me there with my legs crossed.

"But Jesse's doing just fine," she returned. "I swear he just like that boy."

"That's good, Miss," I said. "I hope he stays here a mighty long time."

"Well, where's he going?" she said sharply.

"Nowhere as far as I can tell, but who knows the workings of young boys' hearts."

"Ain't nowhere else for him but here," she demanded. "We always treats our negras good. And you know this, Bernie."

"I agree, Miss," I said. "I just worry Mr. Kern sure gonna grow tired of that noise all the time. He's getting older and his health ain't good like it used to be."

"That noise will be done soon enough," she said, her eyes alive with thoughts that failed to fall from her lips or impart the sights she'd seen all those times when she'd sat alone inside her room. "And Jesse can return with Floyd in the fields soon enough," she added.

"Mr. Kern may tire of him before that time," I said.

"No!" she admonished. "It'll be done sooner than anyone thinks."

And then she was quiet, her heart not attached to Jesse or the Mister or any devotion to a decent home. She seemed to care for nothing at all, and I was convinced it wasn't love for the boy or some deep-seated wish for a pleasant life that struck her heart, because at least those ambitions required she still love or feel desire toward any of those plans. No, it was hate that hit her as she sat before me detached from the world, unable to love or even care for her own situation. And I knew right there that vengeance controlled her heart. That it guided her actions and motivated her to press forward with her schemes, using Jesse to whatever ends necessary to complete her vision.

"You got me thinking of old times, Bernie," she said somberly. "You sure got me thinking."

These thoughts led into Christmas. The Missus had done a fine job on the house that year with Silva's help, hanging decorations the Missus hadn't seen since Little Rock, pointing out to me the chipped elf, the wobbly Santa, and that galloping Rudolph who'd fallen from the tree so many times that they joked each year of his attempts to fly back to the North Pole. Of all the holidays, Christmas was by far the most pleasant around the plantation. Lights strung up around the main house and stable, those scant decorations placed above the servant quarters by Floyd that hung low from the already low ceiling yet were still festive. For a second it seemed we all quit our petty quarrels and allowed those grievances to heal. A feeling of connectedness joined the house, as Jesse completed the final tasks for that downstairs area, and Mr. Kern marched around happily now that this work was over. Fletcher prepared to leave for school, having been accepted to some program up north, his impending absence bringing a heaviness to Silva's footsteps when she walked. Still, if only for this short season it seemed as if we all could be happy at the same time, as Silva's lonely heart could not sustain a lick of anger toward anyone with the realization that her son would indeed escape Mississippi.

Once Jesse had completed that final downstairs room, Silva and I watched from the doorway as the Missus inspected it. She then sighed and turned to the window and the threat of freezing rain.

"You must love me more than I thought," she whispered, the softness of her voice doing nothing to stop its ringing in our ears.

"Miss?" Silva said.

"Jesse," Miss Lula replied louder, now turning away from the window and toward the boy. "He must love me more than I thought."

"Why, Miss, we all love you," Silva said impatiently, turning to Jesse who looked away guiltily.

"Your boy maybe more than others," Miss Lula said. "I think he might actually be fond of me. I'm just happy this little project of ours is over so he can return where he belongs and stop chasing me like he's gone mad."

"Miss, I don't understand!" Silva protested.

"Please, please," Miss Lula explained, "Silva, you've done nothing wrong but I broughts your boy in to work and not spend all day harassing me."

"Miss, I never," Jesse said.

"Jesse!" Silva demanded.

"Don't be worried," Miss Lula said, looking at the boy tenderly. "I never showed Mr. Kern your letters."

Silva wound her body like some untamed beast loose inside the forest, her sights a living promise to kill whatever it was she saw moving next.

"Jesse, you answer me right now," Silva said.

"I never ..." Jesse said.

"Jesse," Miss Lula soothed, "I've given you my word that I'll never tell a soul. You can believe me."

Miss Lula removed her hands from the pockets of her dress to reveal the letters Jesse had indeed written over those past months in secret. She held them to her chest just as she did that night at the train station before leaving, and suddenly I knew what that look in her eyes had meant all this time. She breathed a sigh of relief then glanced around when she suddenly spotted me.

"It won't leave this room," she promised kindly, smiling in my direction.

She now turned to Silva.

"But," the Missus demanded severely, "I ask that in forgiving Jesse, Silva you also forgive me for what I did to you all that time ago and allow Fletcher to return to this house immediately."

"Miss, there's no need for me to forgive you," Silva said.

"Yes, Silva," she insisted. "You must forgive me for sending him from the house and away from his family, yourself and Jesse for all this time. A boy needs his family. It's all we got."

"Thank you, Miss," Silva said again. "But you owed him nothing."

"A mother can't help but want to make it right," Miss Lula said, grinding her teeth and seething some exasperated tone that spat and popped from her lips like splintering wood.

She turned a stiff eye to Silva.

"I heard word he was to leave for school," Miss Lula said.

She watched Silva stand stock-still.

"Funny how fast word spreads around here," she continued. "I would just hope to make it right before he leaves."

"He's already gone!" Jesse interrupted.

"Now that's strange," Miss Lula said looking around her. "I could've sworn someone just told me he was still here, or that he might be here soon. But I tend to forget. Things often get lost in translation."

Miss Lula turned to me, then turned her sights toward the window, bringing both Silva and Jesse's eyes directly to mine. She then heightened her attack, saying, "One day we'll get it right."

She breathed deeply.

"One day," she lamented with her sights on that nothingness that existed outside the window. "One day, I swear. Speaking of, one day Mr. Kern almost found Jesse's letters. I can't tell you how much I worried about what he'd think or say and about that anger of his and what he would do to know a negra he'd employed had done him wrong. Once he left the room, I hid them somewhere I knew he'd never see, and I'll place them there again now. And Silva, I will never tell. I promise. But Fletcher can never go back to that school. He belongs here, and he will always be here with his family and those who love him."

Miss Lula returned the letters to her dress, tucking them far from sight.

"Bring him tomorrow so I can apologize in person," she said. "I know it's only a small gesture, but it's the least I can do. After so many months, I don't even think I'll recognize him."

Miss Lula smiled as she turned and left the room, understanding Silva's silence to mean that her son would never leave Greenwood, working unquestionably for the Kern family for the rest of his life. That in the likeness of that server whom the Missus had met on that riverboat cruise, Fletcher, too, might think he's going somewhere but wake only to find that he's returned to the same place he'd just left, having merely traveled up and down that same river to the same ends.

CHAPTER 18

Silva did not bring Fletcher on the next day or the next or any other subsequent day that followed. Silva held to her defiance, emboldened by that apparent refusal on the Missus's part to stand against it. However, from what I had seen of the Missus, she knew exactly when to strike and the manner in which to do so. And so instead she waited, a serpent in the grass who was never anxious or worried as she watched her prey, a lioness who would pounce, but only when the time was right, never in fear that those months of preparation would suddenly fall apart now that victory was in reach. She anticipated the boy's arrival as she would a cake to rise in the oven, checking on it every so often until the moment finally came.

The first of spring seemed to come earlier and earlier each year, and that spring was no different, although it was still a ways to go before the heat truly descended. The plantation still saw no sight of Fletcher as summer began, although the Missus remained in good spirits and did not show signs of concern. It was during this time of standoff between Silva and the Missus that Floyd pulled me aside one day and revealed a crinkled letter that bore Fletcher's name at the bottom and had been addressed to both Jesse and his mother. Right away I grabbed the letter and started to read.

"Dear Mama and Jesse," it began. "You would never think this country looks any different than home, but it does. There's not a flat spot up here and most of my walks to class are either uphill or downhill but never straight. We all dread it as much as the next. It's already cold, and the first snowstorm brought at least ten inches to the ground. Last week when it melted, there was a social and we all dressed up and met inside the school's gymnasium. I wish I had pictures to send. Some of my classmates and I get together once a week to talk about what's going on back home. They've never been to the South and want to see it for themselves how life really is. I can't say I blame them for their shock every time they read a newspaper or hear one of my stories. I miss you all terribly. And, Mama, please tell Floyd and Miss Bernie I miss them as well and Aunt Joanne and Cousin Marcus and Lilly, too. Always, Fletcher."

I held the letter as if that crumpled piece of paper were the actual boy inside my hands. Floyd had several of these letters, letters he had transcribed personally before returning the originals to Jesse. I read each letter alone, tales of late buses through the dead of night, en route from Greenwood to Maine, the stench of sour toilets during a rest stop, the curiosity on a stranger's face who had seen one of Fletcher's books and wondered what black boy could read such heavy works. His words came to me like Bible verses from my childhood when those foreign places seemed almost too strange to ever exist, and so they existed nowhere other than those pages. I saw Fletcher's every footstep in those accounts, where a passing thought at night could so easily bring to mind that library with its moving stacks that slid noisily across the floor or the bells from the chapel that awakened by the simple thought of morning as the sycamore twirled its leaves.

Fletcher wrote to us weekly, the last of his letters coming nearly three weeks before that summer was to start, just preceding the influx of bees and horseflies around the plantation. It arrived right amidst the swells of smoky air from grills that seemed to define this time of warmth and kick-started a feeling of prosperity in people. And although I typically enjoyed these occasions, my contempt for that end to Fletcher's stories made it impossible for me to smile even once as the smoke imbued the air, and I sat down to read that final letter as it was presented to me.

Dear Mama,

    I will surely miss this place over the summer, although my greatest hopes are of seeing both you and Jesse as soon as possible. I cannot say how much I miss your cooking and the smell of cinnamon and nutmeg in the house. The food here is almost like something outside of the United States, and I've lost at least ten pounds from not eating it. My classes are soon to be over and my grades are good, although there's one professor who seems intent on making my experience harder than the rest. There aren't many other negroes here, and so the few of us stick together as much as possible, and they've each had their own experiences with that teacher. I've also made a few new friends, white boys from California. They're different from anyone here and especially anyone I've ever met back home. But I mind my manners when I'm around them. I can't wait to return next year as a sophomore. They say it gets easier then. Can't wait to see you both soon.

                            Yours,

                            Fletcher

This last letter was old by the time I'd read it, and my thoughts possessed me to believe the boy had been home for some time by the time I'd actually seen it. Inside the house, the tension still stirred between the Missus and Silva—passive, though soon capable of boiling over. Yet each letter from Fletcher placed my thoughts at lengths far away from the madness, elevating me to some height only experienced by the cloud walkers, as we called them in those days, those tall women who left their presence down the aisles of planes, giving off whiffs of rose water and vanilla when they passed, their charm able to captivate any man and leave them stupefied in those women's wake.

That summer would prove to be of a milder nature than the previous year, yet there was still no guessing as to how long the calm could last. The Missus had once again resumed her throne as the honeysuckles and jacarandas made their presence known, their sweetness lingering into midafternoon despite the humidity. There were tidings of cooler air that poured in from the base of marsh trees and sent that coolness directly to our doorstep. The air held hints of pond water and tree bark in its sting, and the Missus took it all in from her perch, exhaling loudly as she looked around at the restoration this summer brought, as though a vibrant energy descended through the greenery and blue skies that penetrated the Missus as well.

"Bernie!" she called forcibly, as if I were not seated mere inches away and could not land my hand directly on her shoulder with nothing more than a simple reach.

"Yes, Miss?" I replied.

"See I should get a handful of those awful treats you all love to eat," she said.

"Some fruit, Miss?" I asked.

"Yes," she replied. "I wanna taste them. See what all the fuss is about."

Knowing Floyd would never pick a single bud for the Missus unless it be poisonous, I stood and gathered the fruit myself from the back tree, picking the small crabapples that had just ripened and blushed a deep red with green underbellies. When I'd returned, Miss Lula had already forgotten my mission and looked about her wildly to see me hand over a cleaned piece of fruit to taste.

"How do you even know where to begin?" she fussed.

"Just bite it, Miss," I said.

Following my instructions, she did, immediately spitting the sour flesh from her mouth for Silva or myself to clean up. In truth, Floyd had never brought crabapples to the house because of their bitterness, yet the persimmons were not yet ripened, and my concern over the Missus's mood had all but vanished since she revealed her plotted revenge. Like the others, I cared very little if she experienced more heartbreak, as she gave it quite well. The Missus shooed me away, and I smiled, hearing her curses follow me inside the house.

The Missus sat quietly for several more hours before she found the energy to stir again, the sun just descending and the bustle that had started the day now diminished into a mere simmer of tractors performing final rounds in the fields. A few birds chirped passively as closed windows dampened the crickets' calls.

"Silva!" the Missus shouted from her sunken chair.

There was a long pause, time enough for Silva to make it from the kitchen to that outside area when the Missus called again. She waited, then cleared her throat. When Silva finally showed, she brought with her a contemptuousness that showed on her face as well as within the bowl of cornbread she mixed so vigorously and persistently she seemed to pound it into nothing.

"Yes, Miss?" Silva sassed.

The Missus remained focused on the plush flowers all around them. She took in a deep breath then sighed.

"What do you make of this good weather we've been having?" the Missus asked.

"It's fine, I guess," Silva said.

"That's all you got to say today?" the Missus chided.

"Ain't nothing else worth saying now is there?" Silva swore.

Silva stood there stone-faced, her temper just as feisty as the Missus's in that moment.

"I guess you hard of seeing nowadays, just as bad as you are of hearing," Miss Lula fussed. "But I thought you might like this weather, especially with your boy out there. Guess we all makes mistakes though. Shame it won't be here for long. Gonna change once fall gets here pretty soon, I bet."

Silva waited impatiently for the purpose of this speech, the time ticking just as those drops from her spoon into the wide-mouthed bowl. Still the Missus did not hurry, watching the fields in contemplation of a thought that remained unspoken.

"Since Christmas I've wanted to make this house complete, get some good weather and get it done," Miss Lula finally said. "Now that Jesse's completed the inside beautifully, there's just the outside. Weather's good enough, so might as well go ahead and get it done. But it seems it'll never be done—that is, unless I force it."

Silva was truly a demonic force at that moment, a woman comprised of failures and shortcomings, and some would say a few successes if you counted her boys. And here was the Missus, trying to ruin them.

"What is it, Miss?" Silva said in a low voice with her eyes cocked toward the crown of the Missus's head.

"Now, I've given you long enough," Miss Lula said. "You pay attention good. That boy of yours won't be going back to that school, that's for sure, not to that school or any other. We need him around the farm out there with Floyd. Now, I've allowed him one year and said nothing about it but that's enough. How many does he need? No, he should be here with us and not abandoning his home and way of life like those other negras. Besides, he's family and should be with family, not running off getting ahead of himself like you lettin' him do. Now, you bring him at the end of summer for the harvest when the new workers come, and we'll keep him on from there."

Miss Lula handed Silva one of Jesse's letters, which Silva read silently.

"Not a day before or after," Miss Lula said. "I means it, Silva. Don't you find yourself having this conversation again."

The Missus said nothing else, returning to her previous thoughts as Silva left the porch.

The sun seemed not to set on its own that evening, requiring several shoves from my willful thoughts to send it across the sky and past the horizon. How long that day seemed to saunter and sway toward some concrete finality that was not soon to come. How torturous it proved when a bird's song or a cool breeze upon my cheek blew that flame away and it was finally tomorrow, yet still I lay awake in view of it all. And when that truth allowed not a civil thought or cause to enter my mind, and fatigue made me as restless as an infant who refuses his bottle or the breast, I abandoned these efforts at civility and instead chose contempt for the Missus and her departed child from that day forth.

CHAPTER 19

Fletcher wasn't due to return for another week, yet the Missus still sat delighted as ever in view of the sunshine outdoors, a contentment built upon her face that I thought would surely reach its peak the moment Fletcher was delivered to her custody. Her color was deeper, and she now appeared a shade I'd never thought her feeble skin could muster. Sadly though, I had settled into the ways of that house, acquiring that bit of anger that touched everyone, and I feared it would stain young Fletcher as well. This restlessness had risen in us all, as no one knew exactly what to expect of the Missus and her plan or from each other anymore. With Jesse's part of her schemes completed, he was released and returned with Floyd in the fields like some dog with its tail between its legs. I don't think that boy was ever happier, surely, looking back on those days when he'd fought to be inside the house and wondering how he'd ever fallen for it.

There was a quiet period that followed Jesse's absence, our routines falling back to that time before Jesse knew the insides of the house, and the Missus only that insolence she bore, as this silence somehow masked the trepidation that was to come when I think back on it now. When Fletcher arrived on that morning in preparation for the harvest, Silva held him close, delivering him directly to Floyd.

"You watch after my boy," she said strongly.

Miss Lula had been asleep when the boy arrived but somehow sensed his presence as she now rushed into the kitchen where Silva prepared breakfast.

"I knows it's not easy," Miss Lula soothed to Silva whose back sat toward the young Missus, that proud servant unwilling to turn a single cheek in the Missus's direction in good weather or bad.

Just then the light curved into the room, bathing the Missus in warmth while leaving Silva as cold as night.

"He's better off here," Miss Lula assured her. "You'll see. It's good for him."

"My boy deserve to be at school," Silva said with her back still turned.

"Your boy's right where he belong," Miss Lula admonished. "Poor Elizabeth never even had one year of schooling. Your boy had plenty. Now he can give something back and be of some use to his pappy. It's all he deserves."

Silva stood erect, her hand clutching the knife that Miss Lula did not see. The Missus turned decidedly toward the brightly painted doorframe which sat within the light.

"I swear this place sure looks nice," she said. "Sometimes it even reminds me of home, negras and all."

"Lord willing, you goin' reap what you sow," Silva said. "And I just pray that you live to see the day His judgment fall on you."

"Darling, you don't know what judgment is," Miss Lula said bitterly. "But one day you will. It comes like a thief in the night and it's gone before you even know it. But for just one glimpse at seeing that boy suffer, I'd die happy even if I had to face my sin in the afterlife."

Miss Lula watched her meanly, then left the kitchen and made herself presentable upstairs. Mr. Kern knew nothing of the boy's arrival as he entered the dining room. He had indeed been oblivious to the boy's impending return from its onset, never hearing of the exit letter Fletcher wrote to school and the program's remorseful response. The Missus kept it all quiet as she eased downstairs and delivered a kiss to Mr. Kern's cheek. She then sat beside him and was as pleasant as the day he'd met her.

"What's this mood?" Mr. Kern asked. "I don't think I've seen it before."

"Don't say that," she teased. "I'm always this good."

"Not since Heck was a puppy, and now he's grown with kids," Mr. Kern laughed.

"Well, if you keep that up it won't last for long," she said.

"Don't mind me," he said. "That harvest gonna take it outta me this year. I don't know if I got the strength for it no more."

"Why don't you let Floyd handle it then," she said. "He knows it left and right. That's what you pay him for."

"I just like to keep an eye out," he said.

"Well, let me," she offered. "I've seen 'em workin' before. I'm sure I can do it just as good as anybody else."

Mr. Kern grimaced not from her words but from some deep pain inside that had steadily worsened and could be said to be brought about by those years in the fields or possibly that loneliness he felt in his heart. Either way, it pained him and was not soon to diminish no matter the length of time he battled. Miss Lula understood that tiresome expression for what it was as she now placed her hand upon his wrist and sighed.

"You make me so angry sometimes, George," she said. "Stubborn as a mule and cunning as a fox. I hate seeing you in pain even if you won't admit it. Now let me be your wife and take over while you rest in here. If not, I'm inclined to call the doctor and see what he says."

"No, no," Mr. Kern barked. "I'm not gonna be some tree stump."

"You *will* be if you run yourself into the ground," she sassed.

Mr. Kern thought about these words and smiled.

"I guess a little rest might not kill me as fast as none is killing me now," he said, bringing a smile to Miss Lula's face as she patted his hand, awkward thumps that showed no affection yet still seemed tender if you didn't know her.

She then stood and quit the dining room, passing Silva as she left her food on the table uneaten and delivered a sly grin that conveyed the workings of her heart. Once outside, she found Floyd by the stables. He had heard nothing of her approach, only turned to see her standing there with quills for eyes.

"Where is he?" she said directly.

"Miss, I never even see ya there."

"Fletcher," she demanded. "Mister's not feeling well, so I'm taking over for him today. Wanna welcome him back."

"I already got 'im workin', Miss," Floyd said.

"Ain't no need of playing coy," she said. "I told you I need to see the boy, so go get him and send him to the stables."

"Might take a minute," Floyd said.

"Takes all you need," she replied.

Floyd did as he was told, sending Fletcher inside the stables, although not without his company. Upon hearing them, Miss Lula looked up to see the boy, spotting immediately those eyes she could recognize, no matter how tall he grew, the familiarity overtaking her as she watched a younger Mr. Kern stare back at her.

"He's fine, Floyd," she said. "It's just me. He knows me since he was little."

"I'd like ta stay if it's work related," Floyd said. "Make sure he behave."

"He don't need a chaperone," she insisted. "I'm sure he's just fine. A young man can walk and talk on his own nowadays."

"If ya insist," Floyd said, bowing courteously as he left the stable.

He found me outside the door as he pushed it closed, though not fully latched.

"Lord knows what she wants," Floyd said, taking his business elsewhere while I nudged the door just slightly to keep it open.

The Missus walked closer to Fletcher, who remained a figure of chaste beauty, and although he wore a simple shirt and tattered shorts and bore hands dirtier than that of an oiler, he still appeared as refined as any gentleman you'd meet on the streets in a suit and tie. His height likely surprised her, although nothing else seemingly did, for he was always this handsome and possessed of those most admirable traits of Mr. Kern, like that old man's unbending eyes beneath his broad forehead. The sternness Mr. Kern held in his face was also present in Fletcher, yet so was the gentleness Mr. Kern revealed at the faintest moments, that gentleness which Fletcher removed on this day.

"It gets to everyone their first time back," she said, looking around the stable at the work Floyd had done.

"I know why I'm here," Fletcher said.

"And that is?" she asked.

"To be your slave," he answered.

"Never, Fletcher," she commanded. "I own no slaves. Everyone gets paid equally for the work they do here."

"Then let me go," he said.

"You can leave whenever you like. It's not me who keeps you here. It's your mother and her alone who makes you work in the fields."

"She makes me because of you," he said.

"That's nonsense, Fletcher," Miss Lula said gently. "You should be nowhere you don't wants to be."

"Then I shouldn't be here," he said.

"You talk as if we've wronged you. By giving your mother and brother and you work here, we've somehow done *you* wrong. It's by our work here on this earth that we work toward the kingdom, young Fletcher. Never forget."

"I didn't ask for this work," Fletcher said.

"But you received it and should be grateful to be so blessed. You should go to sleep every night with your lips to God's ears speaking words of thanks and gratitude. You should pray it never fades because, trust me, many people would want what you got."

"And what's that?" Fletcher asked.

Miss Lula paused in recognition of some thought that had troubled her mind for a while now and bore saying or else it might trouble her always. Her eyes found Fletcher's stare as she continued.

"Tell me, Fletcher, do you remember my daughter?" she asked.

Fletcher looked at her, confused.

"My daughter, Elizabeth," she reiterated. "She was your age, or would be your age now."

"No," he replied sternly. "Should I?"

Miss Lula was an empty vessel, a starlit sky that showed all the possibilities beyond this world, so translucent and clear that I did know all of her at that very moment, and I could not help but pity what it was I did see. For surely it was at that moment that her heart broke, reforming into whatever misshapen monstrosity it remained as until she died, her eyes watery and her lips quivering like a babe.

"No, Fletcher, you're not my slave," she said. "But you are my employee and you work for me and will always work for me. All of you will until the day you die. And that's how you will be remembered by those in this house, and no one outside these walls will remember you or ever know you existed, and you will hate it until you die, young Fletcher. A boy of such promise. No, no one will even know your name outside these walls, I swear to it."

She grabbed hold of Fletcher's arm and squeezed it. Fletcher watched her fearfully. He saw the conviction in her eyes, the savagery that such a small body could hold. She woke suddenly, confused to find his wrist inside her hand as she now eased it from her own.

"Never grow tired of home," she said. "You had your first steps in this house, and I watched you take them. And you'll have your last here. I swear to it."

She turned and left Fletcher at the stall, his eyes a blank stare that for the first time became aware of the brutality that controlled this house and indeed the Missus's role in it.

"Now hurry back to Floyd, or else he'll be mad at us both," she said. "Your place is with him now, not with me."

And with that salutation their conversation ended, Fletcher returning to the fields and Miss Lula to that porch where she watched him, along with the other workers, for the remainder of the evening, her throat never parched as she frequently called for iced tea or lemonade, her stomach never lacking the heaviness of a sweet roll to curb her appetite until dinner. She later retired to her bedroom and would remain there, needing nothing until the next morning when she woke and requested eggs Benedict and a cup of coffee, if there was any creamer left, and that the English muffin be lightly toasted and buttered with an extra pad on the side. Needless to say, Silva refused this request, and the Missus ate oatmeal like the rest. Still, she didn't complain, biding her time here, just like the rest of us.

CHAPTER 20

The pain grew in that certain part of Mr. Kern, deepening that summer, though the prideful man mentioned nothing of it until Silva discovered him half alive in his parlor one afternoon.

"Sir, we gots to get you to a hospital," Silva insisted.

She tugged at his near-lifeless form, feeling his hand slip from her fingers as her insistence was met only by a wave of his arm and she, no longer caring of any outcome inside that house good or bad, merely continued with her duties and paid no further attention to the man in the room.

My response, I must sadly admit, was of the same resignation, as I did not fetch the Missus or even call the doctor when I'd seen the old man in such dire straits. In fact, I did not concern myself with the Mister's death until the plight posed by the Missus's unmitigated power bestowed by that untimely occurrence finally hit me, and I knew his death would confer upon her the one thing she had always wanted: her freedom. And it was then that I acted.

The Missus displayed no visible sign of concern over the Mister's absence during dinner, not that it was expected she would. In fact, upon hearing of his illness at the onset of her meal, she carefully finished her portion then sipped her coffee slowly between bites of sweet roll, before stealing off to his parlor room where she reproached Silva for not informing her sooner.

She found the old man on the floor when she entered, lifting him to her breasts like a newborn.

"Somebody get Floyd!" she yelled.

Floyd was the only one strong enough to carry Mr. Kern to his bedroom, where he ensured the old man was still of this world before he left for his own quarters, saying to him, "Ya gotta kick that demon," and hearing Mr. Kern grunt back, "If it don't kick me first."

Mr. Kern appeared as feeble as a wayward ghost having returned to earth for a spot of unfinished business, his hair ivory and his skin gray-green, like the tint of an overcooked yolk, his eyes deep pockets that were dim as the shadows that hung around him.

"Promise me, sir, if ya don't kick it first, ya better run like hell if ya see that white light comin' for ya," Floyd said.

Mr. Kern grinned, although even that small gesture seemed too exhaustive in his state as he soon lay back with his head on his pillow and closed his eyes. The doctor arrived by nightfall and brought with him an assistant who seemed more interested in the Missus's delicate smile than actually caring for Mr. Kern. Lucky for us all, there would be no need for some lengthy hospital stay, the doctor assured, as the Mister's condition had been brought on by a pesky bug and prolonged periods of dehydration. Still, he would need ample rest and would miss the remaining weeks of the harvest, a fact that ailed him more than the fever he bore.

Miss Lula remained outside during his recovery, never necessarily walking amongst the workers, just checking with Floyd to ensure things were run properly and that the boy was there. According to Floyd, she did not bother Fletcher anymore after her initial harassment, leaving him to toil and sweat and ache and slog out amongst the cotton for days and months and years, as that image alone brought more joy to her mind than actually having to look into the boy's face and see the eyes of Mr. Kern. Elizabeth also shared these eyes, that familiarity glaring back, a familiarity of things she'd lost when Elizabeth accepted the grave.

Other than that first day inside the stables, I hadn't seen Fletcher following his return. With Silva obliged to do nothing while Mr. Kern died, I spent most days in that upstairs quarters where he lay, nostalgia growing, as a spark does to a roaring flame, as I recalled the time with the Missus nearly two years prior when her illness took hold and we formed such closeness. Although he rarely spoke or even noticed my presence, Mr. Kern drew gentler during those passing days. Whether attributable to that inevitable shrinking that occurred in the elderly that caused those once-tall giants to appear like infants or that resolution that came when so close to the end, Mr. Kern was changing and visibly so. He spoke softly in his requests for this or that. He smiled more frequently although never quite long enough to savor it for even a moment. Surprising all of us, Mr. Kern did not die as some had expected, although he never fully recovered from that illness either. His was one of those rusted hearts that lived on out of spite or repetition, merely completing the same sequences day after day with his coffee, newspapers, and walks around the grounds if he had enough strength, finding this consistency to be a vehicle that allowed him to live forever in the humdrum that existed yet never stirred too high or too low.

What started out cooler had turned insufferably hotter as that season progressed to a rapid end and compelled upon us a show of brute force, as not to be labeled inferior with summers past. Just after noonday on one of the summer's hottest, I caught sight of Fletcher for the first time in weeks, Floyd having brought the boys around back for a spot of relief. It was there that I noticed them in conference by the side porch, dangerously close to the Missus, who sat at the front house. Jesse stood by the weak screen door with his back toward my sights while Floyd stood in front of him and Fletcher just off the main path, where only his arm was visible. From that vantage, I could assume Silva was right, as the boy's color had indeed grown darker, although it still paled in comparison to the other workers or even that of Jesse and Floyd. And unlike those other workers, Fletcher's color would not last past this season and would surely once again fade to display that indelible difference that existed between himself and the other workers, that differ- ence that was always there and that stretched deeper than color. The boy was tough, and that grace he showed wrapped tightly about him as if it were a part of his own skin, yet still, one had to wonder just how long it could last inside this house.

For four years nothing seemed to happen except for the weather. The cotton grew and was picked and chopped and harvested and sold. The workers came each year, then left that plantation just as desolate and solemn as before they arrived. The land constantly changed from white to brown to green with each passing season of those cotton fields, yet it was all predict- able. Each day, Floyd and Fletcher pastured the cows out by the long fence line and kept the chickens content within their coop. Jesse tossed slop at the hogs and tended the Missus's garden, where she grew patches of tomatoes, peppers, onions, and some okra. And nothing occurred on that plantation that the Missus did not oversee or dictate or decree, at least while her strength was with her.

Jesse had married a girl from Sidon and with that union became a wiser man. He worked efficiently now, never too hard yet never leaving a task undone. He was quieter and did his hours only in anticipation of returning home to Elise. There was nothing else about him, it seemed, his wife and love for her the only things that kept him alive. Fletcher, too, was a quiet presence, much as those snapping turtles that were seen then went unnoticed for weeks at a time, the boy's eyes always a mystery and that smile no longer visible unless he was caught in conversation with Jesse or Floyd, which was seldom. Some evenings I would see him working the far reaches of the fields, a tall figure that would stand, stretch, then bend once more as he continued. Looking beside me on the porch, Miss Lula watched him as well, her pale skin no longer taking on color as it once did. No matter the length of time she spent outdoors, her color was always the same as when I'd first met her, when it seemed as if her skin could tear by the wind's touch alone.

Maybe it was a lack of sleep or approaching illness that pestered her, but the Missus's eyes had grown darker. She appeared ghostly as she slipped through the house and onto the porch then retired to her quarters without a single word to anyone. Some nights she appeared to be almost maddened as I would catch sight of her wandering the hallways. I found her one night just as Silva left the main house for the evening, and the plantation sat quiet.

The kitchen was dark and everything put away as I'd ventured to Mr. Kern's room once more before retiring to sleep. Sleep had not only touched Mr. Kern but the Missus as well, as the entire upstairs quarters sat silent and bleak beneath the shade of midnight. I eased into his room and made final arrangements for my own rest, as most evenings my bed consisted of a chair beside the Mister's bed. Some nights when Mr. Kern proved quite capable to sleep on his own, I would find my room out in the servant quarters with Floyd just as I'd left it, a small ten by ten space with a bed and a window, that's it. Mr. Kern's breathing had worsened as of late and was quite labored on this evening, causing me to prepare a blanket and pillow in the chair beside him as I closed my eyes and drifted to sleep.

A noise woke me around three in the morning as I opened my eyes to see a presence in the hallway. Begrudgingly, I shrugged off that final layer of sleep, feeling my mind once again connect with muscles as I stirred in the dim space that seemed oddly recognizable, as if fully lit. The strangeness of this place was so familiar—the sadness of that lonely corridor at night when outside sat the dark peak of nocturnal bliss; the buffing of an untrafficked floor by Silva or myself, so godforsaken yet innate that it no longer provoked despair; those halls as peaceful as Eden, as they sat empty most days and never had a single smudge on them. I knew these halls well, that setting pressed upon my memory, for they had not changed in four years, although they could sometimes seem as foreign as those thoughts I'd felt when winter came to Greenwood and I dreamt of my former home in Clinton with Henry.

Drawing from the room with heavy footsteps that slid along the floor, I searched for that sight I'd seen outside the Mister's door, my figure taking on the gloom of the hallway as I lurched. I started in the living room, a site dowsed in affirmation of Jesse's work, as those walls still appeared as crisp as the day they were painted. From the high windows hung drapes that the young man had indeed measured, rodded, and secured to the wall. In the air was a smell of lacquer that never quite faded and still infused the room with bitter hints of its presence. With no sight of that ghostly being, I stole into the kitchen as low and measured as before. Upon the wall hung the Missus's clock that ticked every night and could be heard throughout the house like Morse code calling some far-off place. From the corner of my sight, an ethereal presence like that of a sheet cast in blowing wind rushed past the open door. The air was cold, the wind rapping against the window's seams and now pushing its way through the hallways as it made that narrow space as frozen as the Missus's icebox. The light lasted as I followed its trail upstairs and watched it stop just inside the Missus's doorway.

Fear settled upon my heart like some ironclad appendage whose weight rendered it useless. I leaned forward against the doorframe, that hardwood floor seemingly better than any cushion of my bed as I rested. Still, this fatigue did not present itself as something physical, some ailment that could be remedied by sleep or a good meal. No, it was altogether different although still capable of robbing me of my strength and that bit of consciousness I had at this time of night. Fearing I would sit there forever if I did not stand, I finally entered the Missus's bedroom. She stood at the window, her nightgown blowing like a sail set free of its sheaves.

"Miss," I called to her back, my voice lost in the wind.

Her murmurs raised and lowered yet never really reached a decibel where they were actually audible. I approached and placed my hand on her shoulder, applying loving strokes that caused her head to fall and her arms to sway limp at her side.

"Miss," I repeated. "It's me, Bernie."

Her white face turned to me with plum lips that trembled.

"I see you," she said. "Mama sees you."

Her eyes looked into mine yet I was sure her vision was that of a dream as she continued her nonsensical speech, and the wind kept up its fuss from the open window, causing her hair to fly wildly about her head. I closed the window and led the Missus to her bedside, her body easily manipulated like that of a tired child as she had little control over her faculties and stayed wherever I placed her. She lay down to sleep with the same murmurs as before, her skin a cold mass of ice and her eyes deathly.

CHAPTER 21

This bit of madness was not an infrequent occurrence with the Missus. It had indeed worsened during those four years of isolation amongst the cotton and its endless cycle, growing stronger as Mr. Kern grew more ill and that house increasingly lonelier with only the marsh surrounding us on all sides as company. Her hysterics now manifested in a vacant stare that lasted most days for hours and incited that same trepidation I'd once had, fearing she'd fallen into one of those seizures. Yet no seizure came of these episodes, and she just remained that way for days at a time with no amount of attention capable of waking her.

And so it occurred one day as I ventured into the kitchen from an afternoon reading Mr. Kern one of his favorite books that I saw Miss Lula at the kitchen door facing outward, as stiff as a corpse standing upright.

"Bernice," a voice called just as I moved toward the still body.

I turned to see Silva standing at the stove.

"Just leave her," she said.

"How long has she been there?"

"Long enough," Silva replied. "She done gone mad after all these years, and I don't blame her. Serves her right. Crazy ass heifer. She been standing there mumbling something for the past thirty minutes. Then she started playing a game with her little imaginary friend, the only one she got."

"Elizabeth," I whispered.

"That child ain't no more thinking about her than a man on the moon," Silva said. "But if she is I'm glad, because at least she can keep the Missus out of my hair."

"I don't know who's got more sense left in them," I said. "Mr. Kern or her?"

"She ain't never gonna be the same again," Silva swore. "Something done placed on her heart and it won't let her go. She goin' see that child and what she lost and what she did for the rest of her life, God willing."

We stood there watching the Missus for another half hour before Silva finally tired of the Missus's presence and ushered the woman back upstairs to her quarters. Silva then returned and continued her work while I crushed Mr. Kern's medication.

"I swear she can live like that forever and it wouldn't bother me," Silva said, exhaling a loud breath.

"I honestly don't know who'll go first," I said.

"He's up for the challenge," she said. "That one's not."

This was the longest conversation I'd had with Silva since that dinner at her home nearly five years earlier. It was likely the longest conversation Silva had spoken with anyone inside the Kern house since Fletcher's arrival, yet there was no need to expect she would have a desire to continue. Since my previous sighting of Fletcher outside that house with Floyd and Jesse along the back paths, I had neither seen nor heard a lick from him either, the young man somehow sensing my attention to this detail when he found me one day soon after as I worked the stables beside

Roxy and Corrine. He was a solemn shade, like a tearing of artichoke leaves until one reached that center heart. He had become a creature of habit, using no other endowments other than what he had been taught for work in the fields. He was stripped of that promise he had, lowering his head as he approached and speaking like a servant would, although his tone remained that of royalty.

"Miss," he spoke softly, "Mama sent me to help with the gathering."

The gathering he referenced was to take place at the pecan groves on the outskirts of Mr. Kern's land, that floodplain area where the soil was as fertile as if planted in God's own hand. I walked him to the field where Floyd had been working since dawn, commanding this marshland that took center stage once the cotton harvest was over, where among the seventy-foot giants, workers stretched for miles as they each filled their sacks with the green husks that fell to the ground. Floyd made quick use of our labor, pointing to our designated area and issuing us each two sacks before sending us amongst the muddy trunks.

Fletcher worked close beside me, not intentionally yet the drupes were so numerous that neither he nor I could collect them all individually in one passing. He had never held much weight on him, growing taller than wider each year, and it was now safe to conclude that he would never be a stout man. Not long after we'd started, his slender frame had already buckled and could no longer support the weight of his growing sack as he sluggishly dragged it over the fractured husks and muddy ground. Although he had worked for four years now in the cotton, he was still just as weak, his skin still just as reflective of his young age and not showing of the laborious work he'd done. He was still mild-mannered and his temper never a notch above a simmer, although that kind quality often doubled as complacency. It was as I thought of him during his younger days that he turned to me with eyes that seemed to grieve for that former life and caused me to know immediately that I was surely looking at that innocent boy and no one else.

"Miss?" he now uttered as we bent amongst the groves and his forehead beaded with sweat.

"Yes, Fletcher?" I said.

"How are we not slaves?" he asked.

This shocked me more than anything he'd ever asked, although I did my best to answer.

"Because we're not," I replied simply.

"But how?" he insisted, returning my thoughts to that conversation he'd had with the Missus in those outer stables.

"Because no one keeps us here," I said. "We're not slaves to riches or fortune or any man or woman ..."

"But circumstance," he said. "We're slaves to our circumstances."

While it was true that at times I'd blamed the Missus for our woes and at other times the Mister, and then sometimes during my lowest, rightly or wrongly so, I'd blamed Mississippi for the way we were, I could not think of a single sufficient answer to his question for truly I'd wondered the exact same thing, if every home came with such vengeance, anger, sadness, and scorn. Maybe it was the land, I'd considered during an earlier time, as I'd looked out upon that prideful cotton bloom. That white gold was all we worked for. It was all we ever cherished, each year toiling for its perfection, and it was all we ever did. We did not seek God during those days or His love. We did not thank Him for the land He'd provided or the sky or the birds or the animals. No, we just did what our minds and our sights and our pride urged us to do, and we worshipped our sin like gods. That's all we did.

"But, Miss Bernie, I know no one keeps me here," Fletcher continued. "But I still feel trapped. Like I wanna go somewhere and can't. Like I wanna do anything else sometimes but this. But is that wrong? Am I crying over something I shouldn't?"

"No, Fletcher," I said, lifting my sack onto my shoulder once more and watching him follow. "But no man's circumstance is perfect."

"How about yours, Miss Bernie?" he said. "You and Floyd are so different yet you're still here in the same place."

"Because we're both of the same spirit," I replied.

"I don't understand," he said.

Here, I dropped my sack to the ground, as did Fletcher whose sack was nearly to the ground already.

"You see, Floyd had no schooling growing up, while I was taught my lesson every day," I explained. "While he worked in the fields, I served in the house, where I had time to read and kept a book at my side. Daddy insisted I go to school for at least twelve hours a week while Floyd didn't need any schooling because, according to Daddy, there was no reason for him to get an education when all he needed to know was out there in those fields. But we both grew up as workers, and Floyd's knowledge gained in the cotton was no different than mine inside that house or inside those books. We both have a similar spirit that leads us to the work we do. It's just something that's in us."

"Does that mean I'm supposed to work here forever too?" he asked.

"Only if you want to," I said. "You're only a slave to your circumstance if it's a circumstance you don't want or one you can't change."

"But there's no way to change it," he griped.

"There's no way you've thought of yet," I replied. "Fletcher, do birds remain in winter when that cold threatens their livelihood? Do migrants stay in one place where there is no food left to keep them?"

Fletcher considered these thoughts in silence, his sliding sack the only noise between us for several minutes.

"Mr. Kern likes you," he said. "Why?"

"He tolerates my care," I said. "But he likes no one."

"Especially not me," Fletcher acknowledged. "He saw me the other day for the first time and was so sick he couldn't stand upright. And when I tried to help him, he yelled and shooed me away like I was a dog or worse. But somehow it was like he didn't even see me, and his hands could never reach me so he just stood there swinging as if he had seen a ghost, and so I left him just the way he was."

"He's a man who's spent his entire life out here amongst the fields," I said. "He's entitled to a few gripes every now and then. Would you say?"

"But he loves Floyd and you and Mama too, but not me."

"His heart is heavy and bears a weight neither you or I can understand," I said. "Old age comes with many prices, and we all have to pay for the sins of our youth. You can live your whole life as a wolf, I swear, but one day you'll be a sheep, I promise you."

"So, you don't hate it here?" he asked.

"No," I replied. "But my time here isn't forever, and neither is yours. It's all but a season, my dear, and then we move on. You see, Fletcher, while Floyd and I are of the same spirit, we're still different people and as such he'll likely stay, although I won't, at least not forever. Same can be said of you. You'll do your time, learn what this place has to offer, and use that knowledge and strength when the time comes for you to move on. But you'll never forget what you've been taught. Remember, only children sulk in their condition and don't see the promise that lies ahead, and it's only because they know no better."

"But I can't go back to school," he said.

"And you won't need to," I promised. "You're stronger now and smarter and that comes from your circumstance. No amount of education can teach you to be a man."

It was with this conversation that I knew Fletcher's life would not be as easy as I'd once imagined when he was a child, watching him run amongst the cotton in those days, as if that crop were not the poisonous slayer of his dreams, as if it did not wait for him so patiently as he grew to lure him back so deceitfully into its trust with those white blossoms that appeared so harmless before. How in those days he drew closer to the stalks with childlike curiosity and discerned no more danger in their charm than he would a rose, so delicately meek, failing to notice the thorny bristles that now left his fingers scarred and rough from picking. I now knew he would struggle and suffer like everyone else, a pain I never wished for him, merely because he was so special and kind and giving and sweet— yet none of that mattered, as it would not spare him from the harms of this world. He could be as bright and talented as I'd imagined all those years before and possess that spirit that invited people into his arms without reservation, yet he was still a negro and, as such, would face the same challenges we all bore. And indeed, his road would be tougher, for it was always that way for wayward souls, those gifted ones amongst us, as we saw it, those ones with a mark upon their lives placed there by God's hands alone.

"Some men were just made to work," I later told him. "And some were not."

CHAPTER 22

"The stages of life are simple," someone once told me in a place I can't quite remember. "It's just the in-between that mucks it up."

True words, if ever I'd heard them spoken a day in my life, words that I attributed to Fletcher and his youth.

The young man was alone now, his thoughts kept mostly to himself, those weighty concerns worked out amongst the fields in silence while he pounded the rusty hoe. Maybe Jesse still blamed himself for Fletcher's return and the boy's loss of his former life, but either way Jesse had grown increasingly distant during those years, and indeed that time after his marriage to Elise, no longer laughing and wrestling with Fletcher as they'd done in those shaded areas out by the backhouse. They didn't talk or tease one another, finding their time on the plantation a beckon for work only. Still, Floyd and Jesse remained close, similar spirits of similar ambitions, in agreement that a decent life for themselves and their families was all they could ever hope for and that hard work made it so. But Fletcher wanted more than a life on that plantation—he'd made that clear to me. He desired more than the toils it demanded and that routine cycle ingrained in our bones.

Miss Lula had her good days and bad days too. For that bit of pleasure she gained in Fletcher's constant anguish, which he never showed and she never looked too far to see, she also lived with its downfalls, for her spirit grew weaker each time she spotted him there and saw young Elizabeth in his eyes. Fletcher's presence had indeed brought about nightmares for the Missus and her screams could be heard throughout the house at night when the silence was a sea and we all adrift in it. Her mind was some days with her and some days not. She would be spotted out by the peat soil and soft-stemmed marsh, only to be led back by Floyd or myself and placed in her room like a child who'd been put down for a nap.

"I remember it all seemed like a game," she once told me before that illness took over and maddened thoughts became all she ever saw. "All us parents and friends and family sitting in that waiting area together as one by one they'd call our names, and we'd walk into that side room where the doctors were waiting. Each family jumped up when their names were called as if they had won something—some type of prize, you know—and I'll tell you, I did the same thing when they called ours. Elizabeth was in that corner room by herself, but they didn't take us to her. No, you had to go to that side room first. I swear I could tell you every crack and every smudge, every misaligned tile on that discolored floor. It was so dirty, like they never mopped the thing a day in its life. Elizabeth had started to breathe in that labored manner and that mask was constantly slipping from her nose. She was too small for all this, and I wondered how her body even knew how to fight so hard. But, Bernie, she tried, I can say that. I knew what that side room meant. It meant we had to make a decision about whether she lived or died. George made the call. They said we could sit with her, and we did until the end. I let her know her mama was there, but I swear, when she went a part of me went with her. Hell, maybe all of me left this world, although I never quite made it there to the other side. But I left this earth, that's for damn sure."

These were her thoughts for days and weeks and months before she went down, stuck in that purgatory limbo, yet just like before, that vengeance would come roaring back and she would look around with renewed vigor to ensure her world was the same as it had been before her absence. For indeed, she was a strange presence around the house, either a contributor to its harshness or a soul lost to its brutality, I could never tell. Nonetheless, Silva and I made a promise that we would keep that house going for our own sakes and not that of Mister or Miss Lula. They could rot away for all we cared. Through their insolence they had brought the rain that now descended in buckets and just like the land that sat saturated by its intemperance, it was the best we could do in our situation to keep afloat.

This pact was essential for me to make, as I was to leave Greenwood for one month and travel east to Norfolk where my sister, Gloria, was raising Janice and Steven. Surely, if I did not make this arrangement I was certain to return and find the Mister and Missus both dead.

I left on the early bus from the city, my first bus ride since coming to Greenwood in 1966. There was always that gut feeling that came with going somewhere, that feeling of nerves and excitement and just wanting to get there already, yet this journey resonated quite differently within me, as I cared very little for the destination and more for the actual journey I took. The city was just waking as the bus jerked to a start and immediately met the countryside after that narrow row of downtown shops. I remembered those same cotton fields from my arrival in Greenwood as they now passed outside the window, and it was indeed good to see them go.

When the light cast through the window, how it did bend and break and spread itself over us and make us warm. America appeared to be someplace special when viewed through passing windows, as if anything could be claimed or owned or built or done here if you really wanted it. Yet only when you finally settled in one spot did you see quite clearly that things were not as simple as they'd seemed, that the land and opportunity you saw was not as vast, and that the earth you passed belonged to someone else, and even if it didn't, you were never going to own it, not as a negro. Not in this country.

For the long part of the ride, I thought of the house and of Floyd and Jesse and wondered if Silva had killed anyone by now. I thought of Mr. Kern and Miss Lula's antics and pondered what quarrel they might have next, maybe an incident involving a flattened fork that the Missus would surely never use, as it had lost its curve and wasn't suitable to serve a dog with. I clocked when breakfast was served and the dishes washed, when lunch was prepared and appeared on the table, and when dinner was all but left on the Missus's side, as Miss Lula took pride in picking over her food then retiring to her upstairs quarters with barely a bite in her stomach (unless it was one of her off nights, when she was enraged and ate like a fiend). I wondered if anyone missed my presence, then hoped they didn't as I questioned if I would not stay away forever, thinking of only Fletcher as a reason to return.

Gloria awaited me when I arrived in Virginia. Glori-Mae had been that one beam of light who'd shown all of us girls growing up how to be dignified young women, even if she was fast herself. Norfolk was asleep when I stepped from the bus, a dismal picture of lights here and there with wet streets and a continued threat of rain throughout the night. It was this talk of the weather and conditions where I'd come from that we started with first as Gloria loaded my bag into the car. From there, we made brief conversation of Floyd, whom we both adored as much as one could an older sibling, and then it was a retelling, although much shorter than this current rendition, of my time in Greenwood and the mess that had brewed, simmered, and now overflowed. Gloria demanded we both get out of there as soon as possible, or at least that I leave and come live with her in Virginia if Floyd would have no sense. I would be lying to God Himself if I said those thoughts did not stay with me the entirety of my trip, and especially during those quiet times when there was little to do but think about my situation and the relief I found had settled in my bones from being far away from that place.

Still, only home feels right, where even the dysfunction is somehow familiar enough to make you want or prefer it over the prickliness of a stranger's bed, that coldness that never quite fades or those sheets that never fully soften throughout the night. Even the nighttime sounds seem increasingly haunting far from home, where a floorboard wears at some outlandish hour from a stranger's foot, a light creeps in from the bottom of the door from God knows where, and all of a sudden you're worried about who's coming in and who's going out. Then odd voices filter into the room by morning and you're still not awake, that bed somehow gentle enough now to warrant another round in it. Then smells of breakfast, and not just any breakfast but a good southern meal, invade the room to inform you that you've slept in too long and that everyone else is awake and stirring about the house. And so you exit the room to find that reheated plate of food and feel ashamed and lazy, even if it is your vacation. No, I was just fine where I was, I assured myself.

That month was a blessing and a curse as I considered the Kern house almost daily. I would often wake convinced that I was in my bed in Greenwood under that stained ceiling until my eyes opened to the foursquare window at the foot of the bed, white and bare, the green leaves outside glossy with rain and the glass streaked from the tree's passing touch. The air sat thin and harsh to breathe as if no air was actually there at all, and I felt this was indeed how I would die. Even my shadows stood as nubby strangers, since there was little chance of sun in the coming days or weeks of my time in Norfolk.

If the clouds cleared even once, I swore I would leave that front porch and go for a walk, fleeing the confines of that twelve-foot expanse where I had remained for several days now in observance of what little happened on those back roads of Virginia. I swore not to be one of those people who was said to have visited a place yet only saw the inside of a house or the seat on someone's porch. The neighbors had each come and gone, ventured off to work and to school then returned, creating a bit of routine that I easily fell into as they'd wave each time they passed, and I would wave back. Still, when the sun did appear on that sixth day and there were birds circling the front yard, I found myself too tired, or my mind too preoccupied, to stir from the state I was in and move about the brief pleasantness, instead choosing to wallow in my condition like those silly adolescents who found love to be a curse that struck daily and crippled their every move. For in truth, young Fletcher had prevailed in my thoughts that entire morning, his life a tragedy I watched play out each day, a casting of lots dictated by those who sought to have their way for good or bad, leaving him trapped by the restraints they'd created, his life a whisper stopped short of heaven's door, arriving to find the mat rolled up, swept, and having been beaten by that broom out on the lawn.

Gloria sat for a few hours and the children as well, once they returned from school, taking my mind briefly away from the thoughts of Greenwood and Fletcher. There was a naturalness to their lives in Norfolk that I hadn't experienced in years, that now made me feel unmannered and ill-suited for a place like this or, indeed, any place outside of Mississippi. I had no words to offer most times, sitting quietly as the family chatted away. I felt that when I chewed I smacked and when I spoke it was too loud for everyday conversation. I smiled when I noticed their attention on me, but it was nothing more than obligation, as those innate feelings had long perished from my being.

"You find some peace today?" Gloria asked once the children were off and dreaming.

I shrugged shamefully.

"Well tomorrow's just as good as today," she insisted. "This your vacation, child. Do with it what you please. It'll come. Just remember Daddy didn't find it till the grave. Don't wait that long."

I knew she was right, yet I still spent the remaining weeks of my vacation in similar fashion, each day seated on the front porch with time a slow trickle of cool breezes and walks to the refrigerator for ice water. In the afternoons, I played games with Janice and Steven who were oblivious to a single thought outside of Norfolk and their home and their aunt who had finally come to visit. They behaved as children often do with that idea that everything in this life was made to please them, and Gloria did her very best to ensure this continued, for when Janice cried from having received a smaller slice of cake than Steven one night during dinner, Gloria promised the girl she'd receive a bigger slice the next night. And when Steven found himself alone and pouting over a mean thing Janice had said, Gloria swore the little girl would never say it again. And when the boogieman threatened to come from their closets at night to eat each of their toes and they came running to our bedsides for protection, Gloria swore she would chase him away each time.

A sense of fairness resided in this world, a feeling of order and decency, even if that concept existed nowhere outside of these walls and somehow prepared those children for many disappointments once they'd ventured out into this place called America. After so many years in Mississippi, I could not help but willingly accept this lie, even if it was manufactured for only our enjoyment in this one home alone, as nowhere else did that type of love exist, even if Gloria and I hoped it would be so.

CHAPTER 23

My return to Greenwood was met by signs of trouble. The loud whines of the cicadas raised and lowered under the deep stretch of midnight. The rains left a slow and crackling flow, forming streams that reached the stables just past the garden. The house relinquished its color and faded from snow to old lace. While inside the house, I arrived to a sight that no time in that home or time away had ever prepared me to witness, as Miss Lula lay near death with the Reaper standing above her.

I gasped when I saw her, feeling that weight fall from my throat into my chest, where it burned like some scalding item I'd eaten. Floyd drew me into his quarters and described to me the events surrounding the Missus's downfall, stating it occurred on that third day following my departure when Mr. Kern wandered off by himself. He'd made it as far as the Missus's garden before suffering a nasty fall and, according to Floyd, he remained there helpless for hours, although no one knew the exact time before someone finally noticed him, and it just so happened to be the boy. A scuffle ensued as Mr. Kern figured that kind hand belonged to a worker and as such the old man rebuked the boy's efforts, putting up a fight his feeble arms could not win.

"Get 'way from me, boy!" Mr. Kern was said to have yelled. "Stay back, you hear? Don't touch me!"

This noise was so loud that it drew Silva from indoors and even attracted the Missus from her seat on that porch as both women rounded the corner to find the old man securely fastened within the boy's grip.

"He fell!" Fletcher said when he saw them. "I don't know how long he been here. He was here when I found him."

"Your imagination, boy," Miss Lula demanded as she rushed to Mr. Kern's side and stole the old man from Fletcher's arms.

She cradled him like a baby, soothing and whispering in his ear like some doll she had groomed and pampered into some extravagant fashion. She scoffed at the three faces staring back at her, rolling her eyes so much Floyd feared they'd become stuck that way.

"If he fell, then you should've left him," she said nastily. "Last I checked your duties were in the fields and not here causing trouble. If he's broken something, you've only made it worse."

Mr. Kern watched with slow recognition as the Missus guided him inside. She sat present at his bedside like a good wife for as long as his recovery took, never moving an inch unless it was to beckon Silva to bring water or supper upstairs. Floyd was sure to mention that neither he nor Silva were allowed to see the Mister during this time and that they were quite certain by the time the Missus emerged the old man would be dead.

Surprisingly, however, Miss Lula's intentions were not to end her own suffering by ending Mr. Kern's life, at least not at that present time, but to keep him alive for as long as it took for her to fulfill whatever plan she had next, her motivations leading her to take a front-row seat to the Mister's suffering. In the wake of

Fletcher's unfortunate timing and decency toward the Mister, Miss Lula assigned him duties farther out, placing him at a distance where he was just barely visible in view from the house, although one could still make out his slim figure, Floyd said, recalling how he once saw the boy along the horizon like one of the trees, never knowing it was him until Fletcher finally moved.

Still, Mr. Kern recovered quickly enough, and as a treat of the most malicious kind, Miss Lula kept him by her side, dragging him outside each day like some abandoned puppy she'd found and nursed back to health. With his strength slowly returning, they walked the muddy grounds, venturing amongst the cotton and swampland, yet always returning to that porch, by her insistence, where he sat dutifully. And so it was her fault that it happened at all, Floyd insisted, for Miss Lula had not observed Mr. Kern's wandering eyes during their time together, concluding that his presence beside her for the whole of the day was enough to stave away any knowledge of the boy. She figured she had placed the boy far enough that Mr. Kern would never see their identical faces or have that warmth return to the old man's heart. And so it occurred one day near the middle of my departure that the Missus relapsed into another of her episodes and was locked inside her room for three days in such bad spirits that no one dared offer her food or water, merely placing these items outside her door and collecting the dishes once she had finished. It was during this time that Mr. Kern was left to walk by himself, and sure enough, he caught sight of the boy once more, just as he had each of those times beside the Missus, and the knowledge of the boy's identity reawakened his sleepy heart.

Mr. Kern watched Fletcher from the marshes on this particular day, the old man's thoughts remaining to himself as he stared with those dark eyes and that aging expression that had removed most of the sternness from his face and left him tender and exceedingly helpless. Mr. Kern stood for what had to be hours in this confused state, reminding Floyd of some story the old man had told about his cousin from Atlanta when they were younger and her offer to one day show him her rabbit fur and that look on the old man's face as he described the horror when she finally did. And so it was here that Floyd laughed, stopping his story completely before regaining his composure to add that the old man watched in the same manner on this day without a word, waiting for the boy to move, leaving only when the boy left for the evening and returning the next day when the boy arrived. He watched the boy throw the hoe in silence again and again, yet still the old man breathed not a word. It was after some time of this ritual that Fletcher finally noticed a presence in the trees and stopped his work abruptly.

"Who is that?" Fletcher asked. "Floyd? Jesse?"

Fletcher moved toward the sound, sticks, and gravel all moving at once as Mr. Kern now revealed himself.

"Fletcher," the old man said softly, his body fully exposed from the willows and vines that clung together like nets around him, his voice a soft pucker that if materialized into a structure of mass and weight would not be substantial enough to hold him up. "Don't mean to scare you. It's just me."

"I'm sorry, sir," Fletcher said. "I thought you were Floyd or Jesse playing a joke on me."

"No, no," Mr. Kern said, the nicest he'd been to Fletcher since the boy could remember, "just having a walk that's all. Nothing like fresh air."

Their interaction was clumsy, like two strangers made to

share a space but not sharing a similar language. It came with long pauses and glances at nothing, stares into the open space of the plantation, where branches and leaves held their attention for minutes at a time, then their bowed heads remained lowered until one person moved and the other looked up to see. One sighed and the other held his breath. One flinched and the other let not a single muscle in his body move. Fletcher eventually forced his face into a smile—or the best expression he could muster in response to the old man's kindness—which, although not as warm as Fletcher would afford to his mother or Jesse, seemingly unlocked a chest of emotions in the old man, who stood animated with an enthusiasm or curiosity that was plain as day to anyone who might view this chance encounter—as Floyd did.

This led Floyd to comment that he thought it nothing but the hand of grace that love could hibernate in one's soul for so long yet never truly fade—how at any moment it could reawaken and lead our hearts to bleed again. For Fletcher was Mr. Kern in younger skin, Floyd insisted: the handsomeness, the charm, the reserve. It was all there. Surely whatever thoughts drip through the consciousness of those who have loved and lost, yet get the chance to love again, were in Mr. Kern's heart at that exact moment, for how he did stare and linger and find joy in the place of his sorrow. How he gawked for millennia and never grew weary of his position, until finally the old man reached out his arm, saying gently, "Help me to the house, Fletcher," accepting of Fletcher's arm like a debutante to her white knight.

"Yes, sir," Fletcher replied, immediately dropping his tools and guiding the old man in the right direction, which was ultimately a considerable distance from their current location and took some time to reach.

Mr. Kern admired the boy's smooth skin, the firmness of the boy's jaw, the subtlety of his eyes beneath eyebrows that sat low on his forehead, downward cast as both men surveyed the fields in unison; all those muscles and tissues and pieces of Fletcher that worked together as one and made him complete, that had grown from a little boy into a man and were reminiscent of that passion that grows inside all young men of a certain age. Fletcher's skin held story lines of a younger Mr. Kern when that same passion had led him to Miss Lula's doorstep (but truly to Silva, if he'd had the courage to admit it) and now caused this white man to love this negro just as he did during Fletcher's youth. In truth, he'd never stopped loving him, as Fletcher's reflection cast sparks of himself and Silva alike, and made the boy's rounded nose and thicker lips somehow beautiful. Floyd likened this passion to that adrenaline that rushed through them both with a big catch down on the lake saying, "It's that slight flinch of tha line, that deep gulp it takes, an' then ya know ya got 'im, reelin' an' pullin' like crazy till it comes flyin' from tha water." That uncontrollable force that even the fish could not explain, he went on to say, that inability to manipulate the air so easily as it did the water.

It was this passion that consumed him and caused Mr. Kern's entire body to cease moving, sending shivers that left him stranded in this moment as the two stopped to rest. The old man's face sat in the direction of the boy's smile and did not move at any moment during this episode, and even if he did blink or rear his head it was only in the direction of Fletcher.

"You okay, sir?" Fletcher asked.

"Just catching my breath," the old man replied gruffly. "You'll have many a moments like this when you my age. You'll see."

"I believe you, sir," Fletcher said. "Sometimes I already feel it in my legs."

Mr. Kern smiled, surely aware that the boy's young body had never felt the creaks of old age a day in his life, and if it did it was only a passing heartbeat. Mr. Kern knew Fletcher was strong and could bear the weight of those fields for a hundred years without ever fainting. He could sustain that plantation and the life Mr. Kern had always known, giving spirit to it once more.

When Mr. Kern felt of good-enough mood, he gave in to the pull of Fletcher's arm, allowing the young man to ease him toward the house. That it all spoke of that love he had for the boy, that all of the anguish and pride and shame and remorse were all gone, and indeed that those feelings of fear and uncertainty or of wrong and right were all vanquished, too, Floyd swore at his most animated. That love made him forget it all.

The minute lingered between them as Fletcher walked oblivious to the old man's mood. Floyd swore it was destined the two of them meet like this. My vehemence fell in stark disagreement, but it was one of those moments you just had to see to understand, Floyd said.

The two of them met again that next day, which was the third and final day of the Missus's fit. He recalled it happened out back by the shed and garden, where the Mister had previously fallen.

Mr. Kern was of a particularly decent spirit that day when he first spotted Fletcher.

"Seems like the weeds get us every year before the flowers," Mr. Kern said.

"Every time," Fletcher acknowledged of the flowerbed nearby, turning to see Mr. Kern and smiling a soft grin. "Might as well grow the weeds and forget the flowers."

"Might as well burn the whole lot," Mr. Kern agreed.

Mr. Kern drew closer, an easiness he now had about him and indeed felt with the boy that allowed him to look directly into Fletcher's eyes and forgo any feeling of regret or grief at the years he'd lost. The boy's humor was duly noted by the old man as well, a frequent occurrence between boys and their fathers, I'd noticed, that when those men now of full lives look upon their seeds they see a certain pride at the men they've become and take joy in those telltale signs that make those boys likely to attempt the same schemes those men tried in their youth. And, in this manner, those men became young again.

"How is it today?" Mr. Kern asked.

"Just fine, sir," Fletcher replied, keeping his answer short.

In truth, you didn't say much in those days, and Fletcher knew it. Still, Mr. Kern was of a quiet spirit too, soon disappearing inside the house and returning with a jar of ice water, which he handed to Fletcher.

"No, thank you, sir," Fletcher protested with an insistence he'd been taught by Silva to display toward such strange acts of kindness. "I just use the barrel."

"You need it," Mr. Kern said, his life seeming to fade with every word he delivered. "A hard head sure makes a soft bottom, especially out here in the fields. That sun can take you before you know it."

Fletcher watched him for a moment then reluctantly drank, thanking the old man kindly as he took the glass, managing to forgo any further fights. The boy sipped the water until it was empty, every single drop, feeling strangely, I was sure, to return a glass to his employer, let alone a white man, let alone Mr. Kern. But Mr. Kern smiled, accepting the glass willingly as he then placed a locket into Fletcher's hands. Fletcher recoiled, pulling back his arm as if he'd made contact with fire.

"Sir?" Fletcher questioned.

Mr. Kern touched the wet parts of Fletcher's palm, saying simply, "That there's my family stone. You been good to me, and I can't take it wit' me. Makes a damn good marble too."

"I can't, sir," Fletcher said.

Mr. Kern barked, "You'll learn to accept good things when they come to you. It don't always happen this way. Don't have to be a reason, just is."

He then left Fletcher alone in those parts with the locket still in his hands and the old man's lesson stamped upon his brain.

This final story concluded Floyd's account and made Floyd laugh, a snicker that grew into a resounding chuckle at the Missus, feeling that Mr. Kern and Fletcher had somehow won this battle. Still, no good deed in that house ever went unpunished, and joy could be recalled at a moment's notice here, in this most direst of places, with the marsh that stretched like seaweed into the nothingness that went forever. I hated this place, and rightfully so, for I knew there would be retaliation for the Mister's kindness, and I hated him for his goodwill and despised even myself for feeling such bitterness and trepidation toward it. I knew what the Missus was capable of and, as such, I feared her retribution.

CHAPTER 24

The Missus learned of this encounter by her own means of scrutiny, spotting that bit of cheer that existed between Mr. Kern and Fletcher as clearly as Floyd had seen it. That morning had been of a cooler disposition, the kind that roused the squeakiness of rockers and encouraged a spot of coffee or heavier jacket before venturing outdoors. The countryside sat white with frost, a crunching of the ground beneath their feet that sent no lack of hurried footsteps toward any particular destination. The sky was clear of clouds or smoke or anything that was not the soft blue of heaven's basement above their heads, and for a time it seemed that only this plantation existed, the lark singing a gentle song as Floyd started up the tractor and the normal sounds of the workday returned to life.

From what Floyd told me, the Missus emerged from her bedroom having relinquished that bit of madness that had consumed her. She was stealthy in her mood, remaining quietly observant and making no perceived actions or comments that would alert anyone of her attention. She was actually pleasant, Floyd insisted, and seemed of a new spirit that was more welcoming than the last. She found Silva's company and took a seat near the half-closed kitchen door, saying, "If I live one more day, I'm sure it'll be a crazy one. So, if anything, I'd better die today."

Silva looked up from her dishes, startled for a second at seeing the Missus in this condition, then resumed her fighter's stance as she replied, "No, Miss, you're not crazy. A crazy person don't know they crazy. You know exactly what you do."

The Missus smiled, as she and Silva had felt each other out a long time ago, and she knew every card Silva was likely to play. And so the Missus moved to trump her, replying, "You're right, Silva. There's nothing wrong with me except for all I suffer."

"And what's that, Miss?" Silva asked.

"The usual wears and tears that come with life on the plantation, although I seem to have more. Housewives usually do. It's the burden we bear for our families."

It was impossible to tell whether the Missus believed this or not, but she did not waver a second in her delivery and was never in fear of smiling throughout the remainder of their conversation. Silva shrugged it off, leaving the dishtowel draped over the faucet, wrung of all water, as she limped toward the stove and the biscuits that cooled there.

"I bet mothers make it to heaven first," Miss Lula continued.

"What would you know about that?" Silva replied under her breath.

Yet heaven was no joking matter, and once Silva had collected her senses and prayed that God would settle her heart, she turned to the Missus once more and said, "They have to be there to take the little ones in."

Miss Lula embraced these words, her eyes a deep well that showed no bottom, her face thin now from months of neglect, yet still there was a beauty that shone through the sunlight that hit her at just the right angles to make her attractive. She exhaled a deep breath that forced the air throughout the room then made herself comfortable with these thoughts, as if the words were spoken directly from God to her ears.

Once Silva had finished her duties, she left the kitchen, leaving the Missus seated there alone. Outside, Miss Lula found the company of Mr. Kern who had managed to walk from his parlor to that front porch where he now sat bundled beneath several layers of clothing that made him appear to have regained some of his former size. He had become a peaceful man in his old age and sought not the vindictiveness of his younger self, when he'd pursued nothing but indifference toward the Missus. He was now kind to her and indulged her moods more than ever before.

"Quite cold out here if you gots the patience," he said as she sat beside him.

"I got about as much as the next," she replied. "Ain't seen a cold one like this in a while."

"Sure shake the leaves from a tree if it got any left," Mr. Kern said.

There was a moment following these words where they both watched the trees, as in them they saw the coldness that left those trees stripped and brittle and bare, the branches stretching high like lifelines drawn out amongst the sky in streams of decay. Then she saw him—that line out there mixed with the trees that stood and fell then stood again. And she looked up to see Mr. Kern's eyes upon him as well, and she knew that warmth had returned. And it was there that she watched this show for minutes, if not hours, if not days, before she finally stood and would have no more of it. Floyd swore she shot up like she had fire ants at her tail and found the boy by the marsh as he took respite by the sunny veil of the outer fields, where the warmth had collected around the once-harsh edges of swampland.

The boy sat planted on the ground like the very seeds he'd sown when she approached.

"Fletcher," she said kindly, her eyes drawn immediately to that spark from his hands that he'd quickly covered, making that object all the more recognizable with its light gone.

"Yes, Miss?" he said, placing the locket inside his pocket then turning toward her.

"Don't hide it, Fletcher," she said. "I knows you didn't steal it."

He sighed.

"Mr. Kern gave it to me," he admitted. "Honestly, I don't know why."

"He's old and trying to buy his way into heaven," she said. "Don't pay him no mind. Besides, who can blame him? If you can't get there the right way, then do it the best way you know how."

She took a seat beside Fletcher in the grass, allowing her feet to bathe in the sun, her hair a reflection of that persistent light.

"You know what it is?" she asked.

"He told me it's his family stone," Fletcher said.

"It is," she whispered. "That there locket is a kernel that represents this family's place in the world, its heritage, that last name literally meaning seed or kernel. And now it belongs to you, the seed of both your mother and father. And one day, you'll bear seeds of your own, and they'll plant seeds into this very ground and the cycle will continue."

Fletcher studied the locket as the Missus spoke, the young man's thoughts replicating wildly at that moment, as was evident in his eyes that jittered back and forth.

"You keep it, Fletcher," she said. "It's worth a lot of money and could help pay for anything you need."

"Thank you, Miss," he said, more confused than appreciative of her kindness.

"You've grown a lot in these past years," she said. "I'm just happy to see it so. You made a lot of friends here, even if you don't know it. You're a part of this house, a part of this family. Tell me you still think of school?"

"Not anymore," he said. "There's no need to, is there?"

"There's always a need if you want it," she replied.

"You took it from me, or have you forgotten?" he said adamantly. "And you brought me here. I'll never forget it. Ain't no amount of lockets can undo that."

"And you done good here," she said.

"I've done your bidding here," he replied sharply.

"Fletcher, all I did was bring you to your family," she swore. "If that's my bidding, I won't apologize for it."

"Because it serves your purpose alone, Miss," he declared, rising from the ground.

"Young Fletcher," the Missus soothed, easing him toward her and back to his seat. "You think everyone has done you wrong except for the people in your life who actually have the ability to do it. You live with your head in the clouds, I swear, boy. Now, if I've done anything wrong by you, it was to take you away from that school and place you here where I knew you belonged, around your family. Boy, that's all that matters in this world. So, surely if I've done you wrong, then your mother has committed ten times my sin by sending you away."

Fletcher rebuffed her lies, seated with a cold expression that did not warm even with the climbing temperature around them.

"Fletcher, it may sound wrong to you and it may be too late for an apology," she said, "I get it. But sometimes those hurtful things people do are the best they *can* do. And breaking your heart was the only way to do it. You see, coming back here was what you needed, but they were never gonna tell you. No, they would rather you wander forever, just as lost and confused as you ever been. Let you wonder why your brother always got the best of things and why Silva love him the most. Why it is she protects him like she do, over you. But some things you just gotta know."

Fletcher sat unmoved, and Floyd insisted he almost jumped in at that moment but had no clue what he'd actually say or how the truth could be delayed any longer, and so he allowed it to happen, watching the Missus rise to her knees and stand over the boy while Floyd remained in the trees.

"Fletcher," the Missus continued, "George give you that locket because he's your daddy, and you're his only surviving child, and so you continue his bloodline."

Fletcher's face was a rehearsed reaction to her words.

"It's true," she said.

"Miss, my daddy died a long time ago," Fletcher said.

"The man you call your daddy did die when you were little but not the man who really was. Just look at your skin, Fletcher. You never wonder why you look so different? All this time, why you weren't like your brother. Why your mama love him more. I begged them to tell you. I wanted you to know your people and be back in this house where you belong, but they insisted you go away. They wanted you off at that school and away from here so you'd never know. While all I wanted was for them to tell you who you were and where you came from, even if it broke your heart, but they couldn't."

"Why would I believe you?" he said.

"Because I'm not a friend," she answered. "You know better

than anyone else that I've not a friendly bone in my body toward you. But what I did was more of a friend than anything they've ever done, because only I was willing to break your heart if it meant telling you the truth about yourself.

"Fletcher, I don't have to lie to you. I'm telling you the truth because you deserve to know. Every child deserves to know their mother and father. But Silva and George don't have the heart to hurt you. They know the truth could make you crazy after all this time. That it would hurt you too much. But you have to forgive them and not be mad. It's what any parent would do to protect the ones they love."

Fletcher looked at her squarely, his eyes set in stone. Yet when he spoke, he sounded far away, lost in some dream he couldn't shake. "I'm not mad," he said. His voice drew dimmer. "If it's true, then I hate them. Just as much as I hate you."

"Fletcher," she soothed, "they both had no choice. George could never come out and accept you as his son. You're a boy so you don't understand, but a negra being raised by a white man, well, it just don't happen around these parts, never mind whether it should or shouldn't. He couldn't love you, so he had to turn you away. But he did the best he could. Your mother and him both did by keeping it from you. They had to."

"Then he's a coward!" Fletcher fumed. "And I don't need him or anyone, and I don't need his damn presents either."

Fletcher removed the locket from his pocket and glared at it with his hand reared back to throw.

"Don't give up your home," she said, grabbing his hand before he could release it.

"This ain't my home!" he said. "It's yours and Mr. Kern's but not mine. I'll never live here. I'll never call this place home."

From the Missus's eyes dripped delicate honey that cleared any saltiness from her face.

"You have more power than you know, Fletcher," she said, releasing his hand from her own. "And they can't take that away from you as long as you live. Only you know who and what you are."

Miss Lula stood completely and dusted the blades of grass from her dress as if shaking out an old rug. She then removed her shoes and walked barefoot across the chilly soil toward the house that was some several fields away. As soon as she'd left Fletcher's side and the coast was clear, Floyd rushed to the boy.

"Pay no attention ta a word she says," Floyd insisted.

Fletcher looked at him with eyes as lost as a single seed planted amongst a world of hemlocks and clovers.

"Is it true?" he asked.

"Ya pappy was Mista Johnson likes ya know it," Floyd said.

"But was he my daddy?" Fletcher asked.

"He was all the daddy ya had an' as close as ya were gonna git," Floyd said. "An' loved ya more than a little. The goodest man I ever know'd. Raise ya an' Jesse till he die. That's enough."

"No, Floyd!" Fletcher said. "It ain't enough. You see, I got no one. I got no mother. I got no father. I got no friends in this world. It was all a game, and they played me. None of them ever loved me. They would all let me die out here. Each and every one of them."

Word reached Silva quickly. She was in the kitchen when Floyd entered.

"Tha boy knows," Floyd said. "Missus done told 'im."

Silva rushed out the door and found Fletcher still seated by the marsh. He hadn't moved for some time, shifting his position along the ground to wake his one numb leg in order to allow the other to sleep, firmly settled inside the groove he'd inched deeper and deeper with each passing minute.

"Fletcher, don't you go behaving like this," she said once she saw him. "Your daddy was Mr. Johnson, and you knows it."

"My daddy was a white man who didn't care about me," Fletcher protested. "And would have me work his fields until I died and never care a thing about that either. He would curse me for calling his name or even looking his direction. He'd insist on never seeing me again, and you would let him."

"Fletcher, you watch your mouth," Silva said. "You've been loved by everyone except that mean witch you go listening to now. You a good boy, and Mr. Johnson loved you till the day he died."

"But he wasn't my daddy!" Fletcher said. "And nobody told me any differently till now."

"Boy, your daddy would roll over if he heard you talking like this," Silva said. "He loved both his boys and loved you like crazy too. And you know it."

Fletcher's eyes muddled like a cloudy day horizon, eavesdropping from one field to the next. His sights appeared haunted as he looked up, saying faintly, "I'm not sixteen anymore, Mama, and I ain't crying over Mr. Kern not wanting me and making me stay away while Jesse get to come. I don't want him just like he don't want me."

"Fletcher, you tell the truth and shame the devil right now," she said. "You only had one daddy your whole life and that's why you never needed to know. Mr. Kern was never your daddy. No, you had a daddy who gave you everything he could and made sure you didn't want for nothing. Worked every day out there to gives you food and a roof over your head."

Fletcher stared toward the end of the fields. He watched the trees that divided Kern land from wilderness. Then he wiped his eyes, his body appearing hollow, a shell of a man who had no soul left within him. The sky seemed to stretch even wider out amongst the trees as he took it all in. Then he turned to Silva, eyes wide, barely able to get the words out.

"But you, Mama," he said. "Why didn't *you* tell me?"

Silva looked around for whatever she could find to garner the strength to put forth her reasons. She then spotted something in the brush just aside from where the two of them sat, although Floyd could not tell exactly what it was she'd seen as she soon closed her eyes and continued softly.

"You were gonna have a hard life no matter what," Silva said. "Knowing Mr. Kern was your daddy would only make it worse. Believe me, I thought about it, seeing you always wondering why you were so different, why you didn't look the same as your brother. I know it hurt you. But how was your life gonna be any easier with people knowing your daddy was white? You had a better life this way 'cause no one gonna see a colored boy and treat him special just 'cause he come from a white man. You can be as pale as you want but you still colored, son. Your skin make them hate you, and they always will."

Fletcher sat with these words, drawing from his mouth once enough time had passed for his thoughts to somewhat settle and his eyes to dry of his tears, "Jesse know?"

"No, baby," she said. "All he knows is you're his brother, and that's all he should ever know. Now, I know you're mad, but it's hard for children to understand the ways of this world and how far we go to protect them."

"Why Mr. Kern don't love me then?" he said.

"He does," Silva insisted. "He loved you since you were born."

"Then he kicked me out," Fletcher swore.

"He kicked you outta nowhere," Silva fought back. "Miss Lula the one that made you leave, and he the one that wanted you to stay. He ain't never done nothing wrong by you a day in your life, although I know it's hard for you to see. He give you opportunities you never even know. Now, Fletcher, you choose your lot in life, but you don't get a second chance at it. And all the things we did, we can't take back. It's the best I can say."

Fletcher found solace in tears, leaning on Silva's shoulder as if his head had grown ten times heavier and did not have the muscles to hold it straight. He remained in this position for some time and did not move until Silva indeed lifted him from the ground and with Jesse's help carried him toward the house. The sun was well on its way, although the sky still sat filled with light and the world seemed at once calm. Silva did not enter the house that evening although her duties remained plentiful. For the first time she left dinner unprepared and the Missus to reheat whatever leftovers she could find, although the Missus's appetite was not with her at present, and Mr. Kern proved too sickly to eat even a cracker that evening.

CHAPTER 25

Fletcher did not show the next day, just as the Missus had hoped. Still, the Missus was not as cheerful as one might expect when she appeared downstairs, as she had suffered a seizure during her sleep that was brought about by that three-day period of her madness when she refused to eat large-enough portions and never took a single pill. She had stayed awake the entire night following the episode, afraid to close her eyes again in fear that another attack might strike during her sleep, that most vulnerable time when her faculties were not with her even if she could somehow fight the monster. The Missus had suffered several more of these episodes by the time I'd returned and indeed lay helpless in her bed when I'd found her, her hair in loose shrivels that fell over her forehead, wet sheets that clung to her body like children fresh out the pool, in her eyes a wildness that I'd never seen from her, although in this state she was susceptible to anything.

"The medicine's just gotta build up in her," Silva insisted.

"How many has she had?" I asked.

"Maybe three but not big ones," Silva replied. "I've seen her have worse. Missus just nervous they'll happen again. She'll be fine."

And with this Silva left the room calmly, her mind a steady

focus on circumstances that did not involve the Missus or her health, her tone a return to business as usual. Given Silva's disinterest, I took charge of Miss Lula's care alone, easing that sad creature's concerns of slipping into another episode with constant taps of my hand on her shoulder, assuaging that fear that swore to her the end was near. For during that time the Missus swallowed whatever pill I gave her, no longer a fighting bone in her body.

That evening I ventured downstairs for more water and the Missus's supper as she lay asleep in her bed. I would wake her upon my return with whatever food Silva had prepared as I did each night and force the meal down her throat, which she feared would seize up before she could have a chance to swallow. Then I would end with that pill as I always did, and she would close her eyes and drift to sleep, leaving the room silent and dim as nightfall arrived.

The kitchen was empty when I entered and no dinner upon the stove. I prepared a glass of water then checked the back shed for Silva, but she was nowhere in sight. When I'd returned to the kitchen, the water was still cold and so I carried it upstairs to the Missus's quarters. The room was dark as I entered, yet just as I slipped past the doorway I saw her there, the shadow of Silva near the window as she pulled an unopened bottle from the top drawer of the Missus's wardrobe. Silva then removed another bottle from her apron and placed that new bottle atop the dresser. With great precision, Silva emptied the unopened bottle of pills into her apron and refilled the bottle with pills from the new bottle she'd brought with her. She then closed the bottle and returned it to the drawer of the wardrobe and left the room just as quietly as she'd skirted in, as I slid into the corner and away from her sight.

The Missus still lay asleep in bed when I brought her water.

I quickly placed the glass onto the dresser and retrieved the pill bottle from the drawer. There were only a handful of pills that remained in the Missus's current bottle and matched those same pills now in the unused bottle, useless things I'd been feeding the Missus for days while wondering why she was not improving. There was indeed no chance for the Missus to ever get well, as it was now Silva's hand that controlled the wheel.

While it was true that servants often bore a heavier load than others, at no other time did that weight feel so burdensome than when I watched the Missus suffer and slowly die in that room alone as I wondered to myself exactly where my loyalties resided. For truly, there had been lots of suffering in that home, too much to consider in one night's ramblings as I sat beside the Missus's bed and attempted to add up all the harrowing accounts that now extended to include me. When the count reached numbers my two hands could no longer tally, and these thoughts turned to nightmares that no sight nor sound could ever resolve, I finally quit my state and sought out Silva in the downstairs area where she stood gathering her purse to leave.

"Silva, you'll kill her," I said when I entered.

"Bernice," Silva replied calmly, "God and you both know no man or woman can take a life. Only Him."

"Yet you're trying," I said.

"Maybe she deserve to die," Silva admitted. "You ever think of that?"

"In God's time and not ours," I warned.

"If He allows it ..." Silva said.

"He allows many things that aren't His will," I admonished. "And you know it."

"Then I pray He allow this," she said, leaving the kitchen.

"Our prayers are only suggestions to His ears, Bernice. I only pray this suggestion He hears as clearly as any other. It's all I got left."

Silva hummed a gospel as she walked.

"God help her," she swore staunchly before she closed the door.

"God help us all," I whispered.

———

I found Mr. Kern alone in his parlor, his eyes a mix of tragedy and yearning.

"The Missus's condition is worse, sir," I told him. "Seems we might have to take her in."

He nodded yet remained quiet, leaving those decisions to me, as convulsions begot hysteria and suddenly we lost her, not to the grave but to the mania that persisted. It happened quickly and within a week's time the Missus slipped into a period of uncontrolled seizures the doctors labeled some fancy term: Status Epilepticus, a condition which left the Missus bedridden and saw her hospitalized for several weeks at Greenwood Leflore Hospital, some ways from the plantation. The Missus did show some strength as we drove to that desolate place, although feebly, her will allowing her to open her eyes long enough to see that plantation fade and that building where Elizabeth had also lain until the time of her death now emerge at the horizon where the crop was just beginning to grow.

Good news walks slowly, whereas bad news travels at a gallop, as within a day of the Missus's hospital stay those Arkansas relatives had already arrived in Greenwood and descended upon that hospital. Along with the usual crew also came an uncle, whom

I'd heard stories of from his days in the war and of those coyote fighters who'd nearly wiped out his entire troop on that journey home along the French countryside. With them also came a cousin I'd never met who felt a certain connection to my obligated kindness and was compelled to talk more than any stranger looking to acquaint himself with a fellow wanderer. Every word from his mouth was an uninstigated tale of his life in Little Rock and that job he had at the chicken factory just outside of town. Everyone else had given up on his stories a long time ago, which left him with only my company.

"The fence around it is more like a prison than a factory," he said to me as we sat inside the hospital room for the first time. "You get vertigo from just looking up at the barbed wire top. That first day it made my legs and stomach go weak and nearly landed me flat on my face from the disorientation. Two guards at the security booth had to stand me up, both angry men that I had to wait for to finish their cigarettes, playing a game of who could look the meanest the longest before they showed me where to go. 'You new?' the losing guard said. 'Yea,' I told him.

"And you know what, I must have stared down that clock on the wall because it was close to eight. And so they got a clipboard from beneath it and flipped through the pages before stopping at a part with color printouts near the middle. 'Packaging or prep?' he said. 'Prep,' I told him. 'Name?' he asked me. 'Jackson,' I said. Then he looks at me for a minute, as if there's a right or wrong answer to his question. 'Take it to Sector Three,' he says, so I guess I had passed."

"Jack, you leave that poor girl alone," the mother of those three boys said. "Nobody cares about those damn chickens."

Jackson waved his hand at her chiding, later finding me in the hallway to continue, telling of how the third sector was located at the far end of the parking lot near the highway and how I wouldn't believe its size. How the door buzzed loudly and a tomboy-ish woman met him on the other side. How she was pretty and reminded him of one of those female athletes who were clearly too tall for anything other than sports and whose high heels gave them away each time they attempted anything professional as they stumbled around clumsily. He spoke of her handshake being firm and her painted fingernails slightly out of place on her wide hands and long fingers. He said a man named Mr. Way who had a skillet face and arms like nubs and a wide neck like those wrestlers you'd see on television programs showed him the ropes. He remarked how the man had pudgy fingers and a roll of skin that had folded over the man's wedding band and locked it into place. He commented that the man's wife must have been some former cheerleader who was sadly unaware that marrying the wrestling team captain would come at such a hefty cost. But that maybe she had let herself go too, he considered, her face most likely caked with cheap makeup and her wearing way too much perfume. Then his thoughts drifted to the chickens, telling me how there were four long rows where, at the beginning of each one, suited workers would grab hold of the chickens as they neared the belt, gripping the chickens' necks as those workers then wrung and beheaded each one before passing the bodies along the line of workers who then removed the feathers before tossing them aside as they then reached for another. He told of the chickens' passage through that huge magnet that pulled any metals to the surface and how that son of a bitch was the loudest machine you'd ever hear and how it left the chickens' skins red from the tearing of metals from their flesh. The chickens then came to him, where his job was simple, to divorce the chickens, which amounted to nothing more than separating each chicken that had become conjoined with another during the process. That was all. Every day.

———

Inside the room, the Missus sat in bed as helpless as before. There was no cheering her up, although the presence of her family did place her in a slightly more agreeable mood than when they were absent. Jackson finished another story and, if only for a few seconds, seemingly the entire room became alive again with hesitant laughter that trickled from the lips of each person inside as we personally resolved that it was okay to have laughter once more. Embracing this foreign concept, our breaths circulated the room like games of tag where one must wait for another to be touched before he or she can stop or go. Although brief and not in the slightest bit awe inspiring, this momentary glimpse of normality was imperative to our fragile states, and without it we would have surely imploded from the pressures of looking so stern for so long.

Yet just as quickly as it came it left, back into the vortex that stole most joy, leaving us with only the dismal reality we knew seconds before that moment arrived. We sank like splits inside the cushioned plastic chairs, not really moving until a twitch stirred inside and someone either scratched or stretched or yawned. We remained as still as possible, settling into the space like roots inside the ground. It wasn't until this game was over and no one else felt the need to call out further, not even those last abrupt chuckles that often finish off a good laugh, that we each fell silent once more beneath the humming and beeping of hospital machines. Like anything other than the stillness that sometimes lasted for hours inside the room and the uncomfortable glances at the Missus in the bed who did not move, this beeping of machines was more than welcomed.

The Missus's brother held his head in his hands. His palms nearly bled from the prick of his own nails pressing the insides of his clenched fists, as the idea of death and its finality reemerged inside the room just as quickly as it left, ushering away that levity so discretely beneath the heavy air that swallowed the room in thirsty gulps like a monster.

Mr. Kern left for the night, as did the rest of the family, leaving only me at the Missus's side to care for her needs until morning. The room was a dark abyss around midnight when she woke, the last of the evening having faded in brilliant arrays and fiery bursts that once invaded the room with light but now left it void. The Missus hadn't suffered a seizure the entire afternoon and seemed in better spirits, although far short of a full recovery. She glanced around the darkness, expecting that pit of silent stares and halted breaths to await her. Yet once she'd felt certain that only I sat there did she finally speak her heart.

"Bernie," she whispered, her voice a soft crackle that lurched from her throat, "you know he would've given him the world if I'd let him."

I looked into her weak eyes.

"Ain't never seen a hair in five years and soon as he does he melts," she said. She snapped her fingers. "Just like that."

"It's in their nature," I said. "Boys and their fathers."

She shook her head.

"Fathers and their bastards!" she shouted. "I've never knowed a sight so horrible in all my life that a man would give up his own wife and daughter for a bastard he never knowed. Sure, at first I just wanted that boy gone so we could forget him and move on. But when I saw that look in George's eyes all those years ago in that kitchen, loving that boy like his own, more than he did any of us, I wanted that boy here so he could pay for what he did, showing his face here again and causing this family so much pain. But I never wanted to hurt George with all of it, I swear, not until I saw that last look in his eyes when he watched that boy out in those fields. He still loved him, and so I vowed I would make that boy hate him. And George would never feel the love of Silva or his bastard ever again."

"But you can never stop Mr. Kern from loving him," I said.

She looked at me viciously.

"But I can stop that boy from ever loving him," she said. "And that's a misery George could never take. It'll kill him."

The Missus trembled so violently that I feared she'd returned to one of those miserable states. However a fit did not ensue as she merely lay back with her eyes open and her mouth wide. She still feared resting during those times, worried an attack would come during her sleep. And so instead I entertained her with stories of my trip to Virginia and the different people I'd met there. I spoke briefly about Clinton and the loveliness of that place in spring when the earth appeared as it must have during the days of Eden as children played around the fountains at the town center.

"From wilderness to Eden," she said.

She lay with a smile on her face as she pictured those sites, and we remained this way until morning with neither of us closing our eyes for even a minute. We'd been at it for hours by the time our stories finally ended.

It was midafternoon when the family returned. The sun poked through the holes in the blinds, dotting the floor with light. Throughout the morning there had been calls for nurses over the loudspeaker; however, they were meant for other rooms, not this one. The constant motion outside the door now seemed so distant, as if, in this stillness, our lives had been transfixed by some dreamlike state where we no longer engaged in this world but instead watched helplessly as scenes unfolded around us. In this state, we each watched with tired eyes as life continued in rooms just next door, as this dementia robbed the lives of each person inside and not just the Missus in the bed.

Frightfully, we looked at each other for the next step. No one moved more than they already had, for monotony seemed somehow more consoling than the unknown pressures of ending a person's life and being the first to suggest it. I can replay it a hundred times, and it still feels like some kind of nightmare, and maybe it was. Maybe the seizures had not worsened that day and caused the Missus such shallow breaths that oxygen could no longer reach her brain. Maybe Silva had not replaced the Missus's medication all those days or even weeks inside the house and precipitated this bad event. Maybe I had not gone along with Silva's plan and said not a word of her deceit in order to protect that servant's secrets, and by some twisted logic of my own compromise also protect Fletcher from the onslaught of more pain.

Notwithstanding, the Missus died just after noon on that day, no gasps, no jolts, for she was already dead long before that time. The Missus's brother appeared panicked, his knuckles red and his fingers wrestling a paleness that pushed back the frustration that swelled like nausea at the pit of his stomach, for indeed how he cried faint tears when he thought no one was listening, how he seeped out heavy sighs that each person in the room felt as clearly as the next yet made no mention of.

With her eyes locked on the tasks at hand, his pudgy wife folded more blankets, more newly knitted scarves by the Missus that still needed recipients, more mittens for the boys (not that they ever wore them). Once this was done, she turned from the door with more pillows and sheets that needed folding as she placed them in a well-structured order beside the window. She packed the duffels and arranged the sheets from largest to smallest, along with the Missus's socks, shirts, pants, and toiletries on top in the largest bag, because as everyone knew you didn't leave a hospital or hotel room a wreck. John and Simon stood at the door with one foot inside the room and the other foot out, both boys turning nervously to face their mother once she had finished her chores and everything was packed away. With these tasks now completed, the room was static. Mr. Kern looked up from his seated position bedside Floyd and for once seemed the most uncertain of us all. The Missus's brother took a step closer to her bedside and squeezed Miss Lula's hand, fooling no one but himself into believing that this grip was anything other than a last-ditch attempt at keeping her there.

"I'll get the bags," John said.

"Let's pray," his father interrupted.

And so with our heads bowed and our eyes closed or facing our shoes or those cracks along the floor, the Missus's brother in a low voice paid homage to a God who had taken his mother, father, and now his only sister, whom he loved more than the world. In between his huffy breaths the room sat silent, a suspenseful emptiness that made our eyes sting and our noses run. It caused our hands to shake and that sad man's voice to quiver until he finally let go and sobbed as John patted his back like a good son would do and Simon nibbled at some piece of candy he'd found inside his pockets, lifting my hand to his mouth in the process, as our fingers were interlocked in prayer.

"Brave faces, everyone," the boys' mother said in the awkward silence that followed as we each departed the room one after the other.

The Missus's brother was still tearful, although he had managed to wipe most of his tears onto his shirtsleeve and collar, tears that seemed impossibly heavy as they crashed to the floor and created craters upon their impact with the ground.

The house was unchanged, tiny daffodils and decorative rocks lining the front path to the door. There were still roses surrounding the oak tree in the yard as well as those long limbs that always ruined the paint on that side of the house. I'd climbed the last step to the welcome mat when Silva approached bearing a smile that no amount of bad news could erase, her presence stopping me from moving any farther.

"It's finally over," she said with an expression that was more tired than relieved.

"It ain't over until we in the ground," I warned.

"I know, but deliverance is deliverance, Bernice," she swore, a look in her eyes that showed concern not for the living but for the dead, wanting to know for sure that it was true and that the Missus had not somehow survived, as was that woman's tendency to bounce back from these types of conditions.

"She went with the Lord, Silva," I confirmed, "but we're just beginning to see the trees in front of us. Even with the Missus gone, ain't no clearing for miles. That forest is as far as the eye can see."

"Bernice, you don't get it," she said. "That season is finally over."

"Tell that to the May flowers, dear. Even after the April rain, the storms still come."

She sat with these words then said defiantly, "Our blessings can finally begin, Bernice. It only takes one person to stop those generational curses, one person bold enough to say it ends here. Never again. God goin' bless us. You'll see. He only lets us endure so much for so long. He knows all our hearts can take. I believe it, Bernice. God goin' see this through."

Still, Silva looked at me strangely, somehow aware as I was of the difficulties that could lay ahead, even with the Missus gone. She paused for a minute longer, allowing that glint of hope to slowly burn away. She then leaned her head onto my shoulder and wept, exuding all that was left inside her in mournful stares and uncomfortable bites of her bottom lip. That warmth she once possessed was seemingly no more, that fire somehow extinguished, as even her hands were now cold and in her voice was a weakness that mirrored the Missus's own decline. Inching along the porch, she walked with that strained limp that everyone dismissed as being typical of older age, yet only she knew better and could define that pain as something quite different, something that existed on the inside, beyond flesh and bone.

CHAPTER 26

That Mr. Kern lived long enough to see the Missus die inside that hospital room was a reality that surprised us all once we'd found time to digest the events some years later. Those Arkansas relatives returned home shortly after the funeral, although there had been some talk late at night of the Missus being buried in her hometown of Little Rock. Mr. Kern had objected strongly, saying she would want to rest beside Elizabeth even if that meant her staying in Greenwood forever, putting an end to that conversation just as quickly as it began.

With her death came a constant looking over our shoulders, as the Missus's presence in that home extended far beyond anything physical and could now be seen in the distrust we each had for one another. Nevertheless, that bit of cathartic relief from her passing did still persist, a proverbial weight lifted from our shoulders, although it still remained in the things we did and did not say, as I would see the Missus at night in visages that came to light quickly, woke me, then fell away into nothing just as soon as they'd appeared. She would taunt us from the grave, I feared, her face just as lovely as it was in any of her schemes.

Our hearts were heavy during that time with crying and

laughing and screaming all in lieu of those same pains we'd endured at the Missus's hands and that eventually came of our own with enough time. Her life remained only in the projects she'd ordered around the house, thoughts of her coming to mind only when I'd notice Jesse's work on the kitchen or fixtures in the downstairs bathrooms. These projects were the one good thing anyone ever attributed to the Missus even if they were born of her spite.

Neither Jesse nor Silva nor Fletcher attended the funeral, but Floyd and myself took a seat near the back where a few other stragglers had congregated, Floyd in his suit coat and brimmed hat with a silken thread around the base that tied into a flattened bow and me in my finest Sunday dress from that time in Clinton. Not many people showed for the event other than those few older church-women, who showed at every funeral that was close enough for them to pay their respects. They brought with them crumb cakes and pecan pies and dressed in their gaudiest Sunday hats, gossiping all the way from the house to the sanctuary doors, as these were the only times those women ever left the front porch.

I had not seen her nephew Matthew since that earlier time of the family's visit, as his mother shielded him from the Missus's decline and only sent for him once the Missus had passed. He was eleven now but still had not met that growth spurt that would level him off with the other boys, although his maturity showed in other ways. His face displayed a firmer jawline, and those large eyes and large head had grown proportionally with the rest of his body. Although thin, he was built solid and his boyish features, a button nose and wide forehead, that once made him appear so innocent and sweet were now the early signs of handsomeness. He didn't remember me like the other two who came rushing up to greet me, not necessarily in a loving manner but in the way children often do when there's activity and they look to be a part of it in any way possible. It was clear to them I was an easy target as they talked of Little Rock incessantly. Matthew was a spitting image of Miss Lula, a similar version of how I imagined Elizabeth would be had she grown to be his age. He was fair-skinned and easily bothered by the sun, as his ears sat red at that very moment and his mother fussed at him not to pester them. However, he possessed a temperament that was altogether different from the Missus, for he was kind even if easily affected. He was soft-spoken and peered around the room shyly where, if caught, he'd look down immediately until the threat was over and he could once again spy unnoticed. This led the boy's father to comment just after the service ended that his boy was so similar to Sissy when she was a child, a fact I tried hard to forsake when I thought of that boy's future and how easily one's life could change if given the right set of circumstances, just how quickly that humanity could fade and return us to those primal ways.

The family departed soon after the service, loading their arms with whatever mementos they could gather—their spree lasting hours as they picked through hats, scarves, dresses, pictures, and the Missus's needlework—the absence of those items creating a strange sense of disorientation that lingered inside the house where the void left by their previous placement seemed more off-putting than their presence ever could—that idea once taught to me, to keep your friends close and your enemies closer.

After the Missus's death, those letters from Jesse had been a priority pushed to the forefront of my mind, as I had searched to destroy any knowledge of their existence. Those Arkansas relatives had left the room ransacked and impossible to navigate for days, keeping me at a distance as they stripped it piece by piece,

and I feared they'd find the letters and disclose that informa-
tion to Mr. Kern as soon as they'd come upon it, or even worse,
they'd handle it themselves. Yet as luck would have it, their eyes
remained on loftier prizes and so on the day of their departure
when Mr. Kern had settled in his parlor, I snuck into the room.

I removed the first dresser drawer and started there. These
drawers remained cluttered with items no individual, not even a
family member, would ever want to take, things like the Missus's
old brushes and powders and lipsticks. There were a few hair
clamps and claws that still held strands of the Missus's hair.
Inside her wardrobe I found mostly the same. There were a few
old dresses the family had not gobbled up and some scarves that
were not as extravagant as the ones they'd found in pearl boxes
atop her vanity, and so they left them tossed at the bottom of the
cabinet along with some of the Missus's less exquisite shoes and
purses, cheap items left tucked in the corners, stacked on top of
each other to either scratch or bend out of shape.

I turned from the closet and in my line of sight was that one
drawer of the wardrobe where the Missus's pills were kept. Aware
that the letters were not inside, I moved toward it anyway and
indulged my curiosity. The seals of the drawer were of a certain
firmness that made them harder to open and when they finally
did break it came with a pop as if opening a jar of pickles for the
first time. The pill bottle was just as I'd left it. The Missus's ghost
was there, I could tell. Her presence watched me as I opened the
bottle and spilled its contents inside my hand. The normal pills
had been returned to the bottle, their size and color just slightly
different than those impostors. I buried the look of surprise from
my face, not wanting to tempt that ghost into fury, merely replacing the pills and bottle back inside the drawer and resuming my

normal duties outside the house in silent resignation that Silva had controlled the Missus's downfall from the very beginning and had tied up any loose ends now that it was complete.

Still, there were certain variables that Silva could not so easily control, like Mr. Kern's reaction if he found those letters. I'm quite sure she'd tried to find them just as fervently as I had, eventually settling for the joy of the Missus's death without them once she failed to recover a single one.

Jesse arrived at the house on the second day following the funeral. Mr. Kern was in tolerable spirits, and so I was released to sneak outside for a breath of fresh air. Jesse stood at the wide-mouth barrel with his hands cupped as he drank. He'd grown more cautious over the years although never impolite or mean-spirited in his vigilance. He was still a gentle giant although his affection remained reserved for his wife and no one else. And as such, he gave nothing more than a wave in my direction when he'd spotted me by the side door.

"You gotta do better than that," I chided.

He laughed, now sending another wave with both hands.

"It's nice to see you too," I said.

Jesse walked to the side door where I stood, wringing his hands of water as he walked.

"Good morning, Miss Bernie," he said. "I would hug you but my hands are still wet."

"It's fine, Jesse," I replied. "How's Elise?"

"Real good," he said. "She might be pregnant, but we don't know yet."

"That's excellent news at a time like this," I said.

"There's no other time I'd want my child born than with that woman gone," he insisted. "I never want it to know that type of evil can exist."

192 | EDWARD A. FARMER

"But that type of evil is all around, Jesse," I warned. "Life causes us to do some strange things sometimes."

"If it ain't of God," he said, "then I don't want it."

Elise belonged to one of those evangelical churches on the outskirts of town, one of those 'speaking in tongues, throw you into the river' type of places where they met in a tent some five to six nights a week, and their shouts could be heard for miles in both directions, always with that sign out front that read in blazing red letters: Sinners Welcomed! She was in no way lukewarm about her faith and refused an engagement with Jesse unless he be fired up too, confessing his devotion to that church just as she had done years before. And so one night during that summer's revival, the confused boy rose and took hesitant steps down the aisle through the crowd of staring, praying faces, as Elise nudged him with the back of her heel and caused his feet to get to moving. Jesse had come to the Lord some several months after Fletcher refused that church's invitation. Fletcher in fact had been the one to tell Jesse about the tent and its followers and encouraged him to attend to see for himself. Jesse spoke like them more often now, although we all were of a different spirit, good or bad, following those years with the Missus.

"I won't see the horrors," Jesse continued. "I won't see it come to pass again."

"And Fletcher?" I said. "How's he?"

"He's just fine," Jesse replied. "He won't come back here, but he won't tell me why either. I know it got something to do with that woman. Always has. He spent a few nights with me and Elise but now he back home with Mama. I guess they had a falling out or something. He don't talk much now. Just sit around looking."

"You take care of him like you always do," I told him.

"Yes, Miss," he replied.

There were hints of warmer weather to come yet none had arrived, leading Jesse to return to his work in the stables as I returned to the house to find Mr. Kern seated in his parlor with a cup of whiskey in his hand. The sky was of such a gentle shade that I suggested we sit outdoors and enjoy the color, but the old man refused.

"You go ahead," he barked. "Then tell me about it later."

I had experienced many moments like this with Mr. Kern as of late, depressing encounters where the old man seemed to have no spirit left in him, sitting there with that God-awful expression like he was ready to die but God just wouldn't take him. It was what the Missus had always wanted for him: a life of desolation and agony where each day his heart grew lonelier and he hated this home even more than the pits of hell, if he could ever reach it. In those coming days, he saw no sun from the outside unless it came through those parlor windows. He heard not a shuffle of the wind's fuss and was not of decent enough mood to even bear a visit from Floyd, whom the old man adored more than any of us, save for Fletcher.

One day the Missus's ghost must have roused him, as he stood from his rocker and left the parlor quickly. Mr. Kern walked with a drunken lurch into the Missus's former quarters. His presence had not touched that room in all of its existence yet now he walked amongst it with a familiarity that led him from the dresser to the wardrobe to that veiled window that allowed no light or obstructions from the outside world. Mr. Kern rested in the Missus's old chair. He stroked its arms affectionately even though he still appeared as grumpy as a child given a sweater on Christmas. His breathing remained heavy although consistent enough to lull him into a gentle sleep. He did not wake from this condition for several hours when a cradle, mahogany-laced and strapped tightly with shiny casings of plastic that mirrored its form, caught his attention from the corner of the bed. This was its lot, this shell that served no further purpose, placed now amongst those other items also stored and locked away inside this very room, a corner of one of its four legs bearing the initials ELK that over time had weathered to just faintly show the indentations of that gold-plated mass. One leg appeared to be of a smaller diameter than the rest and served as the weaker side that respectfully sat propped against the wall for support. It was tragic to witness, holding my attention like an accident that is impossible to turn away from. It broke my will to be angry anymore. Still, Mr. Kern remained unbothered by this monstrosity, his nature now akin to those monsters that had, over the course of time, beaten him into this most helpless of states, his eyes downward cast, his tail tucked between his legs, that flinch appallingly noticeable whenever the master cracked his whip.

Mr. Kern abandoned these sights when a chest once belonging to young Elizabeth caught his attention from beneath the bed. He stood and bent painfully at the edge to retrieve the item that sat partially tucked beneath the bed skirt. The chest was small and within it were some of Elizabeth's old dresses and infant shoes. There was a rag doll and teddy she could never sleep without, once given to her by that uncle in Little Rock, Miss Lula had told me. There were photographs but none of Elizabeth, more clothes, then at the bottom a strange pouch that Mr. Kern dug at until he'd pried it from its locked position and it rested flat in his hands. I'd seen this pouch before in Miss Lula's possession but never thought much of it. Many times I'd observed it inside her carrier or upon her nightstand, then it'd be gone within a matter of minutes.

Once he'd removed the pouch, Mr. Kern returned to the Missus's chair, where he sat and opened it. The light fell heavily over his brow, which blackened his eyes and made his entire face grim. His stare remained steady, his color an instant change from pale to red to scarlet to some shade that appeared to be the intensity of fire, it burned so brightly. One-by-one he pulled the sheets of paper from the pouch, stacking these items on the floor each time he had finished one, his chest heaving a ruckus up and down that sounded much like the grinding of gears. Then, after he'd read each one, he sighed, picked up each unfolded page and moved with deep breaths across the room where he refolded them gently. His expression was toxic and he grunted once more, moaning quite miserably as he quickly grabbed hold of the bed frame and used both his hands to prop himself up. He stood there with weak legs, feeling that unquestionable pull at the back of his knees that threatened to topple him at any moment. He replaced each of the letters inside the pouch and returned it to its original position within the chest then closed it, positioning the box beneath the bed in its former resting place before he stood and left the room. Downstairs he found Silva just as dinner was halfway to the table. He sat in his usual chair, and the food was placed before him like always. There was no one to talk to, and so silence prevailed as if that nonexistence of sounds were actual conversation. There was no place to look other than down or around, although it was the same sight he'd already seen over hundreds of meals. He ate quickly, just to get it over with, leaving his plate and the dinner table before dessert was ever served.

Silva returned to the dining area and scoffed at the sight of that empty table as she held a bowl of Jell-O in her hands. Still, she couldn't blame him for being the man he was, just like the dust in the air couldn't help its constitution and so often became stuck in one's eyes and irritated them. Just like the sun that sometimes burned too hotly or the nagging cockroach whose presence in the house sent shivers down her spine. So was Mr. Kern a man whom she had grown to love and accept over time for the man he was and not someone she'd hoped he'd be.

If Mr. Kern was angry or had plans to seek his own revenge, I couldn't tell, although I was sure he'd pondered every option. The days of an eye for an eye were not long gone from this place, and to expect a change in his heart would be to wait for the earth to rotate in a different direction, I knew. Those letters likely burned a hole in his mind as he considered that negro's declaration of love to the Missus, and he now plotted a swift revenge.

Mr. Kern was a pigment of death as he wandered the halls, a cursed soul left to dawdle and wait in insatiable hunger. He entered the downstairs area, where he stumbled inside the kitchen. He passed the preserves atop the newly built shelf, rubbing his fingers over the jars contemplatively. His body rose a little higher. Inside the dining room he looked upon the lacquered floor, its shine like that of new pennies. Then, with that shine in his eyes, he crept past the accented doorway and his body seemed to raise even higher. He stopped inside the living room, where those curtains made the entire space appear like a floral garden from the boldness of their prints. He watched it longingly and, although he still slouched just slightly from that inability to stand completely upright, his muscles seemed to work harder than they had in months as they reawakened from the coursing of his blood within his veins burning hot, and he stood as erect as he could. He boiled, and that sweat on his upper lip returned to prominence within minutes. All of a sudden he was a man of color, a pink complexion that arose on his cheeks, similar to that color those servants down in Louisiana saw in the shrimp they cooked. In his parlor, a globe sat atop a rusted cabinet of nicks no Pledge could remove. The wall was a water-damaged stain that dripped from the top of the ceiling to the very bottom, stopping at Mr. Kern's foot as he stood in anger, tapping his sole to the ground.

He looked like a man about to conquer the world or see it fall, roused and vicious as ever and ready for anything these peasants could throw his way, when suddenly the Mister fell into a fit that landed him on the floor in the most precarious position. His legs spread in opposite directions, and his mind seemed to be anywhere but here. And with this silent revolt he was defeated, spending the next month at Greenwood Leflore Hospital in a room dangerously close to where the Missus had spent her final days, laid in a bed with trays of cornbread and buttermilk served to him by nurses in powder-blue scrubs and triangle hats. Following his stroke, Mr. Kern was left without the ability to walk or talk, partially paralyzed over most of his body, his care left to Silva and myself, as if the old man were a beggar inside his own home.

CHAPTER 27

In this new world that existed with the Missus dead and Mr. Kern halfway there, I wondered what Fletcher would do with his blessed freedom. Would he move to some faraway city and join a cause? Would he dash back to school in such haste that none of us would even have opportunity to say goodbye? Would he remake his identity into that of his own choosing and live by that deliverance it gave? The world was truly before him like never before and, for once, it seemed that no one held him back. So it came as a shock to both Floyd and myself when Fletcher returned to the plantation with his bags in hand that spring, the leaves a supple green behind his head as he stood on that front porch.

Fletcher took Mr. Kern's old room, as the old man was now confined to a wheelchair and unable to manage the stairs on his own. Because neither Silva nor I could carry him, he remained downstairs permanently from that day on. Fletcher declined to change a single detail of the room, from the opened box of baking soda that sat on the dresser to the old man's boots lying on the floor beneath the window. Even the bedsheets were left as they were, the shredded curtains remaining parted at the exact same measurements that he'd found them, only the wind changing their original position once he'd arrived.

From Fletcher's window the young man could look out and see the shaded area near the backhouse where the shed and stables sat, a comfortable spot situated between two trees where Silva and I would roll Mr. Kern in the afternoons so the old man did not spend his entire days alone in his parlor, which he was quite content to do if we'd allowed him. During these times, whatever we thought was good for him stuck, as he could not argue in opposition, although he did wiggle and grunt as a child would. While seated there with Mr. Kern in that outside area, it occurred to me more than once that I'd glance up to that second-story window of Mr. Kern's old room and catch sight of Fletcher seated there with his eyes set on the Mister, as if trying hard to draw a connection between himself and the old man, attempting to find any emotion that would show one was father and the other son.

Nonetheless, Fletcher was an army of one most times, rarely seen outside of his room during this period of Mr. Kern's recovery. He did not venture downstairs except for mealtimes where he ate slowly and purposefully, both he and Mr. Kern seated across from one another like opponents inside a ring. They ate silently, watching each other before they returned to their respective rooms as quietly as they'd emerged. Fletcher's presence inside the house was easy to forget, as he did not welcome family or friends as others might have, and was not even a pain like the Missus had been with her frequent requests. The young man was a locked box, forgetting us all, including Jesse, whom he'd somehow failed to remember was his own kin. Sadly, the two rarely spoke unless Fletcher had some new directive, which he delivered to Floyd and subsequently had Floyd pass down to the other workers, Jesse included. It was in my snooping that I overheard Floyd once refer to the young man as Mister, his words emerging like some barking dog to my ears, as if Floyd himself had not raised the boy out there and taught him everything he knew about this life.

Even Silva found herself arriving to work on schedule, completing her duties in a timely manner, and leaving by nightfall without a word or even a sighting of her son other than those mealtimes and his sullen presence at that upstairs window. Fletcher spoke to no one during those days and kept his intentions to himself more than a thief before police interrogation. Still, by the time that summer arrived, we had each settled into new routines and that unmistakable rhythm the house possessed. It had consumed us all, its order coming by way of that returned silence the house impressed upon our civility, its watchful eye a soothing matter at the end of the day, as we knew we would never escape this servitude but that this protection kept us alive and breathing even if only to torture us. Fletcher, although quiet in nature, commanded all we did, and indeed noticed everything that took place inside that home, even if he never left that upper room. His omniscience was a sight from God that could notice even the smallest detail of his space.

It was one afternoon that he stopped me at the table. Although he had skipped breakfast that morning of his own accord, as he sometimes did, he looked at me as if he'd somehow seen everything we did.

"I swear something's different about this place, Miss Bernie," he said flippantly.

"Can't be any different than last night," I teased back.

"Maybe I'm different then," he acknowledged. "I don't know if I look different, but something's off."

"No, Fletcher, you don't," I said. "You still look like that same little boy to me."

"But we've all changed," he sighed. "It's inevitable, and I don't doubt things can happen overnight anymore. If God created this world and everything we know in it in six days, who says He can't change it in just one?"

"Now there you go poking at a Pandora's box," I said. "Don't open what you can't close."

Fletcher smiled, his eyes that innocence that remained from his childhood and would be with him until the day he died, I was sure.

"What makes me think you're talking about more than just moving the bed frame?" he now said, feigning a smile that was no better than a snare.

"No, Fletcher, that's about it," I said, hesitant in my delivery as if speaking to God Himself. "We needed a cool area to put Mr. Kern now that summer's approaching. Silva and I thought it might be okay to place him in there for now."

"Mama knows best," he said, forcing his face into another awkward smile.

He studied the room carefully.

"I think this summer's gonna be hotter than the last," he continued, "but only time will tell. By the end we may all need a cool place to hide. You just never know with this type of heat."

His eyes reminded me of the Missus at that moment, cold and distant, always perpetuating some secret inside his own mind. Still, the young man was charming, a glint of the old boy I hadn't seen since he'd moved inside the house. He was just as lovely and pleasant as he'd ever been as he now looked around wistfully in recollection of this place from his youth.

"Seems I got my wish then," he said, not seeming to direct

these words at me as much as he directed them inward, although he awaited my response nonetheless.

"What's that, Fletcher?" I asked.

"I got my wish," he repeated. "You remember when I told you out at the stables that I wanted to stay here for a long time?"

"Yes," I replied.

"Well, my wish came true," he said cunningly, with a smile that burns me even to this day to remember.

In that moment he was no longer a slave, as he'd once considered, for his existence inside that house was now a circumstance of his own choosing, although he failed to recognize the score of wealthy men who were each slaves to their fortunes and indeed all of those fanciful tyrants who wielded influence over many people yet held less authority over their own lives than the servants they commanded. With every part of my being that was sane and full of sharp thoughts and reason, I believed Fletcher to be insincere in his words, yet part of me somehow knew he was nothing if not truthful. For I had seen that boy remain in constant search of a place to belong ever since that rocky childhood when the lie was first created. That it had started at that house when he was only sixteen years old and told he could not remain throughout the winter like his mother and brother who stayed on to work for the family indefinitely. That he then traveled to Jackson and hoped for a place amongst his family in those parts, only to be sent back to Greenwood and hushed anytime he spoke about his time in the city or how well he fit in with those negroes and their just cause. Still, he'd had school to look forward to as he'd journeyed to that far-off place where he had hoped he'd find a loyal community amongst the intellectuals, yet this reality was stripped away just as quickly as the others when he was summoned back to the plantation for work alongside those negroes who picked and chopped cotton each year, their hands rough and their sights set far away from those enlightened souls he'd known up north. He'd finally lost the tan he'd developed with those workers out there and was now as pasty as the Missus (on her better days nonetheless) while those workers retained their color like the dark shade of midnight when that hour finally came. Then there was that final connection he'd held to the most, that was shattered some million times over with the realization that Jesse was not of his family. And so now all he had left was this house and this family, for throughout his life it was the only place he truly belonged. He had accepted it and would never leave, God help him.

Never had I judged a person so wrongly before in my life, for so long attributing Fletcher's desire to belong as some type of ambition that would lead him to do extraordinary things, when it was in fact nothing more than a chameleon's flesh that covered his coward heart as the boy sought acceptance wherever it was he journeyed. The boy was just another wanderer amongst us who'd desired to fit in and asked for nothing more of this world than that simple wish to bear fruit. He was a vagabond, a soul freed from heaven and tarnished, dipped in this earthly pool and rusted like iron, the scars shown upon his heart like Adam when he'd eaten the apple. But who could blame Fletcher for his preference, to choose a life of consistency over the upheaval he'd endured for so long? Indeed, we'd all sought acceptance at one time or another: Henry in his flight from this cruel land, me with my hopes to one day join him, Floyd in his unwillingness to leave this plantation even as that work killed him, and even the Missus if one considered those forgone hopes she had of one day living alongside Elizabeth, the only person in this world who'd ever loved her, even if that young mouth knew not the words to call it. And then there was Jesse, the stubborn one, whom I feared had all the complacency in the world lodged inside that weak muscle in his chest, yet it was actually courage that propelled him to seek recognition inside the house and a way out of his circumstance in those fields and into a higher position that he might escape the sun and the calluses formed by working the land. He had all the guts yet none of the glory, for that was reserved for Fletcher and Fletcher alone.

Still, Fletcher was nothing if not smart, a stern man who held no strong emotions for one thing or the other. He made decisions based on reason and not a single ounce of pride or subjectivity. He treated others fairly, yet that fairness applied equally when considering both punishment and reward. He was a Kern for sure, and it was becoming more apparent with each passing day, as his silence drew longer and his eyes keenly perused the world around him. This control he had over the house now made sense the more I understood the pain he stood to lose it, that staunch resolve he had to never leave another place again in his life, fleeing once more in search of some distant home he was never sure he'd actually find. No, Fletcher made do with this world around him, and I never feared for one moment that he would not be content inside that house for the rest of his life.

CHAPTER 28

Fletcher still did not speak to Mr. Kern, this trend having continued since the young man's arrival, and in fact seemed quite normal until Mr. Kern regained some of his ability to talk after several weeks of Silva and I coaching him. Although the sounds he made were mere grunts and slurred particles of speech that did not appear to be words at all, they were still attempts that Silva and I honored with words of praise. Fletcher, on the other hand, refused to acknowledge any of the old man's efforts and allowed Mr. Kern's mumbles and attempted smiles in his direction to go unnoticed for weeks at a time. It was cruel, yet he often was—Fletcher could be the nicest man I'd ever met or the most unfeeling and distant person alive. Truly, I never knew which one I was speaking to, a saint or a devil, for he often presented as both on any given occasion.

Confirmation of Elise's pregnancy had reached the house by way of Floyd's constant yammering one morning, and it indeed came to Fletcher's ears as soon as he'd entered the downstairs dining room for breakfast, where Mr. Kern sat grunting some line no one could fully understand, and Silva urged the old man to just sit still while she fed him.

"She's gots a child," Floyd spat. "I never believe it a day in ma life. Boy's gone be a father. Praise God."

"Not yet, but soon," Silva said.

"Ain't but yesterday he was a little boy," Floyd acknowledged. "Don't know which way is up or down. But that'll grow ya, sure will."

All talking ceased as Fletcher entered the room, a not-so-subtle end to all of the joy that had just filled that space. He looked around at each guilty party then took his seat at the table, his face cast as if carved in stone and his eyes a delicate completion to that sculpture.

Just as Floyd tiptoed toward the door, Fletcher said to him, "Don't leave."

Floyd quit his exit and turned to Fletcher.

"You say my brother's having a baby?" Fletcher said with the groans of Mr. Kern growing louder and more agitated.

"Yas, sir," Floyd said, "sure enough."

Mr. Kern moaned more severely as Silva shoved the spoon farther inside his mouth to keep him quiet. The table appeared to grow smaller as the intimacy of its design was immediately and starkly noticeable in the closeness of our eyes as we watched one another.

"Mama, you didn't tell me," Fletcher accused Silva.

"I didn't thinks you'd wanna know," she replied.

"Since when is good news ever not wanted?" he said.

"Since it comes of what you despise," she insisted. "Now, you say it ain't so."

"And all this time I thought Jesse was still my brother," Fletcher said. "And Elise my sister-in-law. That is, until this moment when you let me know differently."

"You *do* have a brother if you want one," Silva said.

"Just like I have a mother if I can forgive all the lies she's told," Fletcher replied.

"You can harvest that anger if you want," Silva declared. "Never getting through your thick skull it's a seed that's gonna kill you."

The truth of their relationship and its downfall struck my heart at that moment as I watched them deteriorate into contempt and scorn, leading me to close my eyes and bow my head as I whispered a plea to God to save them if it was indeed His will.

"I only harvest the things I've come to know," Fletcher replied bitterly, waking me from my prayer. "All those things I've seen done to me that eventually bear fruit, whether you like it or not. You reap what you sow, Mama, but you can never predict the harvest. Even you know that."

He looked around at each person in the room, venom dripping from his eyes that burned when you looked directly into them.

"So you say I have a brother, do you?" he continued. "And these seeds are going to kill me, seeds I did not plant myself. Guess I should be held responsible for that too. I should feel proud to have a father and just forgive him for never wanting me. I should be thankful I once had friends and forgive the Missus for taking them away. I should thank you that I had a family once until you revealed your little secret. I should be happy I once had joy until you made me lose it all. Just like you made me hate this world I live in, Mama. Just like you made me despise everything about me. That what I have?"

Fletcher fumed, the angriest I'd seen him, although still a perfect picture of composure as he soon returned to his meal without a further glance in Silva's direction. God overturned the bucket and poured in a load of sunshine at that exact moment as the room burned hotter than ever before, and every tongue rushed for something cool to drink.

"Fletcher, you give your spirit to God and no one else," I said in an effort to ease his soul. "For He allows many things to happen to us for a reason. Who knows what that reason is sometimes?"

"I do," he replied sharply, surprising each person in the room with his resolve. "I've known it for some time now. It's that same lesson Floyd once taught me out in the fields. How Jesus arrived too late, and Lazarus was already dead. How Mary and Martha cried, and even Jesus wept."

The room sat quiet, each eye aware of the next around it.

"You see," he continued, "there's a time and place for everything. And God can reverse even the sting of the grave and pry life from its cold hands when the time is right."

"Hallelujah!" Floyd shouted. "It's never too late."

Floyd smiled, thinking he understood Fletcher's heart, although none of us truly did. Still, Fletcher smiled in response to Floyd's excitement, a pretentious grin that seemed to pity those around him as he went on to say, "It just takes a while sometimes for things to happen. That's all. Until then they can have it. They can have all they want for now."

Following these words, Fletcher ate quietly for the remainder of his meal. Mr. Kern grunted increasingly more toward Fletcher's end of the room, yet the young man remained unmoved by these sounds and did not take his eyes away from his food or that silver tray that sat closest to him even once.

———

When the infant was born, Jesse named him David. With Jesse at work in the fields and Elise serving a white family somewhere out near the dividing line of Morgan City and Greenwood proper, the young boy was kept inside the house by Silva, his cries reaching that upstairs quarters each day where Fletcher sat.

These cries were to be expected as David had been born in the midst of chaos all around him. That night of his birth bore witness to a terrible storm that descended upon Greenwood, with the threat of tornadoes almost certain in the mix of darkness and lightning that surrounded us—where one's only sight came during those brief flashes of light when there was, for once, a chance at knowing what actually awaited us on the outside. The rain was constant and its splatters a ricocheting of thumps from the tin roof of the shed and back stables. The streams formed rivers, and the puddles were lakes that drowned every crop and made the walkways impossible to navigate. Despite this bit of harshness, the baby emerged healthy and wonderfully plump. He had a head full of hair and one could add up ten fingers and ten toes, all of which Jesse counted as he held the boy for the first time. Silva was also there for the delivery, although Fletcher had not attended, and neither did Floyd or myself, as Jesse had not informed us of the birth until after it occurred, when he recounted the experience minute by minute.

David was a crier, his screams louder than any child's I'd ever known. Not necessarily a burden on Fletcher, whose mood could not be swayed any higher or lower than it already was, but surely a miserable sound for Mr. Kern who, if he could, would send curses at the mere sight of that child inside his home. Mr. Kern's disgust was still visible in other ways, despite his paralysis, as the old man would spit each time he saw the boy, falling victim to the most helpless display of spite. We'd often find the old man in his room with his shirt collar soaked, his loss of those key motor skills not allowing him to spit any farther than his own chin and so it would dribble down and collect wholly at his collar and sit there for hours until we'd cleaned him up. His eyes would be a blistering red and his nostrils a hissing of breaths in and out so rapidly that it seemed he never enjoyed a full breath from that day on, not with that boy inside the house.

By the time David turned two, it was impossible to keep him still and even more difficult for Silva to keep up with the toddler. Together we'd moved most of the fragile items to higher shelves and placed blockades around certain rooms and corners, yet inevitably he'd find some new item not meant for children in the living room or kitchen, and then, just as Silva retrieved it from his hands, her mind ringing with that instinctual pride at having caught the youngster in another bout of mischief, he'd find another and so on and so on, this game persisting for hours each day. Silva's health had diminished at a steady rate since the Missus's death, yet somehow I'd missed it until one evening I looked up to find that limp she had to be increasingly strained and her face gaunt and unresponsive. Her eyes drooped as if her skin were made of black putty and held not the muscles to keep it taut. Her grace was exhausted in stilted legs that caused her top half to slump upon itself and that wisdom, fatigue, fear, and trust in God to now weigh so heavily that she seemed to be forever dragging her feet. Still, David brought a certain amount of joy to her heart that could be seen in the extra care she took for the boy as well as his love for her, which she swallowed up in long hugs and constant pampering that left him completely spoiled rotten but was surely the only thing that kept her alive.

Whether by his own plans or those of Jesse and Silva, for two years Fletcher had not spoken a word to the boy, wiped a single tear, or played one iota of a game with him, the house having returned to Floyd's recollections of that time when young Elizabeth stormed the hallways, yet only by the sound it gave, as laughter sat abound, yet darkness prevailed. The boy referred to Fletcher as "Mista" and knew not a soul who would contradict him otherwise in his understanding that Fletcher was not of his family.

It was on a quiet morning around the plantation that the two were finally brought together, the lark singing a song just outside my window that woke me and had lasted the length of the morning as I stirred from the servant quarters and made my way inside the house. Fletcher was seated in his usual chair by the open square in his room. Silva had just placed David down for his nap when the boy suddenly stirred, regaining in his young body that energy that never fully retired, no matter how long he rested. In an instant, he was fully awake and wandered about the living room unnoticed, eventually finding that upstairs part of the house that he was never allowed to see or at least not without the watchful eye of Silva to guide him. His feet tapped the hardwood floor with the persistence of a metronome's count as the boy navigated the hallways by swaying from one side to the other until he'd finally trotted to the very end, just outside of Fletcher's open door. I spotted him there, the boy's face peering in curiously at the tall figure that sat by the window unmoving.

"You stop right there, David," I called to him.

Fletcher stared at him with an expression that was uncommitted to any particular emotion, his eyes remaining blind to the reach of my arms extending out to the boy's thin frame just before he rushed inside the room. Nonetheless, youth was on the boy's side as he smiled a playful grin then trotted off toward Fletcher, who had not removed his eyes from the boy since he'd spotted him and now watched intently as he came running with unsteady legs and fell directly into Fletcher's arms. David's screams became fits of laughter as Fletcher tickled the bottoms of his feet and behind his ears lovingly. I stood in the doorway, my breath lodged inside my chest and my heart pushing it upward. It was terrifying yet only from the uncertainty I felt in not knowing what would happen next. Then I heard it, the sounds that stopped my feet from progressing any farther.

"So you're the one been making all that noise," Fletcher said in a rough voice that seemed quite strained after so many months of inactivity.

"You're what, two summers now?" he continued, examining the boy by lifting him in the air and twirling him around as David continued his restless behavior. "Hell must be nothing more than a block of ice by now if they let you up to meet me."

He looked down at the boy's hair, curly and thin, tipped over his forehead like a lob of string having fallen from his dresser.

"You got no words either, huh?" Fletcher laughed.

David understood none of Fletcher's words or intended humor, merely looking up to see a kind face before him and laughing accordingly.

"Mista!" the boy said.

Fletcher nodded, settling the boy onto his knee as they both peered outside the window at the collection of leaves between the two trees in that dismal area where Mr. Kern sat.

"You like it here, huh?" Fletcher sighed with his eyes stayed on that plot of land and its emptiness. "Yeah, children always do. They think this place is someplace special. That's what they want you to think though. They make you believe you've gone someplace magical, then you wake up one day and you're out there in the fields just like the other niggas.

"You got a sack and a scarf around your neck like some type of dog tag, a callus that's exploding, and a bitterness in you that might erupt faster. You got a thought in your head that won't leave. It won't leave you alone and it keeps repeating itself over and over until it drives you crazy. It's the only thought you've had in a while, the only thing other than the whip, the only thing that reminds you you're still a man with thoughts of your own. You don't know how to fulfill it though, or even if you should.

"And then the sun, Lord, how the sun beats you every chance it gets, because you're no friend like those other people who lay out to get color. No, you serve it, it doesn't serve you. Then one day you can't hear that voice anymore and that silence seems more maddening than those thoughts ever could. You realize that voice was all you had left. It was all that was left of you, and you somehow let it go. And then you're nothing."

He looked down at the crown of David's head, a pained expression creeping over his face.

"Don't let them do it to you," he whispered decidedly. "No, it never grows on you, no matter what they say."

These words were subsequently met with laughter by the boy, who wiggled free of Fletcher's grasp as he reached for the curls of Fletcher's hair that hung down past his ears in tight spirals. Fletcher had never worn his hair so long, an insistence made by Silva when he was younger, most likely to avoid another noticeable difference between Fletcher and the other boys whose hair had not that silken quality. Fletcher held the boy tighter to his chest as David settled into his arms once more and quit his squirming. Fletcher studied him, the young man's eyes taking note of the boy's nub of a nose and tiny lips, the boy's miniature arms like that spectacle one could see at any county fair.

I steadied myself in the hall, watching them intently.

"You been the one all this time," Fletcher ruminated, now returning his sights to those fields that spread before them. "All this time such a small thing making such a loud noise in my ears."

Fletcher no longer held a direct conversation with the boy as much as he did with himself, going on to say, "I done heard you from day one."

Fletcher trailed off at the sight of David's eyes peering into his own.

"You got nothing to worry about though," Fletcher said. "You'll never be out there. It ain't a place for men, not a place at all. No place for children or even beasts, but you know that. Don't you? Don't ever grow up, David. Stay this way forever if you can."

It was often easy nowadays to forget that Fletcher had such an eloquence about him that he appeared to be too good for this place. To a stranger he'd probably seem to be a saint trapped in a place of sinners and thieves. Yet for us who knew him, he was an uncaring recluse and not some soul ensnared in a world where he didn't belong. To describe him during his stay inside the house was to tell of a man who had the world on a string, too chickenshit to use it and too afraid to let it go. No, he belonged right where he was and nowhere else, we each knew.

"You know you were named after a king?" Fletcher continued with the boy, retrieving that bit of kindness he still possessed, even if it remained tucked so far away that no one could ever see its existence.

His words returned a sense of hope I had in him, somehow reviving, as it always did, that goodness I prayed never truly faded, even if it was nearly impossible to see any goodness in Fletcher nowadays.

"Floyd will tell you the story one day when you're older," Fletcher promised. "Some pretty big shoes to fill."

Just then David wiggled free of Fletcher's grasp and fell to the ground. Fletcher paid no more attention to the boy as David marched around the chair with his arms raised high, pleading for affection once more.

"David!" I called as I now made myself fully visible.

Fletcher turned to the door as David rushed to my arms with no more awareness of Fletcher than he had before he'd wandered inside the dark space.

"He's faster than all of us now," I said, an apology tucked in there somewhere.

Still Fletcher, who never ceased to amaze, allowed us to leave the room without a word or even a smile to the young boy who now waved cheerfully. David possessed that innocence I'd once seen in Fletcher—an unawareness of the world that drew him closer to our hearts and made everyone swear he would do great things, by that unconditional love he gave and that possibility for God to use those types of people for great purposes. We all thought Fletcher would do the same and walk in the footsteps of greatness, yet we were somehow wrong and, as we often did, expected a great deal of those earthly heroes bound by man's fall.

That afternoon, when I delivered the young boy to Silva, I explained of his wanderings and the things I'd seen and heard inside Fletcher's room, as I'd made a conscientious determination to never gossip but also to keep no further secrets while inside that house after seeing the consequences of such actions. Silva took the boy from my arms territorially, a symbolic removal of the boy from Fletcher's reach as well. Although she could not so easily ensure Fletcher's removal from David's reach, as the boy would seek out that quiet man on the second floor each day and find his intrigue immensely rewarded as Fletcher sat with him while he played, the tall man holding the toy lion above his head or the dump truck steady at the wall. Even if the man rarely spoke after that initial meeting, this silence only heightened the boy's interest in this mysterious character who did not smother him as the others did and who remained a static presence inside that house.

CHAPTER 29

As winter approached, Fletcher sat for longer periods of time downstairs following his breakfast, not seated anyplace where Silva or
the boy could find him, but rather locked inside Mr. Kern's parlor,
where we had not placed the old man for several months. Fletcher
found that parlor room wrecked when he'd first come upon it. On
the floor sat piles of cracked and peeled paint. Strips of wallpaper
had bulged then finally fallen following years of the Mister's neglect
and the constant temperature change inside the room from those
opened windows, which would have surely been prevented had Mr.
Kern allowed Jesse to perform work. The air was raw, the mess of
objects crunching loudly beneath Fletcher's feet as he walked.

Dust clouded his sight, thick upon the Mister's books left
scattered over the floor, while the Mister's chair sat covered by a
dingy sheet of plastic that Silva and I had placed over that wooden
rocker in order to preserve it. The mix of dust and soot fell to the
floor as Fletcher lifted the plastic, tossing it aside in one swift
motion, in likeness to a matador with his muleta, which kept any
dust from ever reaching Fletcher and brought a certain peace to
his face. His smile revealed a gentleness that eclipsed any hint of
bitterness and vengefulness he'd held before.

For weeks, Fletcher removed wallpaper and replaced it with fresh coats of paint. He dusted the books and returned them to their shelves as neatly as if placed there by the Mister's own hand. He scrubbed the floor of all paint and laid down an extra coat of lacquer that caused that wood to shine as if it were some fabrication made by man, the smell of lacquer diminishing faster than any application I'd witnessed, given those large windows that never closed. The walls he painted a gentle blue while that outside world sat as a bursting of green tucked within white trim. In the corner of the wall was left a patch of the old wallpaper, kept as a testament to that room's former glory, a square of soft white and blue that showed a white Maltese at play with glasses and shoes and strings and pipes from its mouth and a ribbon tied around its neck that looked like a bow on a present.

Fletcher sat there proudly once this work was done, no more shuffling of bags or broken and unwanted items outside for pickup, no more cleaning and clearing and repositioning furniture inside the room. No, the room now sat as a reminder of what it had been under Mr. Kern's possession but also proof of what it could be under the ownership of younger eyes. With that room complete, there was a sense of resolution to the downstairs area, a finality that the Missus had always wanted to achieve in making that place feel like home. Fletcher seemingly walked with her hand at his shoulder in each detail of his renovation, as if she called the shots while he merely did her will, just as Jesse had done years before. I swear I saw her smile once it was completed, one of the last times I ever viewed her ghost inside the house, walking as if floating on air.

The length of time Fletcher spent inside that room varied each day depending on his mood, not a mere assessment of happiness or sadness, as he never showed either, but rather a determination he made as to whether others were around. For in times when there was silence, he sat for longer periods of time, and when there was noise, he left relatively quickly and without a word. It was during times of Fletcher's presence in that room that Silva kept a greater watch of David and insisted the boy remain completely quiet even though his playfulness was as hard to contain as a yawn around a fellow yawner. That room was the one space inside the house he'd never ventured, only hearing the noise for weeks behind closed doors and being told by Silva to stay away after receiving a few taps on his bottom if he ever ventured too close. And so it occurred naturally that as soon as he got free of her care, the young boy once again faked a nap and hurried inside when no one was looking, his eyes wild and his hands a reflection of that reckless spirit as he tore feverishly at the room's window crank.

"David, no!" I shouted as soon as I'd caught sight of him with one hand tight on the crank and the other pressed against the windowsill for leverage. There was no telling how long he'd been there.

He turned to me then made a run for the bookshelf along the opposing wall, his size a perfect fit between the tall shelf and window as he pressed himself even farther into the gap while I attempted to pull him out.

"David, this is no place for children!" I scolded.

When finally freed of that corner, he still managed to keep an agreeable grip that allowed him to hold on to the sides of the bookshelf tightly, as if letting go were leaving this world completely, along with all of the wonders it held for children his age. He struggled until there was nothing left to grab, and when he felt that corner slip from his grasp he screamed a tiresome screech, kicked at my shin, then let go and ran from the room howling. The world was a daze of sights and sounds as I took refuge in the Mister's chair, falling into it unabashedly while I nursed that bruise that would surely plague me for weeks, if not months. It was as I sat there in my waning anger and pain, and plotted punishment against the boy who would surely get it once I saw him again, that I took notice of the detail of Fletcher's work. There were little things that no passing eye would ever notice in one swift journey past the open door, like the molding on the top wall that was only a shade different than the room's actual color and added a softness to the space; the attention Fletcher took to unscrew the coat hook from the wall and not just paint around it like others would have; the repositioning of the lamp on the table so that it now sat in arm's reach of the rocker and one no longer needed to stand in order to turn it on or off; the arrangement of books on the shelves in alphabetical order where there must have been hundreds if not thousands to comb through. These considerations were of an oddly methodical nature, requiring patience for days to consider and arrange, hours of mulling over details that now left that area as trimmed as a lamb's tail, docked and cleaned with that bit of pine tar. And so, once my shin felt of better health that I could use it once more, I stood and reordered the books dislodged during David's struggle and exited the room as quickly as I'd entered to find the boy.

Fletcher made no mention of my presence in his parlor that evening, although I knew he was aware of it. I could see it in his eyes, the way they lingered on me as he sat for dinner, that stare a sleight of hand that stole from the room the secrets I kept. He chewed his food carefully then looked around with a sense of amusement as that smirk returned to his face with each bite he took. He seemed of some new spirit, utterly pleased by the rigidity he'd created, watching all of us scrambling inside our heads to ensure we met not one of his pet peeves head-on. Mr. Kern was a laughing mess that night, his inability to talk having led him from frustration to disobedience to anger to now pure madness, although I would later wonder which was actually worse. For the old man found himself one day complacent to all that befell him and accepting of his lot in silence, his eyes a heartbreaking tale of all he'd seen and all that he still wanted to say, yet his mouth sat too afraid to attempt and fail once more, and he sat silently waiting to die.

Fletcher remained quiet at the table even with Mr. Kern's hysterics, the differences between them growing stronger each day as Fletcher sat well-mannered and decent before his meal, eating slowly and meticulously while Mr. Kern waved his spoon wildly in the air like a brute and dropped items over the length of the table, and Silva struggled to guide him while attempting to clean the old man's spills and dribbles down his chin. Still, there was a madness to the house that extended well beyond Mr. Kern's antics, an indecency that existed in the loathing we each had for one another and the ways we showed it. In Fletcher's case, he was a quiet observer to the frustrations of others—although he did not add to them directly, he still offered no help and showed his hatred in these indirect ways that grew from his apathy. Silva, on the other hand, was a weakened player in the game. No longer a woman capable of inflicting swift justice on her targets, she now exhibited a passive role as she focused her love and attention on one child and not the other, removing all ties she had with Fletcher, completely unapologetic in her desire to see no joy come his way. Then there was Mr. Kern who, if he could speak a single thought coherently, would surely wish bad fortunes upon

Jesse and that boy of his. Mr. Kern would find some way to tear that boy down and render him useless to a father of such profound strength, for to have borne a son so weak would be a disgrace before God Himself.

Yes, love came from no one inside that home. It didn't pour from the souls of hurt people, spring up from the rafters like Sundays in Clinton, when the Holy Ghost spread like fire, a cascade like the mighty flowing Mississippi River and drowned us all in its glory. It did not take hold like the Gospel and fill us each with its spirit. It did not breathe a stinging yet warm sensation that caused the loins of men to pulsate and become moist with seed to fulfill some divine purpose that was in and of itself love. It instead stood lame, that limp a tiresome trudge up an impossible hill that at the top saw us all standing, separately, waiting and hoping for some light to come our way.

And so it was with these games taking place inside the house and Fletcher once again an active participant, spending more of his time in that downstairs area, that I wheeled Mr. Kern outdoors more often, now that the weather had warmed. Together we walked the same trails the Missus and I once walked, the yellow light of morning sitting hot on the static tops of the white cotton and over the magnolia and sycamore. Our walks took us along the far reaches of the fields and just before that stretch of marsh that extended around the west end of the plantation, and subsequently led to the pecan groves a few miles down. We walked slowly, allowing the sun to thoroughly warm our arms and legs, exposed to its touch, and we walked graciously, the sky a pale blue above our heads, stretched faint and thin.

When a car one day stopped at the side of the road, and a woman of no more than thirty, and of pleasant enough mood, approached and handed us both pocket bibles, (not that Mr. Kern could grab it, and so she merely placed it onto his lap) we both accepted her openly. Her smile was like that of those people whom Daddy hated to see come around early on Saturday mornings with their pamphlets and brochures, trying to make him believe there was some other god in the sky different from the One he knew. Yet still, that day presented a certain calm, and even Mr. Kern sat without much fuss as we again neared the house and made a trip around the tulips nearly four times before settling on the front porch where he read the Good Book in silence.

There seemed to be a call for everyone to be outdoors on this day as I looked to see both Jesse and David out amongst the honeysuckle that grew in the thicket of brush just beyond the trees along the east side of the house. I wheeled Mr. Kern to a stop along the ramp Floyd had built from old plywood, a rickety thing that seemed to buckle more often than it sat straight, but on this day proved sufficient enough to sustain the weight of the chair and me. Mr. Kern remained on the porch for hours uninterrupted while I went to find Fletcher to inform him of the nasty weeds that grew from the marsh and could easily affect the cotton sooner or later if left untreated, as pointed out to me by Mr. Kern in his vigilance.

———

When I found him, he was seated in his parlor as usual, his eyes a speculative stare that conjured thoughts of happiness or feelings so rarely seen inside this house that I dared not believe it. Following his eyes to the sight right outside the window, I saw that he watched Jesse and David as they sat in that area just beyond the back enclosure. The two were big and small, a protection Jesse gave to David's small frame that no one man could seemingly destroy, that was given of God to men for their children. David's smile was of such bliss, his heart so big and joyful that it burst from his chest. He was precious and sweet and surely the sight God had intended when He conceived the idea of little children. Fletcher indeed saw it just as clearly as I did, his face gleaming and his lips quivering, and he was beautiful and serene in his attentiveness.

Fletcher turned to me with a look of surprise once he noticed my presence, a humanly response that reminded me that he was still flesh and blood, a man of height and width and mass even if he lacked spirit.

"I swear no one makes noise around this house anymore except for Mr. Kern and David," he said wryly.

"I'm sorry, Fletcher," I replied, aware that a person's vulner-abilities when consumed by their own thoughts were private moments that should never be disturbed by anyone or watched in mockery, as I had done.

He accepted these words and gave no further chastisement for my behavior, and I wasted no more of his time with apologies or constant gawking, starting in immediately on what I had seen in those weeds and what Mr. Kern had advised when suddenly he stopped me, his mood appearing to be like that of the Missus on her good days when she was more than willing to talk.

"Miss Bernie," he now said, having regressed to that intona-tion he once held as a boy.

He sighed and collected himself before he continued.

"When do you think your time is up?"

These words could have applied to a host of things, like my

time here on this earth or my station inside that house. But I knew what he meant, recalling our previous conversation in the pecan groves.

"You once said you wouldn't stay here forever," he continued.

"Yes, Fletcher," I replied. "And I meant it."

"But when?" he asked.

"No person knows for sure," I said. "I surely don't. You just know when your time comes. But rest assured, I'll let you know before I go."

I smiled as I patted his head.

"So where will you go?" he asked.

"Somewhere that's not here," I said.

"Heaven?" he said slyly, bringing a smile to my face.

"No, not that far," I chided.

"And you never told me where your husband went either," he said teasingly.

"I never told you lots of things children shouldn't know."

"Well, tell me now as an adult," he said. "And I'll listen as a child."

I had not considered Henry in years and felt my heart drop like those pecans from the burly trees when I considered him now. Still, Fletcher waited patiently to hear the story, a patience his years of confinement inside that room had taught him to bear alone. For confinement indeed served as a lonely creature, not something you could just rush through, no matter how hard you blocked out the days, that like childhood and the process of growing up you just had to complete twenty-four hours of each day in succession until one day you found that you were the person you'd become, and that long-awaited freedom was finally in hand. Confinement humbles you, a solemn reminder that the lessons of life cannot be fast-tracked simply because of some modest plea uttered before a God, who has a lineup of many others placing their orders. And so I freely told him of Henry, knowing Fletcher also knew of love and loss, and that his heart bled for companionship, even if his head warned him against surrender, that the heart could never exist without it.

"Well, we were married for three years," I began. "Nothing I wanted more at that time than to be married to Henry. He was tall and handsome and spoke like no one else I'd ever met around those parts, sort of like you and Jesse with the spirit he had. He had dreams that were bigger than that place and he actually seemed fit enough to accomplish them. He was a jack-of-all-trades by nature, and I swear he could really do anything. He had a plan for us to go away and he talked about it all the time. He said we were going to leave this place, and I believed him. Then he boarded a bus one day with all of our savings, and I never heard from him again. Never have, never will, as Floyd would say."

"Miss Bernie, I never knew," Fletcher said, his heart somehow broken into more pieces than my own.

"No one does except for Floyd," I replied. "Not even my sister Gloria. She just knows that I'm here. She thinks he died, and I let her because maybe he did."

"People think you're crazy if you tell them and crazy if you don't," he said knowingly, a look in his eyes that understood all those lonely, confused nights I'd faced as if he'd been there with me. "I think they're better off not knowing though. Makes them guess and drive theyselves crazy trying to figure it out. You know?"

"Maybe you're right," I said. "But don't tell me you've driven yourself mad trying to figure it out."

Fletcher smiled.

"That amongst other things," he said.

"Well, since I've told you, it's only fair that others know and not be driven mad as well," I said jokingly. "Just look at what you've become over this secret of mine."

"No!" he reproached. "They deserve just what they get."

"And what's that, Fletcher?"

"A handful of nothing," he replied. "A pocketful of dust and that's about it."

Fletcher smiled, then laughed, then returned to that solemn man he'd become, all of these emotions emerging within a matter of blinks on his handsome face.

"I'm not crazy, Miss Bernie," he now said with a smile. "I know it seems like it, and I don't have the will to convince you otherwise. Sometimes you just don't know what to say, and so you say nothing at all, and that is somehow worse than any words you could've ever said. But I watched you be silent for nine years in this house and no one gave a damn. I'm quiet for a year and I'm a demon. But I don't have the will to convince them otherwise either, especially not when they're the ones who made me this way."

"No one makes us into anything," I said sternly. "What we do is our own choice, but it's a choice that's laden with scars, Fletcher. It's crippled by the things we've had done to us and the things they continue to do. But we always have a choice. It's the only thing we got in this world."

"Well, I guess I've made mine just like you and yours," he said. "Ain't nothing we can do about it now."

Fletcher sat quietly after these thoughts, confused as we all were, looking for a place to begin again, yet finding no one and nothing that could ease his journey. I would be quick to say that his troubles began that day on the farm when he was only sixteen, yet after more consideration I would be more inclined to believe that they began some years well before that day, when Silva first perpetuated the lie that robbed the boy of his identity and sense of self. But truly, Fletcher's story predated the Missus and his birth at all, and even the births of his parents somewhere out near Louisiana in Silva's case, and right here on this very plantation for Mr. Kern. In all logic, I would venture to say that his story began before the founding of this country we all called home, and even the emergence of kings and queens and the kingdoms they ruled, that it dated back to the beginning of mankind himself and that greed that swore this belonged to one man and was no longer God's land but mine and mine alone. Yes, that must be the start of his story—that date when those divisions were drawn and colors selected and men given purposes and others given duties. From there we all fell in line and became sidetracked from our true purpose and made to wander.

Fletcher remained silent before me, quiet and reserved and dignified though cruel.

"What was it you said about those weeds?" he now asked coldly.

I again explained to him the things I'd seen during my walk with Mr. Kern and the need for them to be addressed with great urgency if the crop was not to be affected. I explained the extent of their growth and how they had overgrown once before and nearly cost the Mister the entire season on that side, not to mention the effort it took to clean up. I explained the process for their extraction and the time required if it was to be done right but still he didn't listen, only nodding then turning his head away from me.

"Thank you, Miss Bernie," he said once it was over, my words coming to him as some sorrowful reminder of these duties he still held, which he cared very little for and only performed out of necessity for his position.

He wanted a way out, it always seemed, but would never take it. "I'll have Floyd take care of it," he said.

Fletcher returned his sights to the window and that playfulness that existed between Jesse and David as they both sipped the stems of the honeysuckle they'd collected. Fletcher's eyes had lost that bit of warmth I'd seen just moments before and now teemed with a lion's conviction to pounce.

"Miss Bernie," Fletcher now thought aloud. "Maybe have Jesse attend to those weeds since he has more time than Floyd nowadays. Ain't nearly as busy as he used to be. Maybe you could show him the places you saw them. Make sure he does it right."

"And what about David?" I asked.

"Have him come inside," he replied. "He can sit with his uncle until you get back or until Mama returns."

I watched him sternly, knowing he was fully aware that Silva would have no part of him caring for David and that if she returned from town with groceries and saw David alone in Fletcher's care, there would be need for another trip because she would destroy them all in her fury.

"I'm not crazy either," I said to him in all seriousness. "Now you know quite well how Silva feels about that. Do what you want, but don't involve me."

Possessing a slyness that seemed almost villainous, Fletcher smiled, causing even my heart to seize. Even if his insistence was true that he wasn't crazy, his intentions were still bad, seeping from him now like the sweat from his pores as he faced the same deceit that plagued the Missus and Mr. Kern and Silva, and even Jesse while inside that home, all bearing their miseries from the curses of others and passing down those chains like keepsakes from one hand to another.

"I understand, Miss Bernie," Fletcher said in a low refrain. "Funny, there's something special about a father and son that should never be broken. I would be the last to do that, although that sin happens all the time around here. It's like a glue they seem determined to break."

"No, Fletcher," I appealed. "It holds no matter what."

"I'd like to think so," he said. "Something you just hold on to if you can, I guess."

Fletcher found his way into David's heart, if not that day then during the weeks that followed as that parlor presented itself to David like some shiny new toy, and Fletcher welcomed the boy openly into the brand-new space. Silva was unaware of these meetings, and I had not the patience to disclose each one, having concluded for myself that Fletcher was not a complete threat to the boy's civility as I watched them play each day inside the room without a bad thought between them. The two truly acted like uncle and nephew, Fletcher being the most loving I'd seen him and patient with the boy, who could often teeter between joy and anger at not having his way. Fletcher guided him as an older brother would and showed not a mean bone in his body. He'd even relinquished some of that reclusiveness that swore he could live the rest of his life alone, although his treatment of Silva and Jesse and even Mr. Kern remained unchanged. Watching David in his care, I noticed the likeness between them, as David spoke now with a distinct cadence to his speech that was reminiscent of Fletcher. He sat with a peculiar posture that was not of these parts as well, and he slightly squinted his eyes when listening intently to someone speaking, then smiled with Fletcher's smile. David was surely growing in Fletcher's image, although few others seemed to notice these changes as the boy retained one after the other like genes obtained inside the womb.

CHAPTER 30

With the warmth and calm that descended that summer also came a slight recovery for Mr. Kern, who could now talk a little, although he still remained helpless and required our constant intervention for even the simplest tasks. Given his gradual improvement, our walks now took us farther away from the house and stretched as far as the pecan groves on one side and the graves on the other, although we never quite reached the churchyard during those walks, stopping well short of the Missus's grave. Mr. Kern and I spent hours in this refuge, drunk in the pleasure of bees and dragonflies under the shade of massive trees. It was in that contentment that Mr. Kern seemed the greatest improved, as he would bark madness that slowly formed into words and eventually served as complete sentences once he'd strung them all together. I would clap and then he would continue, entertaining himself as much as he did me for hours.

The railroad tracks sat high in the Delta, safe from those flooded fields and swamps that could overtake them with just the slightest summer rain. On both sides were the distractions of bright yellows and greens while the scorching crackle of brown rocks popped under our feet. The sky was a pleasant blue even though it was still hot, yet just when we'd suffered the worst that sun had to offer, a large cloud would come and shade us from its scorn and the winds would blow cool again in the momentary reprieve that touched our skins. By late afternoon would come the threat of those frequent thunderstorms fueled by the summer heat, filling the sky with ash-colored clouds that relieved none of the humidity in the air and somehow added to its misery. How during those moments every wind gust felt like rain and brought with it a heaviness like thick wool that made the air unbearable and impossibly difficult to breathe.

The insects grew louder, with a sense of cohesion in their croaks and chirps and whistles that climbed the tracks and encircled the trees and landed on us listlessly, lulling us back into our humdrum and wait. In the absence of the rain, the ground burned when touched, although it could rain every day out here and still feel the same way. At sunset, the tracks continued into the haze of trees that blurred into one vaporous mess out at the edge of existence as we knew it, that spot where we couldn't see the continuing land or sky anymore yet knew the tracks continued on, straight as pencils, laid flat for miles alongside the steamrolled land. The tracks reflected the blistering up above in likeness to a peach slightly grayed on top of our heads and orange as fire in the distance.

We'd passed the shaded coves carved by the tress where we lay sometimes and those wicker bushes that were a burden to navigate if one ever became tangled, all of those quiet places where Mr. Kern and I found peace during our time away from the house that summer. Then I'd roll him onto the front porch, and he would sit there for hours taking in those sights not observed by younger eyes who knew this world awaited them day after day when they woke. Mr. Kern had no such assurance and, as such, sat consumed by each thing he'd seen.

Fletcher was a nod to his former self during this time, a reawakening of that spirit he once had, now positioned within an even handsomer body. He spared no lack of smiles or kind words. And like Silva, he also reaped the joy and energy that came from David's presence. He treated the boy like his own, David's soft eyes a reflection of Fletcher's own kindness, the boy's small hands and nose attributable to Fletcher's own creation. Yet like any other occurrence that took place inside that home, there could be no good without the bad, and with David now absent more often than not from Silva's company, she seemed to fade before our very eyes, her faint presence seen in that scarf tied around her head that loosely fell, her housecoat a lazy smock that reached just below her knees and sank with heavy pockets, her socks clinging just above her ankles in tired rounds, her shoes a worn mix of soft leather eased with saddle soap and cotton, her face a staunchness of years that showed, the narrowing of her right eye from the effects of glaucoma and its persistence over time. At the top of Silva's housecoat was a white lace collar that matched the trim along the sleeves and those two pockets that sat along the front at her waist, this lace and trim the only prettiness that coat had to offer and indeed all that Silva bore.

David played out back around the shed and stables on this day, where Jesse could keep watch while Silva rested inside, the boy's feet perched on top of a tire positioned alongside the wall so that he could better peer over that short barrier and into the pigpen where Jesse worked. The boy was all legs, his linen shorts having been hemmed so that they easily grew with him and could be lowered as needed, and anyone could see that it was definitely time again for the stitches to be popped and resewn. Jesse held the catchpole while one of the workers who had been released from his field duties for these few hours restrained the fighting hog. The worker placed his weight on the pig, using both knees to press down at its throat. Jesse then grabbed the ring and secured it to the pig's snout. David was unimpressed by this struggle, having viewed it many times and, as such, losing interest as soon as the pig was released from their care. He stood there for some twenty minutes in this vacillation before he finally tired of barn chores and hopped down from the tire to return outdoors where the sun awaited him.

The light emerged in one burst, over and under and through until his blinded sight finally made out Floyd's tall stance, the boy's hands shading his eyes as he ran to Floyd in the nearby field. Floyd's jumpsuit showed a faded thinning of years and had changed from a khaki gray to that color of cinders from a fireplace in winter. His starched white shirt peeked from his opened collar, just barely, and his shoes sat caked with mud, crumpled at the toes as if they were able to become wrinkled like a shirt or a wadded piece of paper. In his eyes was a distant sight known only to his mind, a sadness that caused me pain to ever consider what thoughts he might have pondered as he stood there with the stick in his hand and his hair peppered gray and this life on the plantation with Mr. Kern and Miss Lula all he had ever known out here in the Delta. David reached him, grabbing the bottom of his pants just below his knees, which woke Floyd from his dreams and revived whatever life he had left. Floyd embraced the boy lovingly, his large, worn hands placed around the boy's shoulder as he gathered up the youngster and placed him onto his shoulders.

David screamed, howling like some coyote in the fields with his sights set on the barn.

"Ya got away, huh?" Floyd said, snickering with his jagged teeth. "Well, let's see if we can pet tha cows."

Floyd now carried the boy toward a black cow, its temperament calm when compared to those massive bulls he kept in the pen opposite the shed. The cow backed away just as the two of them approached, its black eyes following them each direction they turned as Floyd eased closer while cooing to the cow as if speaking to a baby. Floyd then tapped his stick onto the ground and reached with his free hand to rub the cow's ears gently, which caused the cow to stand completely still and allowed the boy to reach down and do the same.

"Ya got 'er," Floyd encouraged him.

Floyd's gaze was always wise, his mouth always pursed and his eyes always peering around him in omniscience at the things he had seen. He held no judgments yet offered lessons as outright as a preacher, which we all heard as often as the next during his rambles. Seeing that wise expression, I recalled how he had stood with those men at Daddy's funeral, all of them dressed in white shirts and trench coats, their hats removed and their voices raised in song. No man's suit matched from top to bottom other than the preacher, although those men were just as put together as anyone else, Floyd included. Some with their canes and others choosing to slouch without any support at all, they stood, their voices singing loudly around the open pit until, with their arms raised and their eyes closed tightly out of fear of viewing this world while in consult with God, the women joined in and the spirit took hold of some and made others scream out in long cries, while others fell to the ground in fits that no one dared disturb as we praised God for this man who had raised three children alone after the loss of his wife and taught them truly the Word as best as he could. We sang until the crying stopped and then Floyd poured the dirt into the open grave and Gloria delivered a final song, as she had been known to have a lovely voice.

With a child now present on the plantation, the laughter no longer stopped at its edges, refusing to touch the house in journey from one farm to the next. It now exuded from all sides, as David was truly an excitable child, always running from one shiny thing to another. In typical fashion his laughter rose once more as Floyd returned him to the ground, and the boy ran wildly amongst the cows, slapping their hind legs with his stick and fleeing their retaliation while the dust trailed behind.

"David," a voice soon called from the house.

David stopped, looked up, and ran.

Within the living room, David practiced his letters, the boy's voice reaching us on that porch where I sat with Mr. Kern in the sun's residual heat, left after the red-hot day, the remaining warmth quelling any exaggerated movements we had or even thought of exhibiting. The boy's words lingered in my ears as he sat, reciting the same letter over and over, as he had learned no other letters besides that one that started them all.

Soon the voice came again as David trotted off once more toward the sound that called from the other room, my ear leaning to the door as he ventured farther inside the house. When no sooner did he return to that front area with that unmistakable tap of his feet did he run away again, rushing off toward the sound of that voice calling. A swell rose in the cotton bloom that pushed up the white heads row after row until that wind finally shoved the collected dust toward the front step where we sat. The dry ground smelled of rust and grit, all those years of being tended and ruffled now taking its revenge in the form of that vicious sting, that smell

I had gotten used to, like my grandmother's lavender perfume when I was younger, that smell of Mississippi I knew so well in the back of my mind.

The sunlight was a twinkle left in that part of the sky that refused to retire as we sat outside by ourselves on that country road and watched the wide side of America give way to the rising moon, craters and all. Mr. Kern could sit for hours in this heaven, living each day in the tidings it gave with nothing more than the sight of his farm and vast amounts of cotton spread before him, the last of his wishes having come to pass before he died—at home with his son and his land. It was there that I left him to his dreams and returned indoors to assist Silva with whatever preparations were still needed in getting dinner to the table. The house was dark, and the light that did enter from the outdoors was less than substantial to make clear the pathways I walked. From the hallway I could hear Silva's constant stirring within the kitchen and smell the aroma of sweet rolls, I was sure, as that recognition came blessed with what could only be the potency of pot roast and potatoes and carrots and onions keeping warm inside the oven. Her voice caroled through a song, low and husky. "*Steal away,*" she sang, "*steal away, steal away, steal away home. Steal away, steal away, haven't got long to stay here ...*"

David's voice was a recurring sound amongst Silva's song, as through the sweet refrain of her vibrato that sailed then soared then whispered around me, came his indecent howl. His voice emerged again—a tyrant, a brute, a harlot who did not concede the call to worship and instead sang over it with his own song, his voice screeching throughout the halls of the house like children's voices often do, his calls ringing out like some game of hide-and-seek where David was the seeker, counting in preparation for the subsequent chase.

I turned my eyes into the kitchen but did not see him, witnessing only Silva as she stirred the pot on the stove, her hip a protruding mound on one side, where her hand rested, as her face now settled like old clothes that show their wear over time. I returned to the hallway where that dimness sat as a soothing presence at the end of the day yet unsettled my mind as I now considered the boy's likely whereabouts. When I'd finally found him, he was indeed seated on the floor of the parlor with his book spread before him and Fletcher seated in the rocker on the other side. Fletcher flashed a smile in my direction as I approached, a victorious grin that ate away at my conviction that God had somehow touched him and removed all of those cunning ways from his heart. We watched the boy continue his letters, silently and deliberately picking each other apart as Fletcher would look to me then I to David and David to Fletcher as the boy would glance up from the page for reassurance then return his sights to that crayon-marked inscription and all of those doodles added by his own hand. He was Fletcher from every detail of his being, some humorous trick God had played on Silva, given the boy's likeness to that dreaded son. The boy sat on the floor like a gentleman, not sprawled out or tossed on his stomach like other children but instead seated in a cross-legged position as he leaned slightly toward the floor and used his arms to support himself. Fletcher had not ruined the boy yet—on the contrary, he had made him into a sophisticated young boy, David becoming increasingly unrecognizable, especially when compared to his father, who was of a rougher stature and made for work in the fields.

"David, it's supper time," I interrupted.

The boy yelled, protesting with his pounding fist and his eyes toward Fletcher to back him up.

"David!" I scolded.

"Miss Bernie says it's dinnertime, and so it is," Fletcher insisted.

And that was all it took, the boy soon standing from the floor and dragging his body as he reluctantly gathered the book into his hands and paced toward the door. He relinquished his pouting for just a moment to stop at Fletcher's side.

"Can I come back after dinner?" he asked with his eyes a blank slate.

My stomach knotted, turning over itself violently, although I attempted to inject a sense of calm in my voice, saying, "Come on, silly boy," pulling his arm a little harder than any adult should, and indeed hearing him offer a slight whimper, yet it had to be done, and Fletcher did not argue any differently.

CHAPTER 31

Dinner was quiet, although Mr. Kern did utter his usual assemblage of words and sounds in likeness to an infant who was just learning to speak. During those months the old man had indeed progressed from cooing to babbling to singsongs to actual words now and, like an infant, made sounds for the simple fact that he could. Often he slurred words together at the dinner table just because those were the only words he could fully say without restrictions, words like *me, you, at, this,* or *that* as he pointed recklessly with his spoon or fork. He was starved for any attention we could muster, although no one paid much notice to him or his tantrums. Even I had become accustomed to stroking his hand in a half-assed manner as I fell in and out of sleep—the old man and his phantom pains seemed less important the longer they dragged on.

Dinner was a ritual that never changed inside the house, and while David was surely a boy of extraordinary measures, he still was not allowed inside the dining room during mealtimes, Silva's orders and not Fletcher's, I was sure. And so as the sun fought its nodding head against the persistent call for sleep, the boy adhered to Silva's charge that he "gone see his daddy" and he trotted off toward the backhouse where Jesse and Floyd ate. Fletcher made his way down the dark hallway and inside the dining room, the dimness following him into that space, as it had touched the entire house and cast grave marks of light and darkness over the faces of everyone inside. Since Fletcher first laid claim to the plantation and called this place home, this ritual was the same: Silva and I served while Fletcher ate quietly and Mr. Kern was attended to by either Silva or myself, refills were issued as requested by way of raised glasses, and the customary nod of approval was either given or refused by Fletcher to inform us of his tastes on that evening. We'd performed this routine so many times that we did it without thinking. We served the dishes promptly and warm. We poured the ice water, and the sweet tea dripped like honey from the glasses. We cleared the table when it was all over, and all of the things it had just seen were put away and stored. We did as we were told, making the shock experienced on this night, when David suddenly appeared at the table, understandably great.

"David!" Silva admonished, her anger growing even stauncher when she saw the boy cling to Fletcher as a friend would, and she knew the boy loved him.

Mr. Kern grunted and spat when he saw the boy and his display of affection. The old man turned his head away from that sight as Fletcher wrapped the boy within his arms as well.

"David, you come here right now," Silva demanded.

The boy did not move, not necessarily a telling sign of some lack of love for Silva but more revealing of the boy's adoration of Fletcher, as Fletcher now whispered something into David's ear that saw the young boy burst into tears, his tiny feet trudging over to Silva as if leaving his father's side for that of a stranger.

"What have you done?" Silva demanded, holding the boy tightly about his waist.

"Nothing more than treat him like family," Fletcher said. "He deserves at least that."

"You lie, Fletcher," she swore.

"You lie too, Mama," he said.

"You know this ain't right," Silva said. "Don't let your mistakes affect anyone else inside this house."

"The sins of the father are no worse than the sins of the mother," Fletcher protested.

"Too many to count up but still you add another one," she said.

"I'm just trying to do right, Mama," Fletcher admitted. "We so off track nowadays we don't even know what right is anymore."

"This ain't right though, Fletcher," Silva said. "You know deep down it ain't."

"Like you know right. Like you know me or David or even yourself anymore," he seethed. His eyes veered beneath his heavy brow as his face hardened. "You don't know one thing that's right, although I thought you did at one point. When I was younger, I believed you. I said, 'my mama love me. She got my best interest at heart,' and so I did what you said. But you made a fool of me and made me come back here, and you lied over and over. Then you let me believe another man was my father while everyone knew except for me. But I was stupid then, not anymore."

Silva placed her hand on her hip, digging her foot into the floor.

"You see what you want, Fletcher," she said. "But just know I did the best I could. Don't let what happened to Missus over hate happen to you. Don't be that foolish to let it kill you."

"No, it ain't gonna kill me," he said. "Not if I'm taking what's rightfully mine, Mama. Not if I don't let you rob me again."

"You'd dare steal from your brother!" she said.

"How can I steal what belongs to me?" he answered.

The room fell silent to these words, as not even Mr. Kern breathed during those minutes that passed by slowly as we each took in Fletcher's revelation.

"Jesse always gonna be his father," Silva said meanly.

"Because I say so," Fletcher fumed.

For the first time Silva was silenced as she watched Fletcher fearfully.

"You think your wrong is any worse than mine?" he said. "You think I'll let you take what's mine just like you took the other parts of me?"

Silva appeared no larger than a flea, her eyes starting to flutter.

"No one loves him like I do," Fletcher swore. "Because only I can."

"Jesse loves him just the same," Silva said. "He knows no different."

"But he should," Fletcher insisted.

"No, Fletcher!" Silva said. "He should not. He doesn't deserve that type of hurt."

"And I do?" Fletcher said.

He waited for an answer despite the silence that lingered.

"I think we've both done bad," Silva finally admitted.

"And what about Elise?" Fletcher said.

"Her too," Silva replied. "None of us are innocent. The only one is David. He the only one that matters."

David now cried tears that streamed down wildly into his mouth and over his entire face until it was red and scorched like fire, and I fear it was only this sight of the boy in such turmoil, the same as Fletcher had been before the Missus, that returned Fletcher from whatever thoughts he'd had and indeed stopped whatever actions he'd planned to execute at that exact moment from taking place.

"I let you all blame me for so long while you stayed a family," Fletcher said, his body spent and his voice echoing that same deterioration. "Mean Fletcher. Just like the Missus. Only thinks of himself. Nothing like his brother. No, Mama, I'm exactly like *you*. I loved Elise before Jesse, and I love her now. But that wasn't enough. And funny thing is, she loved me too. The only one who ever did. So now it's my son he raises, and I'm the one who's shut out. You all would make sure this house was never David's home, not as long as I was here."

"Fletcher," Silva soothed.

"No, I give up," he said. "Sometimes you do the wrong thing and just hope it'll work itself out, but it never does. Does it, Silva?"

"No," Silva replied. "It doesn't, Fletcher."

"Seems we do this every year," he laughed. "We choose our lot in life only once, you told me. Seems you took my chance away yet again. And you gave it to Jesse once more."

"Fletcher," Silva tried.

"No, Mama, take him to Jesse where he belongs." The boy looked to Fletcher, yet Fletcher turned away. Fletcher's breath purged from his body, crying, "I don't want to see him again. I done hurt too much for all of you so that your wishes might come true. Well, I promise he will never know his father just like I never knew mine. Seems only right, like father like son."

Silva took the boy from the dining room as instructed, David's eyes following Fletcher as he left. Then, in the low, slow trudge of silence that passed, with the heat sweltering both inside and out of our flesh, Mr. Kern leaned forward in his chair with eyes nearly extinguished from all those years of fire and spite. For the first time I'd ever seen, he was crying. And I thought to myself, Floyd was wrong: the old man *could* cry. I watched him and knew he'd reached the end, his body crippled and meek, his journey a savage passage on this earth toward the grave. He drew open his mouth yet could produce no sound then saw it close once more. His eyes fell to the floor. His body seemed to rest there beside them, trembling as if it shuddered to an end. He slouched like this for several seconds then looked up to see his son before him. He pulled his body as high as it could go and in that slurred speech summoned what was left of him, saying weakly, "All these years ... you been mine ... and I ... let you go. Don't ... do ... the same."

He fell back into his chair as Fletcher turned to him innocently. Fletcher looked directly into the old man's eyes and for a moment returned to that young boy Mr. Kern had seen in the kitchen crying over spilled eggs. Fletcher breathed deeply, appearing to take in these words with every breath he took. His body raised and lowered, inflated then fell flat again, repeating this motion several times. Then he dispelled those words just as quickly as he'd accepted them. He released a heavy sigh, turning away from the old man as he stood from the table. Yet he did not walk away, his feet armed to move though his body remained stock-still. He focused his eyes and slowly turned back to Mr. Kern.

"I belong to no one," Fletcher replied. "Not you. Or Mama. Or any man."

Mr. Kern watched him feebly, his eyes a fading streetlight when morning finally came, his mouth a tragic ring box of unrequited love. He forced the words out as best he could.

"I don't ... lay ... claim ... to any-thing ... or any-one ... any-more ... but I do ... try ... to do what's right ... and love you ... 'cause you were my own."

These words emerged as slowly as if he'd taken two breaths between each one he delivered. He closed his eyes and winced in pain.

"You ... do ... the same ... son."

Fletcher stood before him like a boy having returned home from war as a man. Fletcher did not reply, merely returning to that parlor without another glance in Mr. Kern's direction. He remained there throughout the night and into the early morning hours with only a bottle of scotch beside him, which he sipped every so often, yet never enough to become intoxicated. Silva had suspected it from the child's birth, the lighter skin, the dark wavy hair, those eyes that only Fletcher and Mr. Kern possessed and Elizabeth before she passed.

Fletcher stayed awake for days, a ghostly presence around the house that did not eat or drink or speak a word. Yet still he knew wisdom, that hungry child who had eaten what little the kitchen held, who'd prepared dinner upon decrepit stoves for his mother and brother, whom work kept, who'd wrapped the lukewarm half of his meal in aluminum foil and left it there for whenever they returned, who'd stayed awake until he'd heard that latch from the door turn and safely close. He was the same boy now as he was then, robbed by everyone around him, defined by what others told him he would be, left empty and ashamed and unknowing of himself like an infant, his identity no more known to him now than it was when he was first aware of himself, a pale color shaded by all that was around. He lay awake for days with these thoughts until that summer came to a definitive end with that last warm day that touched the water and settled between the rows of cotton, before the lasting light became gravely shorter and we lost the sun for weeks.

In those last days of summer, I walked Mr. Kern nearly every day out amongst the cotton, where the bloom still sat high. The sun was a pestering friend but we took it in stride as we continued on through the jacarandas and their purple court, the bull bays and that white procession of tumbling leaves out amongst the fescues and rye. And all that was beautiful and all that was seen did not matter anymore, for in an instant he had passed, right there in his chair, out amongst the rows of cotton. We buried him that summer by the large oak tree at the end of the road, where his father also lay, clearing the green pecan shells just enough to place a stone and photo, one of the few pictures where the old man actually agreed to wear a shirt and tie, had actually smiled, although it wasn't a large one and had to be captured fairly quickly before it disappeared. No family came and no one said much other than Floyd, who sighed a deep sigh then wiped his brow of the sweat that collected.

I took leave of the plantation following Mr. Kern's death, returning so far south only when there was a wedding or funeral that required my attendance, but at no other time did I come to that house or venture toward Mississippi. Just as I'd lost Henry, I released Greenwood too, and I was content. Henry's hand seemed to lead me to the door and onto that bus that grumbled toward its final stop in Virginia. For the first time, I knew how he felt to leave, and it felt of heaven.

David indeed grew up in his father's image, although Fletcher would never see the boy grow. Fletcher having said it best when he insisted there was a special bond between father and son that should never be broken, yet some things were too ingrained to change and some too minute to save, and so he gave them all away for he left the plantation that autumn as well, leaving some three weeks after my own exodus, when the house lay asleep and there was no one around to see his departure other than the cows that stood witness to the few bags he carried from the side door at that modicum of dawn, Floyd finally waking that morning to find him gone and never seeing him again—nor did the rest of us.

And so it came to pass that after Fletcher had rejected the land, Mr. Kern had left the plantation to Floyd that he might never work for another man in his lifetime, and Floyd then to his son Arnold, who in his short life had borne no children that did survive, that with his last breaths he then left the land to Jesse, and Jesse to his son David, and David to all his generations that followed, and they were a blessed people who went on to accomplish great things, passing down that locket of the Kern family that Fletcher so cunningly passed to David one day in secret out amongst the wide bloom of the cotton just before Fletcher disappeared from that plantation forever. And so it was that the house remained with the Kern family for generations to come and would be that way for as long as I knew it to exist.

ACKNOWLEDGMENTS

I want to thank my agent, Annie Bomke, who saw something special in my work and took a chance on me. You worked tirelessly on my behalf, and I'm forever indebted to you. I also want to thank Blackstone Publishing and their amazing team, including my editor, Peggy Hageman. I am truly the luckiest author ever. After God, I have to thank my ever-supportive mother and brother who believed a book would come even when there were no signs that it would. A big thank-you to my friends Jen Brown, Julian Fray (JT), Laura Schuyler, Michael Hibler, Edgar Martinez, Dalia Guillen, Jamie Biggs, Francisco Tellez, Tonatiuh Juarez, Kai Love, and many more. I am a writer because of you all, although there's one person I owe it all to: May-lee Chai. You are my biggest supporter and the person who taught me to write, query, and never give up. God placed you in my path, and I'm glad for it. I'm forever inspired by you. Finally, thank you to the Amherst College Library staff for pushing me toward writing many years ago. You gave me a coat during the Massachusetts winter, food when I was starving, and an open ear during my toughest times. You listened to all of my ideas and made me promise to never stop my pursuit. Judith, Tracy, and Janet, I am humbled by your friendship.